D. K. Broster

Child Royal

e-artnow 2021

D. K. Broster

Child Royal

Historical Novel - The Story of Mary Queen of Scots

e-artnow, 2021
Contact: info@e-artnow.org

ISBN 978-80-273-4133-7

Contents

To
Miss Jane T. Stoddart

In gratitude, since, without
her book on Mary's girlhood,
this story would never have
been written.

THE PICTURE

Before the flames so lamentably had their will of Garthrose House in 1896, there used to hang in the hall a small painting which caught the eye at once by its unlikeness to any of the more important-looking and better executed portraits of a later date, the Allan Ramsays, or the Raeburn, or even to the dark-backgrounded family pictures belonging to periods nearer to its own. Childish visitors in particular were sure to be attracted to this painting, and their questions were generally identical in substance: "Why is there another little picture painted inside this picture, please?" "Who is the little girl in it?" "Are the lady and gentleman her father and mother?" Or sometimes it would be, not a query, but a request: "Grandfather, will you show us the funny picture?"

And to the questions Sir Patrick Graham would answer: "No, my dear, the lady and gentleman are not the parents of the little girl; they are my ancestors-and yours as well," he would add, if the case required it. Then, if the small visitor were below a certain stature, he or she might be lifted up. "Suppose we look closer. You see that crown on the frame of the picture of the little girl? *Now* can't you guess who she is? . . . Mary Queen of Scots when she was quite small, between eight and nine years of age, though she looks a good deal older, doesn't she, in that stiff bodice and that tight-fitting head-dress? The whole picture was painted when she was a child in France, before she was married to the little boy-the Dauphin-with whom she was brought up, and who became, you know, King Francis II of France."

"Is that why there is a crown on the frame?"

"No, the crown is there because Mary was a Queen already. She had been Queen of Scots since she was a week old."

"Did she have to do lessons, like us, when she was little?"

"Indeed she did, and when you go to Paris you will see her Latin exercise-book in the great library there."

"But did she have toys, too?"

"Yes, and a great many pets, and dresses and jewels, because she was a very important little person, although she was only a child like you."

"And why are those two people with stiff white things round their necks holding her picture like that?"

"Because they both had to do with her in those days, and they were very fond of her."

And the child would gaze at that other child whose name at least was familiar, and perhaps her fate, too. The lady and gentleman in the painting, who were Sir Patrick's ancestors, sat either side of a small table covered with a dark velvet cloth reaching to the floor. They were looking neither at the spectator nor at each other, but towards the oval picture of the little Queen, along the top of which the farthest hand of each was laid, thus holding it upright on the table.

It would probably be an older visitor to Garthrose who would observe further details in this somewhat unusual picture. On the front of the table-cloth was emblazoned a shield with the family quarterings, the scallop-shells and roses, surmounted by the mailed hand holding a rose branch which was the special cognisance of Graham of Garthrose, under the scroll bearing the motto which went with it, *Par heur et malheur* . There was nothing out of the common about this heraldic display, but what was apt to excite a connoisseur's curiosity was the presence on the floor in the foreground of a sort of plaque, showing the same shield traversed by the bend sinister of illegitimacy. Near it lay an open letter across which a little snake was crawling.

And to one such visitor old Sir Patrick said with a sigh: "Yes, some fated natures throw an early shadow. Even as a child Queen Mary was, through no fault of her own, the cause of anguish to those who loved her. We had cause enough in my family to know it. . . . You are familiar with her own chosen motto: *In my end is my beginning* ? I sometimes think it should have been reversed."

"That same thought has come to me before now," answered his hearer. "There is, of course, a story—a dark story, perhaps-in that enigmatical picture?"

Sir Patrick Graham bent his handsome grey head in assent. "You shall hear it to-night, if you care to."

THE STORY

I. ARCHER OF THE GUARD

(June-December, 1548) —(1)

The dogs were still barking down below in the court-yard, so recent was Ninian's arrival. He was not too late; that much he had learnt from old Gib, all a-tremble with agitation and surprise, who had admitted him, and from his young sister Agnes also, now preparing their mother for his visit.

And while he waited in the oriel-windowed chamber overlooking the strath, the wind which had just brought him from France, and which was now sporting with the pennons of Monsieur d'Essé's fleet in the Firth of Forth, buffeted the House of Garthrose with a good will, and, entering by various imperceptible crannies, set swaying on the wall the tapestry of Queen Semiramis and her train, so familiar to Ninian Graham in his boyhood. Staring at it now, on this June afternoon of 1548, he could scarcely believe that nearly seven years had passed since he had been home to Scotland. When last his eyes had rested on those bannered towers upon the wall, squat and formal behind the casques and spears of the Assyrian warriors, the catastrophe of Solway Moss was yet to come, and the disaster of Pinkie also; Leith and Edinburgh had not yet been sacked, nor hundreds of Border villages destroyed, and Jedburgh and Kelso, Dryburgh and Melrose, those fair abbeys, still stood inviolate. Then, also, the crown of Scotland had rested upon the brow of a King, not, as now, upon that of a little maid of five and a half. The queen in the arras, even though in the act of resigning her diadem to her son, still had the advantage there.

Turning away towards the window, Ninian began to detach his rapier, and, passing through a shaft of the June sunlight which, as it poured through the gules of a blazon in the glass, lay upon his shoulder for a moment like a stain of blood, came into a beam of untempered light —a man in the late thirties, spare, springy and upright. There was a faint touch of grey at his temples, but not a thread of it in the little pointed brown beard which left revealed a mouth more resolute than might well have accompanied eyes so reflective. His high boots were muddy with his fast riding from Leith; dust speckled the grey cloak flung over a chair. He had the bearing and air of the soldier he was, a soldier in alien service-though no Scot held it alien to serve, as he did, in the Scottish Archer Guard of King Henri II of France.

Laying down his sword, the returned exile set one knee upon the window seat, threw open one of the small panes and looked out upon his elder brother's domain. Between the soft green meadows, held in place as they were by the gentle hills on either side, shone the river of his boyhood. He could still rehearse its every curve. Rather more of the countryside was Graham property now, for Robert had extended and improved the lands of Garthrose, though without imagination, as a merchant builds up his business. Yet everything in the prospect before Ninian's eyes spoke to him, as it had always done, of his father, that charming and masterful Malise Graham, who had run so royally through his wealth that, but for the portion of his first wife's dowry secured to her children (and but for Robert's careful husbandry) there would have been little left to keep up Garthrose to-day. Catherine Hepburn, Sir Malise's second wife, had been almost portionless-the main reason for her son's entering foreign service. But this marriage, unlike the first, had been a love match, which was perhaps the reason why Malise Graham had always received from that son a devotion which his occasional brutality had had no power to quench. Yes, everything about Garthrose spoke to Ninian of his father, though that father was fifteen years dead. . . . And now Catherine Graham, who had mourned her husband so unremittingly, was following him. It was that news which had brought her son from France to-day.

The sound of the door opening caused Ninian to spring up. It was his half-brother who entered.

About Robert Graham of Garthrose there had never been any of his father's carefree grace and radiance. Stoutish, greying (for he was over fifty), a perpetual harassed frown upon his forehead, he came forward with a quick and heavy tread.

"Ninian! My dear brother!" Despite that troubled look, there was no lack of warmth in his voice as he embraced the traveller. "Ill news has brought you, brother-but a good wind natheless. I'm gey glad to see you again after these many years!"

Ninian returned the greeting as cordially. "And my mother? Agnes tells me ——"

Robert shook his head, the frown deepening. "She was anointed this morning. Indeed, Ninian, we thought she would have passed yesterday. You are but just in time."

His brother stifled a sigh. "I wonder will she know me?" he said to himself. Then aloud: "How does your young brood, Robert, wanting their good mother?" For Robert's somewhat shrewish wife had died a couple of years ago, leaving, besides two sons of seventeen and fifteen, a whole nursery of younger folk.

But before Robert could more than touch the fringe of a complete answer to this question, Agnes returned to the room-the sister in whom Ninian had some ado to recognise the child of thirteen who had sat beside him on a stool at his last visit, asking him so many questions about France that their mother had rebuked her. She was a young woman now, in a wide-spreading green gown.

"The news of Ninian's coming hath not distressed your mother?" asked Robert Graham anxiously.

Agnes shook her gentle head. "Nay, for she was looking for it. Indeed, she has recovered her speech, which a while ago we thought gone. . . . Will you come with me now, Ninian?"

And seeing him glance down at his mud-splashed boots, she added: "Dear brother, *that's* of small account!"

* * * * *

Was it possible to have become so small and shrunken when one was only fifty-three, and had been fair and fresh-coloured, like the miniature he had of her? In the enclosure of the great curtained bed, Lady Graham was lost, like a grey-haired child with watching eyes. She knew him; that was evident. Shaken with affection and emotion, the Archer knelt by the side of the bed and asked her blessing, kissing the thin hand as it slipped nervelessly from his head.

"Ninian, my dear son!" came the murmur; and again: "My dear, dear son!"

After he had kissed her and was seated by the bedside, she scanned him, for all her weakness, with intense eagerness, motioning for the curtains to be drawn farther apart. Then in her echo of a voice she asked him of his voyage, of his own health, of his circumstances; yet she seemed scarcely to listen to his answers, as she ceaselessly studied his face. And at last she said, less faintly:

"You grow liker your father . . . although he was of fair complexion . . . liker than Robert is, or his son James. . . . Doth he not, Agnes? But you scarce remember him, child . . . I mind me, before you were born, Ninian, how we used to ride . . ."

And from that moment onwards she talked more of her dead husband than of either Ninian or herself; talked of incidents and sayings, pathetic at this hour, which her love had preserved, as in amber. And as the flame sank, so did the mind become confused, till she was speaking of Malise Graham as though he were alive, but absent. Her hands were twisting feebly together as she murmured, with her eyes fixed on her son's face:

"In France still, woe's me . . . with my Lord of Albany. . . . Bid him hasten home . . . hasten home . . . Ninian . . . he bides too long there . . ."

Her eyes wavered, the lids sank; Agnes beckoned Ninian out.

"I have fatigued her," he said remorsefully, once beyond the door.

"No, no. But she wanders in her wits more than of custom. I think the end is not far off. I shall send for Father Sandys."

"Yet she doth not wander so much as you think, Agnes," replied her brother gently. "Our father was in France once with my Lord Albany. He was there for a year, I remember, when I was a boy-years before you were born. 'Tis not so unnatural that, since our mother seems to think of him as still alive, she should fancy him to be in France now, as he is not by her bedside."

Bewailing the ills of their country at the hands of the English, Robert Graham paced restlessly to and fro in front of the deplenished supper-table at the upper end of the raftered hall. Ninian sat back in his chair listening to him. The servants had some time ago withdrawn from their own table at the lower end, Agnes had quitted her brothers' side for her mother's, and young James and Henry, Robert's two elder sons, had left in obedience to their father's dismissal.

But not before they had been permitted to question their uncle about the famous corps to which he belonged, and which, it appeared, young Henry cherished an idea of joining one day. So Ninian, smiling, had answered: Yes, the Scottish Archers were all of good birth, and they did always guard the King's person at home or abroad, an honour they divided with the Cent Gentilshommes. Moreover, Ninian told the boy, the Captain of the Archer Guard had the privilege of the nearest place to the King at his coronation, and the coronation robe for his perquisite, and he always received from the King's hands any town-keys which had been delivered or presented to His Majesty. When the King of France crossed a river, it was the Scottish Archers who went ahead to guard the bridge or the boat; when he was in church it was they who guarded the entries as well as his person. Jacques de Lorges, Comte de Montgomery-himself of Scottish descent-was the captain, but would probably be succeeded before long by his son Gabriel, to whom the reversion had been promised.

"So you must not aspire to the captaincy of the Guard when you join it, Henry," finished his uncle.

But now that the lads were gone from the hall, the only company left to the half-brothers were the two dogs watching their master, and Malise Graham looking down upon his sons from his full-length portrait on the wall.

Auburn-haired, assured, a hidden sparkle in the eyes, he stood there with legs planted apart and a hawk on his wrist, in all that bravery of twenty years earlier, which lent so much width to a man's figure. His dark velvet doublet was cut down to the waist in front to show the then fashionable waistcoat, all slashed and purfled, and square across the neck, exposing the base of the throat; his jerkin of fine blue cloth was lined and thickly edged with miniver. Even in the immobility of paint, the suggestion of vitality drew the eye, and half the time, aware or unaware, Ninian was looking up at him.

"And now," Robert finished his diatribe against the English invaders, "now they have established themselves in Haddington!"

"But not for long, we'll hope," responded his brother. "Has not His Most Christian Majesty just sent six thousand men to turn them out?"

After asking Ninian for particulars about this force, with which he had come over, Robert passed on to the internal situation in Scotland. Since Cardinal Beaton's murder at St. Andrews two years ago, things had gone from bad to worse, for his death had been an irreparable loss to the National party. The mention of the Cardinal led him not unnaturally to the subject of his assassins and "the spread of the pernicious doctrines called Reformed." They were troubled with this in France too, were they not? Though he did not deny that there was much corruption in the Church, Robert thanked God that he himself still stood fast for the old faith in these half-heretical days. . . . But he had great difficulties in his worldly affairs (thus he continued to bemoan himself). There was no one to help him with the estate, even now that he had managed to build it up again after their father's —Christ assoil him-after their father's extravagances. James was but seventeen and more bookish than he liked; Henry had this whim for foreign service. If their Uncle John had not died three years ago, he might have been of assistance. As it was, there was no one to whom he could turn.

Ninian expressed commiseration. He was not unaware of what was coming. Sure enough it came. Had he never thought of leaving French service? Had he never thought (if he had put by a sufficient sum) of returning to Scotland, and settling down and marrying? Married or unmarried, there would be plenty of room for him at Garthrose, and a warm welcome to boot.

Ninian read his brother's mind; a welcome, and the unpaid office of grieve. He smiled, not unkindly. It was something to feel that he was needed in the home which he had loved as a boy. He did not blame Robert for wishing to make use of him.

"I am a soldier, Robert," he answered, "and know little of any other trade. And though I am a young man no longer, 'tis a thought early to lay down the tools of mine at eight and thirty."

"Aye," nodded Robert reflectively, "that's true. But, brother, I wonder that at eight and thirty you have not thought of marriage? Or are you perchance wed in France?"

The Archer shook his head. "Neither wed, nor thinking of it."

"You have no fair French demoiselle in mind? You'll have seen no lack of beauties in these years of service about the person of King Francis!" hazarded Robert, with a sort of heavy playfulness.

Ninian shook his head again. Not to Robert was he going to speak of that grave by the Dordogne which had claimed Béatrice des Illiers so soon after the betrothal ring was on her finger.

"The years go so fast now," he replied rather sadly, "and a man thinks himself still young, and wakes one morning to see the grey at his temples. I may not be old enough to sit in the ingle-nook, but I'm over old to go a-wooing."

"Too old! Havers, brother! However, I jalouse you'll have had your distractions; they would come easily your way over there," answered Robert, not without envy. "We have no court beauties here, since there is no court worth the name. Tell me, has there been much change in France since the new King came to the throne last year? You wrote that it was thought he would much curtail his father's extravagance."

"Aye, he began with some measure of reform," said Ninian dryly, "but, though he has been on the throne but a year and a bare three months, there is already more lavish spending than ever in King Francis's day."

Robert shook his head. "And what of that mistress so much older than himself. We hear he hath not discarded her now that he is King?"

"By no means! Save in name, Madame la Grande Sénéschale is Queen of France now."

"And what says the Italian Queen to her?"

"Gives her nothing but fair words and calls her 'Madame Diane,' as though she were royal. They are good friends enough-to the eye-and Madame Diane tends the Queen when she is ill, and spends much care upon the King's children, the Dauphin and the little princesses. But what Madame Catherine thinks in her heart I do not know-there is not a soul knows, I believe. She is like . . . like a figure in a tapestry," said Ninian, suddenly remembering Queen Semiramis in her suspended life upstairs. "Yet some day the wind will blow and she will move."

For all at once it seemed to him that everyone over there at the court of Henri II was no more than a personage in an arras. But that was absurd, because neither the Grande Sénéschale, nor the Constable de Montmorency, nor Messieurs de Guise were in the least figures woven of threads to which only the wind could give life. The King, perhaps . . . ?

He was roused from his brief contemplation of this flight of fancy. "The talk still goes on," Robert was saying, "of betrothing our own sovereign lady to the little Dauphin and sending her to France."

"'Twould be the only sure course to save her from the claws of England," agreed his brother. "And it is no new notion. But there have been rumours of other matches, have there not?"

"Wild tales, with nothing in them. In January it was to be the young Earl of Kildare; last March the King of Denmark's brother. But the French match, as we all know, is the match for Scotland."

"Where is her little Grace now?"

"At Dumbarton, strongly guarded. She has been there since the month of February, when she was brought from Stirling. Before that, save for a few weeks after Pinkie fight, she was hidden in these very parts, as perchance you may have heard-in the Priory of Inchmahome, on the isle in the Lake of Menteith."

"I had heard something of it. I would she were there now, since it is so near. I might have contrived to get a sight of her," said the exile.

"Yet if she be taken to France, brother, you will have your fill of seeing the child there!"

"My fill, no. But now and again I may set eyes upon her."

"Why, Ninian," protested his elder, "you speak as though you were not ever about the King's person!"

"Why, so I am, in my shift of duty. But the King's children are not, and I'm thinking that 'tis with them that her Grace will be brought up."

And he explained that in France the royal nursery was scarcely ever established in the same place as the Court, and small wonder, seeing how extremely peripatetic was the latter, now at Fontainebleau, now at St. Germain, now at Blois or Amboise-always, it might be said, upon the road. Not indeed that the royal children also did not change their residence from time to time, but less frequently.

He had barely finished when Agnes came in again to say that their mother craved another sight of him before she slept.

"Sleep? Is she disposed for sleep already?" exclaimed Robert. "It is not her wont. Is not that of good omen?"

"Of the best, I think, brother," replied the girl. "It must be Ninian's coming that has brought about the change."

"You see, Monsieur l'Archer," said Robert, again heavy-handedly, "that it behoves you bide here at Garthrose!"

Though the eastern windows of the little fourteenth-century chapel at Garthrose were scarcely more than slits, a solitary gleam of sunshine was enough to pale the altar candles for a moment. Soon they would cease to burn at all, for the week's mind mass for the soul of Catherine Graham was just over.

Kneeling there in his mourning garments beside his young sister, Ninian found it hard to believe that the respite had come to an end seven days ago. For a respite there had been; his mother had lived on for five weeks after his arrival. And now there was nothing to keep him longer in Scotland, for he had learnt that he need have no anxious thoughts about his sister Agnes's future. John Crichton of Fentonhill was all eagerness to provide for that, now that Lady Graham no longer claimed her daughter's care. Stealing a look at Agnes now, as with fast-joined hands and closed eyes she prayed for their mother's soul, Ninian thought she looked more like a nun than a bride-to-be.

Robert and his two sons left the chapel; then the servants clattered out. Brother and sister knelt side by side for a while longer, until Ninian, with a sigh, rose and offered his arm to Agnes. They came out silently into the grey, cloudy morning-and to the perception that the courtyard of Garthrose House was full of strange horsemen. Agnes hung back, surprised.

"Ninian, who are these?"

But her Archer brother was for the moment as much at a loss as she, though he saw at once the badge they bore, three red cinquefoils on a silver ground. His memory, rusted by his exile, would not interpret the cognisance. Then a figure ran down the steps and his young nephew James came hastening towards him.

"My father has sent me to fetch you, sir, for my Lord Livingstone is here, and asking for you."

"Lord Livingstone!" exclaimed Ninian astonished. "Lord Livingstone, one of the Queen's Keepers-and asking for me?"

"He is our kinsman on our mother's side, Ninian," Agnes reminded him gently. "He has perhaps heard . . ."

They went together up the steps, but at the top the girl slipped away. Ninian went alone into the hall chamber. There stood Robert with a richly-dressed gentleman, red-faced and grey-bearded, whom he had evidently just induced to seat himself in the high-backed chair of honour.

But the gentleman at once heaved himself out again. "Is this Master Ninian Graham? Kinsman, I hope that you as well as your good brother here will forgive this unheralded visit to a house of mourning?"

He held out his hand. "My lord," murmured the still astonished Ninian, "your presence here at all . . ." For he knew that since the decision had been finally taken to send the little Queen to France without loss of time, Lord Livingstone as well as his fellow Keeper, Lord Erskine, must be immersed in preparations.

"Aye, aye, I have weighty matters on my shoulders these days," completed the visitor, with a sigh not devoid of satisfaction. "Nevertheless, I would have come to Garthrose before, although I had not heard till three days agone of my poor cousin's death. I have but snatched an hour now to ride hither to present you with my condolences and to say a prayer at her graveside. . . . Poor Catherine; I mind her as a lass. I was at her wedding too . . . a fair bride she made, and a loving one."

Lord Livingstone turned suddenly about, as if seeking something, and found it-upon the wall. Malise Graham seemed to give him back look for look; and after a second or two the Lord Keeper removed his gaze.

"My lord," here said Robert, indicating the food and wine which was being hurried in, "you will, I hope, take some refreshment?"

But their visitor, saying that he had recently broken his fast, would accept no more than a cup of wine and a morsel of bread. Ninian served him and then sat down by his side, and found after a while his noble kinsman enquiring how he intended to return to France. He answered that he supposed he should find some vessel or other at Leith, that he must get back to his duties as soon as possible and that he would not have lingered even these few days since his mother's death, but that there were her affairs to set in order.

Lord Livingstone wiped his beard. "But know you where to find King Henry when you land? Was he not about to set out for Piedmont when you left France?"

"He had already done so, my lord. It was on the way thither that I received news of my mother's illness and obtained leave of absence to go to her. And when I reached the coast I was just in time to procure a passage to Scotland in M. d'Essé's squadron."

At that Lord Livingstone threw down his napkin as one who receives illumination. "'Tis in a squadron, then, that you shall return, kinsman! I'll contrive that you shall embark upon one of the French galleys which are to take the Queen's Grace to France. God willing, we set sail in a few days from Dumbarton, for the galleys have already passed the Pentland Firth."

"The Pentland Firth!" exclaimed Robert in amazement. "In God's name, what do they up there?"

The Lord Keeper smiled. "Why, good Master Graham, they fool the English, to be sure, who look to see them setting forth for France from our eastern coast. And while they watch it the galleys with her Majesty on board will slip out of the Clyde."

"By'r Lady, well thought of!" said Robert Graham. "But . . . galleys, my lord, *galleys*, off the northern shores, in those seas!"

Lord Livingstone nodded complacently. "Aye, I believe no galley hath ever confronted them before. But it is high summer, and M. de Villegaignon a skilled and seasoned sailor. So, if they make the Clyde safely, will it like you to sail for France in one of them, cousin Ninian?"

"Nothing would like me better, my lord," answered his kinsman gratefully. "And thus I might chance, also, to get a sight of my sovereign lady, who was not even born when last I was in Scotland."

"I shall contrive that too, if I can," the Lord Keeper assured him. "And you will see that she is the rarest child the sun ever shone upon. I counsel you, then, to be at Dumbarton in three or four days' time."

Armed men, waiting ships, a wide river stippled by the wind, a nursery of five excited little girls to be embarked from the frowning steeps of Dumbarton-and one of them a Queen. In addition, a retinue of nobles and gentlemen, young and old; Monsieur Artus de Maillé, Sieur de Brézé, the French ambassador, full of solicitude and the last recommendations of the Queen Mother, Mary of Lorraine; the Lords Erskine and Livingstone, appointed for "the keiping of our Soverane Ladeis persoun"; Lady Fleming, her "governess" who, being a natural daughter of King James IV, was also the aunt of her royal charge; Lord Robert and Lord John Stuart, the two youngest of the Queen's four bastard brothers, and a number of serving men and women. Most certainly that seaman of experience and Knight of Malta, the Sieur de Villegaignon, had his hands full.

One hundred and twelve years earlier, from this same port of Dumbarton, another child princess of the House of Stuart, but little older, had set sail for her marriage to the future King of France. She left behind her broken-hearted parents, and went herself, all unknowing, to a broken heart. But with the widowed Mary of Lorraine the compensations far outweighed the sorrow of parting with her only child. Her ambitions for her daughter and the strong family feeling which ran in her Guise blood were alike gratified by that daughter's coming betrothal to the heir of France. The marriage would lift to yet greater eminence that ambitious and already very influential princely house. In France the little Mary, France's future queen, would still be under Guise tutelage, for when her grandfather, Duke Claude of Lorraine, and her grandmother the Duchess Antoinette, and her great-uncle the rich and powerful Cardinal of Lorraine should have passed away, there would still remain her six uncles, of whom two were already high in royal favour. So much for the family fortunes. More important still, once in France and betrothed to the Dauphin, Mary of Scotland would be safe from any further attempt of the English to wed her to their young King, Edward VI. and to make a vassal kingdom for themselves beyond Tweed.

Before the summer sunset had ceased to colour the waters of the Clyde, the embarkation with all its turmoil had been successfully carried through, and the French galleys with their passengers were anchored for the night, to await a favouring breeze next morning. The fresh wind of the earlier part of the day had almost entirely died down, but what remained was still south-westerly, and the master of Ninian's galley, the *Sainte Catherine* , averred that he liked the look of the sunset not at all. But, inexperienced and excited, the Scottish lords and ladies of the Queen's train were fain to think it augured well for their voyage towards that Paradise of their dreams, the Court of France.

In a small, richly-decked cabin in the stern of the Queen's galley, the *Saint Michel l'Archange* , the hanging lamp burnt already, swinging almost imperceptibly over a narrow bed behind which was stretched on the bulkhead a tapestry with the arms of Scotland. On either side of this bed were two slightly wider ones, for there was not room on board to give the Queen of Scots a cabin to herself, and she must share it with her four little namesakes and playmates of Livingstone, Beaton, Seton and Fleming. Laid two and two, tired out with the day's happenings, for they were none of them much above six years old, these playmates were now drowsy, save little Mary Seton, who was already feeling sick, and was tearfully proclaiming the fact to the annoyance of her sleepy bedfellow, Mary Livingstone, snuggling away from her companion beneath the bed-clothes.

All at once there was a stir in the central bed, and the Queen of Scots sat up. The embroidered nightcap which fitted her little head so tightly could not altogether imprison her young red-gold hair; her eyes were bright with disdain.

"Foolish little Seton!" she said contemptuously in the French which was her mother's tongue. "This is but the river, and we are at anchor! What will you do when we are upon the ocean?"

"Lie down, your Grace, I beseech you!" adjured the maid of honour, Magdalen Lindsay, who, being at the moment the only attendant on the royal sleeping cabin, had come over to comfort

Mary Seton. And stooping over the whimpering child she said kindly, "It is but fancy that takes you, my dear. Shut your eyes, and think that you are in Stirling or Dumbarton again."

"I wish I were!" gulped the sufferer. "I do not want to go to France in this ship!"

"Not want to go to France!" exclaimed the Queen, her childish voice shrill with scorn and amazement. "Mary Beaton, do you hear that?"

A sleepy sigh was the only response from the other double bed.

"If indeed you do not want to go to France, little coward," continued the royal child, "I will leave you behind. You shall be put into a boat to-morrow morning, and I will tell M. de Ville-gaignon to have you taken back to Dumbarton, all by yourself, and we will sail without you!"

At this prospect the already tried Mary Seton burst into howls. A determined presence with a white coif and wide skirts was immediately in the cabin-Janet Sinclair, the Queen's nurse, who was accompanying her to France, though it was assumed that she would not remain there.

"What's this? Greetin' a'ready? What gars the wean, Mistress Lindsay? And you, your Grace, lie ye doun!"

Her Grace assumed a mutinous expression, but after a moment she obeyed. So did Mary Seton obey a rather fierce injunction to cease her lamentations; and when, some quarter of an hour later, Janet having departed again, Lady Fleming herself entered the cabin, every one of the little girls was asleep. She stood a moment by the Queen's couch, then bent over her own little daughter, curled up unstirring beside Mary Beaton, and smiled.

Mother of six children, widowed of the husband who had fallen at the battle of Pinkie only the year before, Lady Fleming at eight and thirty, in the plentitude of a rich, full-blossoming beauty, was still very attractive to men. And she had a way with her own sex too; at least she had in the past shown her young kinswoman Magdalen Lindsay a marked kindness, for no ascertainable reason. And now she had procured for her the envied post of maid of honour-dignified by that title, though it was rather that of bedchamber woman-procured it too with some difficulty, seeing that the daughters of many noble Scottish houses coveted it, and that Magdalen Lindsay's widowed father would only consent to her absence for a year.

"'Tis to be hoped," said this benefactress in lowered tones to her protégée, "that Mary Seton will not be queasy again, and awaken the rest of the children."

"If she is," answered the girl, "I will take her to my own bed in the little cabin yonder."

The wonderful good fortune which had attended Villegaignon's galleys in the voyage right round the north of Scotland —a voyage the like of which vessels so little suited to such seas had never made before-now deserted them entirely. Almost immediately the weather deteriorated, and though it was high summer the sky put on the gloom of November, and the sea its turbulence. And when, after delays in the river caused by the adverse wind, the convoy was at length launched forth into the Firth of Clyde, between the long finger of Kintyre and the Ayrshire coast, a real tempest snarled about the slender vessels. Having so precious a cargo M. de Villegaignon thereupon put back for safety into the harbour of Lamlash in Arran, behind the shelter of Holy Island.

Despite his kinship with Lord Livingstone, Ninian Graham was not of sufficient importance to be among those who made the voyage in the royal galley, nor, for all his desire to see his little Queen, had he expected such a privilege. But it was here at Lamlash that the ill wind not only brought him the fulfilment of his wish to set eyes upon her, but blew open the gate to all that followed.

It was three o'clock in the afternoon of the day succeeding that on which the squadron had sought refuge at Lamlash. The sea had marvellously abated, but the sky was still angry enough to make it prudent to defer departure till the morrow. Leaning against the bulwark on the poop of the *Sainte Catherine* , Ninian was staring idly at the long, slim shapes of the anchored galleys, built for speed rather than for encountering heavy seas, and relying more upon their banks of oars than upon their triangular sails. A small boat, he saw, had put off from the *Saint Michel l'Archange* , and was pulling towards the *Sainte Catherine* . He noticed it, but no more, his thoughts busy with memories of his mother and of Garthrose.

Some minutes later the captain of the galley approached him. "Monsieur l'archer, a messenger is come for you from the Queen's galley."

Ninian turned, and saw the cinquefoil badge once more. Its wearer removed his cap.

"If it please you, Master Graham, my lord requests your presence that he may present you to her Majesty the Queen."

When Ninian boarded the *Saint Michel* he found his distinguished relative awaiting him.

"Welcome, kinsman," said he, clutching his fur-bordered mantle closer about him. "I bethought me to take advantage of this delay to present you, as I promised, to the Queen's Grace, lest it should not be possible upon arrival in France. But when I saw you tossing about in that cockle boat, I doubted if the summons pleased you."

"Indeed it did, my lord," Ninian assured him gratefully. "For I too have doubted whether upon landing I should have that privilege, seeing that I must hasten back with all speed to the Archer Guard."

"God knows whether we shall ever land in France at all, as things have fallen out," responded the Lord Keeper rather dismally, as they engaged in an alleyway. "Even should we have fair winds henceforward, this delay will have given the English the chance to waylay us. You will find great quantity of people round her Majesty, I fear."

He was right. The long, narrow poop cabin was full of the Queen's train, and Ninian could see nothing at first but a throng of gentlemen and ladies, though almost immediately he heard above their voices the sound of childish laughter. Next moment the nearest group, recognising the Lord Keeper, parted to allow him passage, and the Archer, following him, saw in a space cleared in the centre of the cabin, three little girls in their long stiff kirtles playing at ball, watched and applauded by the bystanders. Yet as Lord Livingstone paid no heed to them, Ninian knew that none of them was the Queen.

But farther away were two others, engrossed with a large bell-shaped wicker cage, containing a couple of quails, which stood on a small chest by one of the cabin windows. The child whose face Ninian could see was a dark-eyed, golden-haired, mischievous-looking little girl of five or six; the other, whose back was turned, had a hand inside the cage and was trying to stroke one of the fat brown birds. Over her bent a handsome lady in the late thirties, and a man, whom Ninian correctly took to be the French ambassador, stood surveying the scene with a benevolent smile.

"Your Grace!" said Lord Livingstone, advancing.

But his small sovereign, murmuring words of endearment to her pet, seemed not to hear, and the lady was obliged to touch her on the shoulder.

"Marie, here is my Lord Livingstone, who would speak with you."

And at that the little hand was quickly pulled from between the wicker bars, and the child turned round, dignity coming upon her as she did so.

"My Lord?"

A short distance behind his kinsman Ninian Graham found himself looking down with emotion at her whom he had so desired to see. Long minorities had been the rule, rather than the exception, in the troubled history of Scotland since the days of Bruce; time after time the sceptre had fallen into a childish hand. But never before into the hand of a girl-child six days' old. On that innocent head, where now the red-gold hair showed bright through the elaborate gilded caul, the crown of Scotland had been solemnly placed when but nine months and a day had passed over it. As he thought of that, Ninian felt oddly moved.

Lord Livingstone addressed this little girl fresh from play, whose head came no higher than his dagger point, as he would have addressed any enthroned sovereign giving audience.

"I crave leave to present a kinsman of mine, your Grace-Master Ninian Graham, who returns to his post in His Most Christian Majesty's Archer Guard, and who hath a great desire to kiss your Grace's hand."

He stepped back, and motioned Ninian forward.

"Master Graham, you are very welcome," said the child, in a clear, composed voice. With equal composure she put out to be kissed the hand which a moment ago had been caressing the quail. And her very humble servant put those small fingers reverently to his lips.

When he rose from his knees the Queen looked up at him, and he could see better her rather narrow and deep-set eyes, reddish-brown like her hair, the straight little nose, short upper lip, small mouth and prettily-rounded chin. The lower part of her face was unusually oval for a child's.

"How long have you been in the Gendarmes Ecossais, monsieur?" she asked, speaking French.

"Fourteen years, your Majesty."

"They are all Scots gentlemen in the Archer Guard, are they not?"

"Everyone, your Majesty."

"I should like to see them when I come to France."

"Your Majesty may be assured that it will be their most fervent wish to see their Queen."

"The Guard goes everywhere with the King of France?"

"Yes, Madame, it has that privilege. A certain number of us are always on duty about his person."

"Then, Master Graham, you have seen Monseigneur le Dauphin, whom I am to marry. Is he as M. de Brézé has described him to me?"

Ninian glanced for a moment at the French ambassador, regarding this colloquy with an intensification of his benevolent smile. How exactly had this gentleman depicted that sickly but high-spirited little boy destined, if he lived, to be Francis II of France? His brush was certain to have been dipped in the rosiest colours.

"I am sure," answered Ninian diplomatically, "that whatever M. de Brézé has told your Grace of his Royal Highness is no more than the truth. The prince is full of promise, and of the most gallant disposition."

"But he is six weeks younger than I am," announced Mary, with a slight accent of superiority. And then, taking a further backward step over the frontiers of childhood, which for a few moments she seemed entirely to have left behind, she added, "Although it is true that he will be a King some day, I am a Queen already!"

And with that, giving a little inclination of her childish head to signify that the audience was at an end, she turned back to the cage behind her and said decisively: "Now, Mary Beaton, we will let them out."

Lady Fleming instantly protested. "No, no, Marie, not here!" She appeared, perhaps of set purpose, to be speaking to Mary Beaton, not to her royal charge, but the prohibition was unmistakable. The little Queen, however, disregarding it, beckoned to a tall girl in a blue gown standing at a little distance.

"Mistress Magdalen, pray set the cage on the ground for me."

The girl came forward, but made no motion to obey. "Indeed, your Grace," she protested gently but firmly, "it is not wise to loose the birds here. The Lord Robert's hound — —"

"He has it on a leash," replied the Queen impatiently. "Lady Fleming, I desire — —"

But just at this juncture Lord Livingstone caught at Ninian's arm. "Come, kinsman, and I will show you my own wean." And he bore him away from this little unresolved clash of wills towards the three children with the ball. "There, that is she-but I will not call her from her play."

It was indeed a pretty sight at which the two men stood gazing, yet Ninian rather wished that his eyes were set in the back of his head instead of in the front. With some idea of being allowed to return to the two children with the quails, he looked about after a moment or two, and began to ask questions of Lord Livingstone.

"The Queen's eldest brother, the Lord James, does not accompany her, I think?" he observed.

"No," replied his kinsman, "only the two younger, the Abbot of Holyrood and the Prior of Coldingham. You can see them yonder; the Prior is he with the dog."

No two persons could have looked less like the bearers of such reverend titles than the two youths talking together a little way off, but Ninian was aware that the little Queen's four illegitimate brothers were not in holy orders, and that they held their respective abbeys and priories in commendation, as had happened before in the case of royal bastards. One of the boys had in leash the large wolfhound to which the maid of honour, Mistress Magdalen Lindsay, had referred. The leash indeed seemed necessary, for the animal's eyes were fixed intently on the birds, in their wicker prison upon the chest at no great distance.

The game of ball now took on a much faster and more general character, for as the little girls tired the younger among the spectators joined in. The ball sped, amid laughter, from hand to hand, and all at once the little sovereign herself, abandoning the quails, hastened towards the group, followed by Lady Fleming and Magdalen Lindsay, and clapped her hands at a good catch, as any child of five might do.

And she was still the child, and a wilful child to boot, when, just as suddenly, after a glance at Lady Fleming, whose head was turned the other way, she slipped back to the chest and the caged birds, by which little Mary Beaton was still standing.

Out of the corner of his eye Ninian Graham watched this manœuvre with amusement, but no one else appeared to be aware of it, not even M. de Brézé, who had left his former place and was talking to Lord Erskine. Ninian saw one child whisper to the other, and then deliberately open the door of the cage. And as neither of its inmates displayed any enthusiasm for liberty, the Queen put in both hands, captured a quail and brought it forth.

Next instant the whole cabin was a tumult of noise and movement. Baying furiously, the great wolfhound in the corner had wrenched itself free from its young master's hold, and, sending the Lord John reeling, launched itself towards the bird. Crying its name, the youthful Prior hurled himself after it, too late; while the bewildered and then horrified ball-players merely got in each other's way. Only the man on the outskirts of their circle who happened already to have his eyes on what was taking place by the cage was able to get there in time-and ever afterwards wondered how he had done so. He flung himself between the wolfhound and its double quarry-for the little Queen, with a cry of alarm, had caught the frightened bird up in her arms, and was herself in equal danger. The dog was enormously powerful, and slavering with desire for the quail; for the first few seconds, as Ninian struggled and staggered, with its great scrabbling paws upon his shoulders, its bared fangs within a foot of his face, he thought he must go down before its onslaught. Then other hands, and many of them, seized and dragged the beast off him, yet not before its terrible claws, cutting through doublet and shirt, had torn their way like steel down his left arm.

Even before the wolfhound, growling and resisting, had been hustled out of the cabin, every soul in it had realised that the royal child had been saved from what none liked to contemplate. She was breathlessly surveyed. Hurt she was not-but was she badly frightened? She was very pale, the little Queen, standing backed against the chest with the terrified quail still clutched to her breast, while its mate beat in alarm about the cage, and Mary Beaton, with her hands over her face, continued to scream.

But Mary Stuart, at five years old, could remember in the face of danger that she was, as she had just announced, a crowned queen; and when the distracted Lady Fleming, even paler than she, rushed to her, flung herself on her knees and clasped her in her arms, the child said, with scarcely a quaver:

"My poor bird is frightened; pray take her, Madam." And then, looking round, "I hope Master Graham was not hurt."

Nobody answered that, of all who were crowding round her with anxious questions on their own lips, with protestations, with solicitude, like the French ambassador, with excuses and pleas for pardon like her brother the Prior, and those of her train who realised that they might have been quicker to avert disaster. Little Mary Beaton, weeping hysterically, had to be removed by Magdalen Lindsay; Lord Livingstone hastened to reassure his own little daughter. And as for the rescuer himself, he was all the time edging as best he could through the press in the direction of the cabin door. The blood from his lacerated forearm was now soaking his torn sleeve, but since his doublet was black it made not too much show upon it, and he hoped that the fact might escape notice. His intention was to leave the cabin unseen and get the hurt bound up.

He was almost at the door when Lord Livingstone caught him.

"Kinsman, kinsman! Indeed you must not leave us thus! The Queen desires to thank you in person-as you most fully merit! And I too. God's troth, if that beast had sprung upon her! . . . What, did it harm you?"

"It is but a scratch or two," answered Ninian, nursing the injured arm. "I do indeed thank the saints that I was in time, for I verily believe the beast would have pulled her Majesty down. — Nay, my lord, best let me go now. The child is too young to see blood."

But other faces were turned towards him, and other voices were speaking his name. Ninian saw that the sooner he acceded to the Queen's request the sooner he could get away. Winding his handkerchief hastily over his sleeve, and putting his arm behind his back, he made a sign that he assented, and was led back by the Lord Keeper to receive, not only his little sovereign's thanks, sweet and oddly dignified, but Lady Fleming's much more effusive ones, the apologies of the conscience-stricken Lord Robert Stuart, and M. de Brézé's congratulations on his good fortune in being of such service.

And all the while he was conscious less of the pain of his hurt than of the fact that his clenched hand, concealed behind his back, was now sticky with blood, and that unless he were soon suffered to depart, the fact of his injury must proclaim itself, at least to anyone in his rear. But as long as the child-Queen did not see . . .

And she, looking up at him with sparkling, red-brown eyes, was making what he knew to be an impossible proposal, flattering though it was.

"I will have Master Graham to be captain of my guard when I am come to France," she had just said to the assembly. "Are you willing, Master Graham?"

"Your Grace does me far too much honour," responded Ninian, bowing. "But I am in the service of the King of France."

"Then I shall ask his Majesty to set you free for mine," responded the Queen of Scotland. "My Lords Erskine and Livingstone, may I not do so?"

Lord Erskine took up the challenge. "If his Majesty gives your Grace a household of your own you might with propriety make the request," he responded rather doubtfully. But from the rapid glance which passed between him and his brother Keeper it was plain that he did not think this condition would be fulfilled. And Ninian himself felt pretty sure that the future bride, of such tender years, would at first be brought up in the royal nursery with the Dauphin and the two little princesses.

Here, to the damaged hero's relief, the scene was cut short by the advent of M. de Villegaignon himself, who, entering the poop cabin at that moment, and being instantly apprised of what had happened, perceived, as he came forward, just what that hero was trying to hide.

"Tête-Dieu!" he exclaimed bluntly, acknowledging the Queen's presence only by removing his cap, "this gentleman needs care rather than thanks. With your Majesty's leave I'll take him at once to have his arm dressed." And he laid upon Ninian's shoulder a hand so compelling that the latter was obliged to withdraw, after a word of excuse and reassurance to the royal child, whose eyes were wide now with concern and, for the first time, with a measure of alarm.

Just outside the cabin the two men all but ran into the tall maid of honour who had removed little Mary Beaton a few minutes ago. At the sight of Ninian's arm, with the now soaked handkerchief crimson about it, she stopped short with a cry.

"Yes," said Villegaignon, "you have this gentleman to thank, it seems, Mademoiselle, that your little Queen was not savaged before everyone's eyes by that accursed dog. And, as you see, he has paid for his courage and quickness. Could you procure us some clean linen?"

"I . . . why, yes, Monsieur. But . . . for the moment, will you not take this?" And Magdalen Lindsay, hastily unpinning the short white veil which hung from the back of her head-dress, thrust it into the Frenchman's hands and quickly disappeared.

In the Sieur de Villegaignon's own cabin, where the commander himself, despite Ninian's protests, acted leech, Ninian asked the name of the donor of the veil which, after washing the injured arm, he was binding round it.

"A Mademoiselle Lindsay, I believe," replied the Frenchman, "some kinswoman of her Majesty's gouvernante, the Lady Fleming" (he pronounced it Flamyn). "She is quickwitted, is she not? But this scrap of stuff will not suffice. —Here, however, if I mistake not, comes further provision for your hurt, Monsieur."

There was indeed the sharp, screeching sound of linen being rent, and in the doorway appeared Janet Sinclair, her hands still busy, strips of white hanging over her arm.

"Eh sirs!" she exclaimed, in a tongue which it did Ninian's ears good to hear in that French vessel, "whit a mairciful escape! I've torn up a shift o' my Leddy Fleming's for ye, my bonny brave gentleman, and had I torn up ane o' the Queen's hersel it wad be nae mair than is due to ye . . . forbye they're but wee bit things, ye ken. God send ye be weel recompensit that saved the blessed bairn!" And here, to the Archer's embarrassment, she reached up and gave him a hearty kiss.

"You say well, Madame Nourrice," observed the Sieur de Villegaignon gravely. "Had aught happened to her little Majesty, whom I am to bring safe to France ——"

"Ye'd likely hae lost your ain heid," completed Janet Sinclair, who did not mince her words. "Best let me finish redding that airm, my Lord Captain; savin' your presence, ye're not ower handy at it. And what's this ye hae happed it in a'ready?"

Ninian explained, Villegaignon with a grin of amusement yielding his place. "Aweel," commented the thrifty Janet, "since the bit veil isna torn, ye'll be able tae gie it back tae Mistress Lindsay in the end."

During the Scotswoman's ministration Ninian was aware that someone else had sought and obtained admission to the commander's cabin. Hearing his own name he turned his head, and beheld a small, withering gentleman, breathing hard, as from hurry-Lord Keeper Erskine. He began at once:

"Master Graham, I am glad to have found you at last. Sir, I cannot enough commend and thank you for your courage and your promptitude. I am your debtor, Master Graham, to eternity! Had my royal charge — —" And here he broke off, as one unable to finish the sentence. "If there be any recompense in my power, sir . . . as for her Majesty's desire to see you captain of her guard —a child's whim as you'll understand-there'll be no such post for a while yet in France, if ever there is . . ."

"That I well understand, my lord," answered Ninian, still unable to free his arm from the hands of Janet Sinclair who, beyond glancing up once at Lord Erskine, took no notice of his presence, but went on bandaging. "Moreover, I am in the service of King Henry II, as I pointed out to her Majesty. Nor do I desire any recompense; to have saved her from possible harm is recompense enough."

"And lucky ye think sae," muttered Janet Sinclair under her breath. "For I'm thinkin' ye'll likely get nae ither. —There, Maister Graham, ye'll need but tae carry yon airm in your bosom for a while, or get ye a scairf. Guid day tae ye, sir, and tak an auld wife's blessin' for whit ye did!"

She made a brief reverence to the Lord Keeper and went out with dignity.

(6)

A light haze hung over the treacherous, rock-strewn Breton coast, for the August morning was as fine and still as though it made a mock of the last seven days' memories of hazard, and even of terror. As the boat from the *Sainte Catherine* drew over the gentle swell towards the little fishing port of Roscoff, which had already received the Queen of Scots and her train, the handful of Scots in its stern rehearsed to each other their thankfulness at approaching a shore which, during those eighteen days on shipboard, more than one of them had despaired of ever reaching at all.

To Ninian Graham also, sitting among his compatriots with his arm in a sling, the sight of port was very welcome. He had had his moments of apprehension as well as another, not only for his own safe arrival, which was a matter of small importance, but for that of the little Queen herself. For, after the convoy had ventured forth from its refuge at Lamlash, the tempestuous weather had returned in full force. There had been one night in particular, not far from the implacable Cornish coast, when it had encountered such tremendous seas that the rudder of the Queen's galley had actually been smashed, and only by the direct intervention of Heaven, as M. de Brézé averred afterwards, had the seamen succeeded in repairing it. Nor had that night of storm seen the end of peril. If ever a captain was glad to sight land, thought Ninian, it must have been M. de Villegaignon with his precious lading. Even then he had no easy coast for a landfall.

The Queen and her immediate attendants had already disappeared an hour ago into the house set apart for her reception when Ninian clambered up the side of the rough seaweed-hung quay. But there were still plenty of his fellow-countrymen about the narrow streets of the little port to be stared at by the baggy-breeched, long-haired, wide-hatted natives, and to stare in their turn at the unfamiliar Breton costume and exclaim at the unintelligible language.

It was Ninian's duty to press on at once to rejoin the Archer Guard, and when he had sought out Lord Livingstone to take farewell, he would have to take steps to ascertain the present whereabouts of the King. In this remote corner of a remote land it seemed unlikely that he would find exact information on this point. These people, of a different race, tradition and speech, were not France as he knew it-nor, indeed, had they long formed part of France. Half fascinated, half repelled, he wandered away from the thronged quay and its fishing boats and walked beneath the overhanging little houses, nearly all bearing a sacred image or painting, until some steps leading down to a tiny church recalled to him his own intention of putting up a candle to the Virgin in thankfulness for the Queen's safe landing and his own after this perilous August voyage.

Inside, the place, redolent of stale incense and candle-grease, was appropriate enough for any voyager's prayers. Rough little votive ships hung from the beams, and the uncouth wooden image of the Virgin and Child before which he said a prayer had a fish and an anchor carved at its feet-Stella Maris none the less, who had surely brought that other crowned Mary to safe harbour through the tempest.

Ninian had hardly stepped out again into the little parvise outside when two hooded ladies came down the steps from the narrow street. Any doubt about the identity of the one was removed by a convenient gust of sea wind which blew aside the hood, and showed him the features of the giver of the veil on board the Queen's galley. He stood still, removing the bonnet which he had just put on.

Colouring a little, Magdalen Lindsay stopped also. "Master Graham, is it not? Mistress Ogilvy, this is the gentleman who saved her Grace from the Lord Robert's great dog."

But Ninian scarcely heard the words of admiration which this speech drew from the comely young woman bearing that name. His eyes were all for Mistress Magdalen Lindsay, whom he had not seen before in untempered daylight. Now he could appreciate the pale, smooth oval of her face, from which the momentary colour had already faded, the intensity and very dark blue of her eyes, above all her expression, faintly remote and pure, as of some saint in a missal, but a saint full of compassion, even of tenderness. At all this he gazed in what he felt next moment must have been an unmannerly fashion, conscious at the time of a wish that he were alone with her-not that he had anything especial to say.

In another instant the wish was all but fulfilled, for a smiling youth came pelting down the steps, and accosted Mistress Ogilvy as one who was in search of her. Amid the chatter that ensued between them, therefore, Mistress Lindsay and the Archer were to all purposes alone.

Her eyes were already dwelling on his sling. "How does your arm, sir?" she asked gravely. "I hope that you consulted the Queen's physician before you left the galley that day?"

"What need was there, Mistress Lindsay, since the arm was bound up with your veil?" asked Ninian with gallantry. "From that moment its healing was assured, and is now near accomplished. And since in Roscoff such ladies' gear is not, I think, easy to procure, I hope you will permit me, should we meet again, to offer you in place of what you sacrificed — —"

"Oh, never speak of that, I pray you, Master Graham!" she broke in, her face losing its gravity, her eyes very kind. "Do you not know how heavy a debt you have laid upon us all-upon all Scotland indeed! Her Grace is not unmindful of it; she still talks of her desire that you should be captain of her guard."

Ninian smiled too. "Bless the child's sweet heart-if it be not treason so to speak of one's sovereign! But I am sure she will have no household of her own yet awhile. Nevertheless, Mistress Lindsay, since King Henry will certainly soon pay her a visit — —"

"Magdalen," broke in the voice of her companion, as she swung round and caught at her sleeve. "Magdalen, come say your prayers quickly, for Master Seton waits to escort us to St. Pol de Léon. There, if you be so minded, you can say them at more length in a cathedral. Perhaps," added the maid of honour (if so she was), casting a look at Ninian, "perhaps Master Graham will also accompany us thither?"

Ninian thanked her, but refused. "I have too long a journey in front of me, mistress, and must set out at once." He kissed their hands, and, young Seton having intimated that he was not for entering the church, watched the hoods and farthingales of the two ladies disappear through the low grey doorway.

"'Tis to be hoped their prayers will not be long ones," laughed the young man, twirling his gaily-plumed hat round and round on his finger. "For my part, I put up enough Paters and Aves on the voyage to last me from here to Tartary. . . . I see you have suffered an injury, sir, at the hands of Neptune, no doubt. My faith, he nearly caused me to break my neck one night. But does it not make amends for all to set foot on the fair soil of France, where other gods have power-Venus, to wit, and Mars?" And before Ninian could make any reply he added, clapping his hat upon his head at a jaunty angle, "For myself, I own it intoxicates me!"

That indeed was the impression he gave, and Ninian's smile as he took leave of him was not unkind. He himself had once been a youth abrim with high spirits and expectations.

7

Habited once more in the white surcoat edged with gold, with the three crescent moons inter-laced on the back, the crowned H and crescent moon on the breast, Ninian Graham was back again among his comrades of the Archer Guard. The town was Lyons, the place the large lower room assigned to them as guardroom in the building set apart for the reception of the King and Queen, and the time the last week in September.

The King had been at Turin when Ninian set out from Roscoff, but the news of the serious revolt in Bordeaux against the salt tax had decided him to return to France, and he had recrossed the Alps in the first week of September. Immediately he was in Dauphiné the Constable de Montmorency and François de Guise were despatched against the rebels, and the King joined the Queen and the Grande Sénéschale of Normandy, Diane de Poitiers, on the 21st at Ainay, thereafter descending the Rhone in a great barge to Vaise, near Lyons, and making his state entry thence on Sunday the 23rd.

And for the last four days the city on its twin rivers had been given up to a perfect orgy of fêtes, processions, mimic water-battles, and pageants-and these were not over yet. To greet its royal visitors it had bedecked itself everywhere, on archway, banner or obelisk with the device of Henri and his mistress, the intertwined H and D and the crescent moon, and with the motto *Donec totum impleat orbem* . Queen Catherine in her open litter had indeed glittered with jewels, while Diane rode modestly behind in her customary black and white, but it was upon Madame Diane (after the King) that the eyes of the cheering multitude were bent.

Many, indeed, looked with interest at the other Queen in the procession, the King's aunt, Marguerite of Navarre, seated in a litter with her fascinating and strong-willed daughter Jeanne, a girl of twenty. And all Lyons knew why there rode by the side of the litter that handsome if unreliable cavalier Antoine de Bourbon, Duc de Vendôme, for he was the chosen husband of the Princess of Navarre-chosen, that is to say, by King Henri and approved by the young lady herself. Not a single smile, however, was Queen Marguerite, that erudite novelist, poetess, and protector of Huguenots, observed to throw to this bridegroom to be, for both she and her husband disapproved of the match, which, besides increasing the prestige of his house (just then sorely in need of this) would eventually give the Bourbon the crown of Navarre. And none of the good citizens of Lyons, none of its school of humanists, were seers enough to perceive that it was not only the crown of Navarre which hung upon this marriage, but that above the young couple was hovering impatiently the spirit of the unborn Henri Quatre, with two hundred and fifty years of Bourbon Kings of France to come pressing behind him.

"Yes, this has indeed been a noble reception of his Majesty," observed Ninian's friend and comrade Patrick Rutherford, yawning, however, as one who had had enough of it. "Did you not admire last Sunday, Ninian, the nymphs who came tripping forth from the artificial forest, and in particular her who, in the guise of Diana, led the tame lion on a silver chain?"

"Graham should have been with us at St. Jean de Maurienne on the outward progress to Piedmont," said another archer. "There the town entertained his Majesty with the most curi-ous and original device you ever heard of. As he entered he was met by a hundred men clad in the skins of bears, who followed him on all fours to the church when he went to hear Mass; and afterwards, making the noises proper to those beasts, climbed about the market place. His Majesty vowed that he had never been so diverted in his life, and gave them a large sum of money."

"But Heriot has not told you," observed Patrick Rutherford, "how they frightened the horses left tethered during Mass, and that some of the townspeople were injured by them."

"Tell me," said Ninian to him, dropping his voice, "why the burghers of Lyons are so set upon exalting Madame Diane above Madame Cathérine? Surely for the city fathers to kiss the Grande Sénéschale's hand before that of her Majesty was little short of an affront?"

Rutherford shrugged his shoulders. "You know who is Sénéschal of the Lyonnais —M. de St. André. Madame Diane had only to inform him that she wished to see her authority recognised in the south-east and he took measures. . . . Whom are you looking for, my lad?"

For a royal page, jaunty yet languid, had just approached the group of Archers.

"Which of you three gentlemen is M. Ninian de Graeme?" he enquired. "You, sir? I am sent to tell you that his Majesty desires to see you at once."

"For what reason, I wonder?" commented Patrick Rutherford; and Ninian put the same question to himself as he followed the messenger up the wide staircase to the first floor, where were the temporary royal apartments.

His two comrades on guard outside the door moved aside to let him pass and the gentleman usher announced him.

The wide, handsome, panelled room, bright with arabesques of painting on wall and ceiling, sumptuously furnished by the city of Lyons for its exalted occupants, enshrined, amid its rich colouring, only two figures, both in their habitual black and white-assumed by the one in memory of her husband, now nearly twenty years dead, and by the other because she always wore it.

The King's back was turned when Ninian entered. But Madame Diane de Poitiers, Grande Sénéschale de Normandie-soon to be Duchesse de Valentinois-sitting upright and composedly at a table with a parchment spread before her, and an inkhorn and pen within reach, faced him as he advanced. If he had not already been familiar with them for years, he would therefore have had an excellent opportunity of studying those firm features, that dazzling complexion, so much extolled, which was supposed never to have known cosmetics, and that small, determined and slightly pursed mouth. This woman, nearly twenty years older than himself, for whom Henri de Valois' affection had never wavered since as a youth of seventeen he had come under her influence (and he was now just upon thirty), was comely rather than beautiful, a woman of business rather than a siren, calm, capable and grasping to the last degree. The thought flitted through the Archer's mind that probably the parchment under her hand was waiting for the royal signature, and was some grant conveying to her or to her kin still more of the public revenues. She wore her usual widow's coif and a gown of black velvet with wide, white-furred sleeves. Smiling, she motioned to him to approach, and extended her hand over the small table for him to kiss.

As he did so, the King turned round, revealing his dark, melancholy countenance. He was wearing a doublet of rich black velvet under a sleeveless just-au-corps of white leather embroidered with two golden crescents clasped together by the H and D of his name and Diane's. Tall and vigorous, an adept in all athletic pursuits and passionately devoted to the chase, he yet looked fully ten years older than his age. He had never shaken off the adverse conditions of his youth, the years of captivity as a boy in Spain, a hostage for his father, the brilliant Francis I, the knowledge that that father's love was given to the elder brother who died untimely, and that father's failure, after the first Dauphin's death, to train him, sullen and inarticulate as he was, for the throne which he would inherit. Whatever he had learned, whatever awakening of the spirit had come his way, he owed to the fifty-year-old mistress beside him whose livery he wore, and whom that age of pseudo-chivalry and the *Amadis de Gaule* could quite comfortably view as merely his *inspiratrice*, but who undoubtedly had his heart, and to whom he was almost unwaveringly faithful-as he was to that other great influence of his life, the Constable Anne de Montmorency.

"I would have sent for you earlier, Monsieur de Graeme," said the King, with the affable address which covered a capacity for occasional outbursts of dark fury, "had I known that you returned from Scotland in M. de Villegaignon's squadron. I learnt of it but this morning from a chance remark of M. de Montgomery's. I am naturally eager for further news of my dear daughter the Queen of Scotland, from one who has so recently been in her company."

Conceiving himself censured, Ninian got out some excuse. He had no idea of His Majesty's wish-he had ascertained that the royal courier had arrived at Turin from Brittany within ten days of the landing at Roscoff. The King cut him short.

"Nay, I am not blaming you," he said pleasantly. "But I have sent for you now that Madame la Grande Sénéschale and I may question you about a child who is so dear to me. Did you make the voyage, Monsieur de Graeme-which I hear was sadly tempestuous-in the same galley as her Majesty?"

"No, sire, but I had the privilege of seeing her when we were in harbour in the isle of Arran."

"Tell me of her then," said the King, throwing himself into a chair. "I have here M. de Brézé's letter full of her praises; no doubt but that you will echo them."

"To do otherwise," observed Madame Diane with her pursed smile, "would in M. de Graeme be disloyalty."

So Ninian, standing there, answered questions, attempted a description of his Queen, and gave by request some details of the voyage and its stormy nature.

"There was also a mention in M. de Brézé's letter," said the King, "of the Queen of Scotland's having been saved-he says not by whom-from some savage dog which was about to attack her. Upon a sea-voyage that has a strange sound!"

Not knowing whether this were a question or a mere comment, and uncertain in any case what to reply, Ninian was silent; but Madame Diane, whose eyes had never ceased to study him, remarked: "Your Majesty forgets that M. de Graeme has just told us that he was only for a brief space on board the Queen's galley, nor was he of her train."

"That is true, m'amye," said Henri, turning towards her. "However, wherever this incident took place the child, thank God, unharmed. —Tell me now, Monsieur de Graeme — —"

The door opened rather smartly. "The Princess of Navarre craves an immediate audience, your Majesty," said the usher in a hurried voice.

And without waiting to learn whether her request was granted or no the suppliant appeared almost at the same instant, swept forward, and entirely regardless of the Archer standing there, began with but a dipped curtsy to the King her cousin:

"Here is a fine to-do, your Majesty? That tiresome Antoine-what hare do you think he has started now? Why, that our marriage may not be held valid because of that contract to the Duc de Cleves when I was a child! And my mother — —"

The King's face grew dark, for he had set his heart upon this union.

"What nonsense!" he said sharply. "It is well known that your former marriage was annulled. Vendôme must — —"

"Her Majesty the Queen of Navarre," announced the usher once more.

Only then, as he perceived his aunt bearing down upon him, did the King give Ninian the signal to withdraw. And Ninian, as he left the room was sure, from the expression of the royal authoress, that it was her prospective son-in-law's scruples rather than her daughter's wishes which had her support.

And he had for a moment a clear picture of that marriage ceremony eight years ago at Châtel-herault, when the twelve-year-old and entirely recalcitrant bride, in her heavy cloth of gold and ermine, had suddenly declared herself unable to walk to the altar where the Duc de Clèves awaited her. King Francis had bidden the Constable de Montmorency carry her there; and Ninian, in the King's guard, had with his own eyes beheld this order carried out. Child as Jeanne de Navarre had been then, and in spite of her all-powerful uncle François, she had set her will then as much against her marriage to Guillaume de la Marck as she had set it now as a young woman upon wedding Antoine de Bourbon. And, with King Henri behind her, Ninian thought that the ceremony would probably take place in the end just when and where it was planned to do-at Moulins, whither the court was next to proceed.

He was making for the staircase, to return to the guardroom, when he heard a cough and a rustle behind him, and turning, perceived an elderly waiting-woman who could only be the Queen's.

"Her Majesty desires, Monsieur l'Archer," she said primly, "that you would come to her, if your duties permit."

"Certainly I will come," quoth Ninian. This was something new. He could not remember ever having been summoned by Madame Cathérine before.

Following the discreet, duenna-like figure he soon found himself in a small room furnished partly as an oratory, but decorated by the tactless municipality of Lyons for the occasion, like every other apartment of the royal suite, with the twined initials of the King and of her who was not the Queen. Here-also with writing materials to her hand-sat the other member of this singular *ménage à trois*, true daughter of the Medici, with the ugly mouth and jaw, almost the long nose of the great Lorenzo the Magnificent, her great-grandfather. Catherine's forehead was high and rounded; her large eyes somewhat prominent; she was no beauty. Her dress, rich but severe, had pearls sewn along the juncture of the bodice with its transparent upper portion, and, at the base of the ruff-like collar which opened to expose her throat, a beautiful stone of the hue of an aquamarine engraved with some device or scene, for she had a passion for cut gems. Of the same age almost to a day as her husband, she was still a young woman, and the mother now, after ten disconcerting years of barrenness, of four children.

She greeted the King's archer with the courtesy and affability which she showed to all. Yet for all that, thought Ninian, as he kissed her particularly small and beautiful hand, her thoughts and intentions were a hundred times less easy to guess than those of her triumphant rival a few rooms away, whose pre-eminence she endured with such outward composure. And though the situation was not new to Ninian, since it had gone on for twelve years, at least Catherine was now Queen. Yet as he rose from his knee he saw that the very chair she sat upon was surmounted by the gilded crescent of Diana. How, being a woman and not a sphinx, could she endure to sit in it? . . . That the same crescent and the same twined initials confronted her on his own breast did not occur to him. It had been the Dauphin Henri's device too long for him to feel it strange when it had replaced the salamander of King François there.

"I hear that you made the voyage from Scotland with the little Queen, Monsieur," began Catherine. "His Majesty naturally received despatches from M. de Brézé at Turin, but I am anxious to hear of my daughter from one who has set eyes upon her. You did so, I suppose, Monsieur de Graeme, even though not making the voyage in the same galley?"

"Yes, your Majesty, I had the honour of seeing her once." (How does she know, he thought, that I was not on board the *St. Michel*, when even the King, apparently, did not?)

"She will now, I think," said Catherine as if to herself, "be nearing Blois or Tours on her way to St. Germain. But as there still remains to celebrate the marriage of Monseigneur de Vendôme to the Princess of Navarre I do not know when I shall be able to embrace the child. Yet I am all impatience to see my son's future bride," said the Queen, as naturally as any burgher's wife. "I would I had a portrait of her."

"If your Majesty permits, I will describe her to the best of my ability," volunteered Ninian.

"You would indeed put me in your debt by doing so, Monsieur de Graeme," said Catherine graciously.

Ninian did his best, and, this being his second attempt at word-painting for the benefit of royalty, succeeded, he thought, not so ill. At any rate, when he had finished Catherine put out that marvel of a hand and took out from a small embossed casket beside her a netted purse of gold tissue.

"I pray you accept this, Monsieur de Graeme, as payment for the portrait you have drawn me. The Sieur Monnier, whom His Majesty appointed last year as painter to the royal nursery, had not made me a better."

Thanking her, Ninian bent his knee once more and kissed her hand. The Queen, he knew, was fond of making gifts, in contradistinction to Madame Diane, who preferred to acquire them.

As he left the room, Queen Catherine turned again to one of those urbane letters in which she was continually seeking to oblige her correspondents by the exercise of such small powers of patronage as she possessed. They were seed cast upon waters which must recede in time; for she had twenty years the advantage of Diane de Poitiers. Then would come harvest. . . .

It was not until he reached the stairs that Ninian began to speculate how she, away in her apartment, was aware that the King had sent for him that afternoon, and why; and how she had so exactly timed his interception by her woman.

And a little later, going down the stairs, he suddenly wondered how the royal child in whose company he had come across the sea from his own native shore and hers would fare in this many-tided ocean of the court. She would be another Queen in the arras now-his thoughts had flitted back to Garthrose for an instant-but, scarce out of the cradle though she was, she had already given signs that she would one day be as living an inhabitant of that tapestry as the young Princess of Navarre, whom he had not long left.

8

The French tiring woman removed the half-made gown about which she had been receiving instructions, and Magdalen Lindsay sat down at a table in her bedchamber in the château of Carrières, near St. Germain. It was rather cold there, so that she was glad to see a shaft of thin autumn sunlight strike in through the narrow window, for it gave at least an illusion of warmth. Already, by this second week in November, the Queen of Scots and her train had been lodged in the château for a month, while the cleansing and setting in order of that of St. Germain-en-Laye went forward. This was now finished, but the move thither would not take place until the King came. His arrival from Moulins was expected now every day.

Magdalen had sat down to write a letter to her father in Scotland, but her pen was idle, and after a moment she got up and stood by the window looking out. She could see little but the sky, of a very pale blue, traversed at a considerable rate by wisps of cloud. Yet there was no sound of wind. After three months it still caused her a certain emotion to realise that it was the sky of France. When she felt thus she would sometimes remember with a pang poor young Seton, so overwhelmed with pleasure at Roscoff, who had never completed the journey hither. Short indeed had been his acquaintance with this fair land, for he had died at Ancenis of the flux. Lord Livingstone, too, had been ill for some time, though he was now better.

The girl's thoughts played once more over that leisurely journey. An affair of many stays and stages, it had taken almost exactly two months. There was indeed no hurry for the little Queen to arrive at St. Germain, since King Henri for all his anxiety to see her was occupied elsewhere. And how enchanted the child had been with all she saw-herself enchanting, too, all those who saw her. Brittany had been for all of them a new and strange world, with its outlandish costumes, so gaily embroidered for the men, so sombre for the women, with its uncouth Celtic tongue, its calvaries at every turn, its little chapels to unfamiliar Armorican saints. The great moment of that portion of the journey had been the delivery of the Queen by M. de Brézé to her grandparents, the Duc and Duchesse de Guise, who had travelled across France to meet her, and whose delight in the child had been patent.

Magdalen had looked upon the father and mother of the Queen Mother of Scotland with a certain amount of awe. She had imagined them older; yet the Duchesse Antoinette, born a Bourbon, was but in the early fifties, and had captured the girl's fancy with her long nose and her amiable and intelligent expression. Duke Claude Magdalen revered for his personal courage; had he not been left for dead upon the field of Marignano in 1515 with two and twenty wounds? She had not been long enough in France to know how much of the Guise greed and calculation were his, along with these honourable scars.

Then had come Nantes, and the slow peaceful voyage up the wide Loire in the serene September weather, with constant song and merriment and the children trying to hang over the sides of the barges to watch the water sliding past, while from the banks one proud castle after another watched them go by. At Tours they had left the river, and proceeded by Illiers and Chartres towards Paris, and thereafter to the temporary quarters of the royal children of France in the château of Carrières.

Magdalen's first sight of the little Dauphin she would never forget; she thought, with a shock, that she had never seen a more unhealthy-looking child. The richness of the costume in which his puny little body was encased only accentuated his sickly appearance. Born with a wretched constitution, smitten by small-pox at the age of three, his short life had been-and was to continue —a perpetual struggle against ill-health. And yet, as she soon discovered-and it made his case the more pitiful-the little boy's spirit was alert and gallant; he longed already to emulate his father's physical prowess and looked forward to the day when he could go to the wars. His greeting to his future bride was courtly beyond his years, and they were soon on excellent terms.

* * * * *

The girl came away from the window and sat down anew to her letter.

> *Honoured Father,*
> *Since I last writ to you there hath passed little of moment. Monseigneur the Dauphin*
> *continues to show great pleasure in the company of her Majesty our Queen, and it is verily*
> *a charming sight to see them together. The King of France and the Queen, and in partic-*
> *ular "Madame Diane" have writ many letters of instruction on matters connected with*
> *the royal children to Monsieur and Madame d'Humières, under whose care they are. My*
> *Lady Fleming continues to show me kind — — —*

The door was flung open without ceremony, and a young, excited Scottish face looked in.

"Magdalen, Magdalen, he is on his way! A courier has just arrived."

Magdalen sprang up. "Who? Not the King?"

Jean Ogilvy nodded. "The courier reports that he will be here in a couple of hours. He says that His Majesty, in his haste to enjoy the company of Messeigneurs ses enfants, and to greet his new daughter the Queen of Scots, is hastening hither with but a small escort, ahead of his gentlemen. Come, there is much to make ready!"

That indeed was the case, and the next hour was feverish. The little Scottish girls were all arrayed in their best gowns and coifs, nor did Lady Fleming omit to embellish herself. To M. and Madame d'Humières the occasion was naturally less perturbing. But the Dauphin was greatly excited, not having seen his father for more than six months.

"Now at last, Madame," he was heard to say to his future spouse, "now at last you will behold the great King, my father!"

At the same time Lord Erskine enquired in an aside of Lady Fleming whether her Grace needed further instruction in the deep curtsey which, except to her mother, she had been so seldom called upon to make. As for her four small playmates, the chamber at one moment resembled a dancing school as they all diligently practised their reverences, with their stiff little skirts outspread, till Mary Fleming, to her mother's mortification and her own, toppled over and sat down.

At last everybody was ready and waiting in the hall of the castle, grouped round the great fire at the upper end. Midway down the long apartment the old tapestries which cut it in two swayed almost rhythmically in the draught. Some distance from the fire, in the background, and near a window with ill-fitting glass, Magdalen shivered, yet not, as she was well aware, entirely with cold, but with excitement and a touch of apprehension, too. She was not yet used to courts. She thrust her chilly hands up the wide, bell-shaped sleeves of her gown; even the fur edging seemed to give no warmth.

Then she forgot her physical sensations. There had come a brisk and continued clatter of horse-hoofs; the King and his escort must be riding into the court-yard.

The Dauphin began to jump with impatience; a flush came into the little Queen's face, and for a moment one hand made a wavering movement towards Lady Fleming, just behind her. Then she folded them both resolutely in front of her. Yet it seemed a long time before the two ushers in readiness drew aside the heavy folds of grey and green, and through the aperture came with his vigorous stride, alone, Henri II in his usual costume of black relieved with white, his short cloak swinging, his high boots spattered to the thighs with mud.

The Dauphin gave a little shout and ran forward; then, recollecting himself, advanced more sedately, bent his knee, and formally kissed his father's hand, on which the King stooped and embraced him warmly. He was devoted to his children.

The stage was now set for the meeting of the two crowned heads. Mary Stuart neither hurried nor hung back, and the two sovereigns, the tall, early-grizzled man, and the bright-haired little girl not yet six, met in the centre of the hall. The Queen of Scots dropped a very respectful but not reverential curtsey, and the King of France, removing his plumed cap, stooped —a very long way-and lifted her small hand to his lips. Then, murmuring, "Welcome, my dear daughter," he kissed the cheek which she presented to him. Holding her by the hand, with his other hand on the Dauphin's shoulder, he then advanced towards Madame d'Humières and his three-year-old daughter Elisabeth, whom he caught up in his arms.

"No more measles, I see, my sweet-no more need of that unicorn's horn of the Constable's! Madame, I congratulate you upon my daughter's looks!"

"Indeed, your Majesty," said Madame d'Humières, rising from her deep curtsey, "her Royal Highness has never been in better health."

"And Claude, the sweet chuck?" He bent over the fourteen-month-old princess presented by her nurse. "How she has grown since I saw her last! And my small son Louis . . . asleep elsewhere, no doubt?"

Both the Dauphin and his eldest sister were now pulling at their father, making innumerable requests. "All in good time, little chatter-boxes," said King Henri good-humouredly, "all in good time!" And then he became the King again.

"My lords and ladies, you may now withdraw. Monsieur d'Humières, will you convey my dear daughter the Queen of Scotland and Monseigneur the Dauphin and the Princess Elisabeth to my own apartments, that I may enjoy their society there. —Nay, first there is a further thing to do. If my daughter the Queen of Scotland permits, my escort, the archers of my guard, all of her own nation, who have ridden hither with me, desire to kiss her hand, which will more than recompense them for their hard riding. Do you consent to this, Madame la reine d'Ecosse?"

"With all my heart, your Majesty," said the child sedately, but with brightening eyes.

The King waved his hand towards two chairs of state which stood upon a small dais against the wall. To one of these Lady Fleming conducted the Queen of Scots, waiting, however, for the King to seat himself first in the other. But Henri shook his head good-humouredly, and merely saying, "Bid my escort now enter," went and stood by the great hearth as though to warm himself, his melancholy eyes fixed upon the scene.

Once more the ushers drew apart the tapestry curtains, but wider this time, and through them came in double file a dozen of the archers of the famous Scottish Guard in their white, gold-embroidered surcoats with hanging over-sleeves striped diagonally with gold. Magdalen Lindsay did not recognise in this unfamiliar garb the man who had taken farewell of her at Roscoff, but Mary Stuart had better eyes, for when all the Archers had kissed her hand, she gave a little cry and stood up from her chair, looked hard at the row of Scottish gentlemen gazing at her with such pleasure and emotion, and next moment, like any small girl, had jumped off the dais and was running to King Henri by the hearth.

"Sire, my good father, I have a favour to ask!"

"A favour? Ask what you will, my dear daughter, and it is yours."

"Yonder in your guard," said the little Queen excitedly, "is Master Ninian Graham, who saved me from the savage dog on board the galley. And if your Majesty is willing, I desire him for my own service."

The King looked somewhat astonished, as well he might. "Saved you from a savage dog? Whose-Ah, I remember, M. de Brézé wrote of something of the sort. But how came one of my Archers . . . nay, I remember that also. Monsieur de Graeme, come forward." And as Ninian obeyed, the King went on: "Why, when I summoned you at Lyons, did you not tell me that it was you who saved her Majesty, for I spoke of the affair, I believe?"

"Because it was nothing, sire; only the kindness of her Grace recalls it."

"No, Master Graham is wrong," urged Mary; "it was not nothing. My brother's great dog would have attacked me, had not Master Graham come between. And he was hurt himself-his arm . . ."

The King looked round the circle as if asking for corroboration. Lord Livingstone stepped forward.

"It is perfectly true, your Majesty. The Lord Robert Stuart's dog was excited by the presence of some quails which were in the cabin near her Majesty, and flew at them and her Majesty. It has been a source of gratification to me, as one of the late Keepers of the Queen of Scots, that it was a kinsman of my own who had the honour of saving her from this peril."

"Tudieu! Perils by sea I know her Majesty ran, but I had no notion there were others! And so" —Henri smiled down at the small royal suppliant —"so you wish me to give up Monsieur de Graeme to you! But, madame my daughter, what shall I do if one of my dogs attacks *me* ?"

"*I* shall defend you, my King!" promptly said the Dauphin, laying his hand upon his miniature rapier. "And I shall defend her Majesty the Queen of Scotland, if need be."

"Then she will hardly need Monsieur de Graeme," replied the King, looking fondly upon him. "Well, we will deliberate upon the matter. Now, my children, we will go to my apartments, and you shall tell me, Marie, of all the other incidents of your voyage to the land which you have made happy by your coming."

9

Early next day, even before the rest of his suite had reached Carrières, the King was off to St. Germain to ascertain in person, such was his concern for his children, that all was now in order for their reception there, in the great pile which his father had built. The château had been thoroughly cleaned out, since the court's last stay, such periodical cleansings being highly necessary, and forming indeed one of the reasons for the frequent royal changes of residence. The report was already going about that King Henri was enraptured with the little Queen of Scots, who was, he had told her gouvernante, the most perfect child he had ever seen. Nor, added one or two observers, had he appeared ill-pleased with the gouvernante herself.

Had not the other eleven Archers who had ridden with the King from Moulins to Carrières been Scots like himself, and rapt to heaven by the sight of their child queen, Ninian might have had to undergo some chaffing about the notice bestowed upon him, and his little sovereign's ingenuous request. As it was, he was an object of envy to them for the privilege of having done the royal child a service. And Ninian himself never gave the request another thought, save to bless the warm childish heart which had prompted it.

And now, for a time at least, Court and royal nursery were under the same roof at St. Germain-en-Laye. This, therefore, was the opportunity to present to Mistress Magdalen Lindsay the veil, of the finest Cyprus lawn, which Ninian had bought for her in Lyons; accordingly one afternoon, when his spell of duty was over, he disposed the little packet in his doublet and made ready to mount to the apartments of the Queen of Scots which were, by the King's desire, over those of the Constable. But his intention was frustrated, for the moment at least, since he was at that very point of time summoned to the King's presence.

Henri II had not long come in from hunting in the great forest of St. Germain, and was in his cabinet with some of his nobles and gentlemen, all discussing the number and ferocity of the boars which had fallen to their spears. He beckoned the Archer to come to him in the embrasure of a window, a little apart. As usual after indulging his master passion, the chase, he was in a cheerful mood.

"I have sent for you, my good Graeme," he began, "because I have not forgotten your courage and address in the matter of the dog which attacked the Queen of Scotland, nor the Queen's request to have you attached to her household, which she has since renewed to me. But even the Dauphin has not yet his separate household, and I wish her Majesty to be brought up, for the next few years, with the Princess Elisabeth in the household of the Enfants de France."

He paused, and Ninian said respectfully: "So one has understood, sire," and wondered why he should have been summoned to the royal presence to hear this.

"Nevertheless," pursued the King, "the Queen has within that household her own particular attendants. Therefore, although I am sorry to lose you from my guard, Monsieur de Graeme, I have, to please my new daughter, decided to reward you by creating a post for you amongst them."

"Your Majesty is very good," murmured Monsieur de Graeme, considerably taken aback.

"I have ascertained from the Queen's gouvernante, Madame de Flamyn," went on Henri, playing with the medal hanging from his neck, "that her Majesty has a great desire to perfect her horsemanship, for it seems that, in spite of her youth, she has already ridden a little in her own country. I know you to be a skilful horseman, and it is my intention to appoint you to the post of Master of the Horse to the Queen of Scotland. The brevet is being prepared, and you will take up your duties on the first of December. For those duties you would do well to consult the Lords of Erskine and Livingstone" (the royal pronunciation was Asquin and Leviston). "Seek out one or two peaceable palfreys for the Queen's use, and when occasion offers, instruct her carefully. I need not urge you, a Scot, to take the utmost care of her royal person. —Does this not please you, Monsieur de Graeme?"

To which Ninian, still in a state of bewilderment, replied: "Your Majesty's will is my pleasure."

"That is no answer, my friend," said the King, clapping him on the shoulder. "I give you leave to be perfectly frank, for I love frankness in those about me." And he perhaps really thought that he did.

"Then, if I may say so with respect," responded Ninian, "it is somewhat of a blow to me to give up my place in your Majesty's bodyguard, and lose the privilege of watching over your royal person."

The King was evidently not ill-pleased at this response. "You will still have a sovereign to guard-and your own. I am but lending you to her service; your name shall remain upon the muster-roll of my faithful Scottish Archers. When her Majesty of Scotland has her own establishment, you shall return; and meanwhile you will be one of the few Scots about her, for in general it is better that she should be served by French men and women, and most of her train I am sending back to Scotland."

"Indeed, Sire, I am grateful for the opportunity," said Ninian. "I need have no divided allegiance."

"Then, my dear Grand Ecuyer, that is happily concluded!" As he kissed the royal hand that title fell upon Ninian's ears with a faintly ridiculous sound. So swelling a name to bear for teaching a child to ride! Yet it was an honour, a great honour, to be thus singled out . . . and the child was the Queen of Scots, whose liege subject he was, whose face he had averred, at Garthrose, that he so much longed to see. . . .

Still half bewildered, he made his way through the laughing groups of hunters to the door, and had nearly reached it when he heard his name called. Turning, he saw that he was being addressed by that young and brilliant captain, François de Guise, Duc d'Aumale, the scar of the two-year-old wound which had nearly cost him his life under the walls of Boulogne, and which had gained him the epithet of le Balafré, livid across his cheek.

"It is you, Monsieur, is it not, who, chancing to be on the galley which brought my niece the Queen of Scotland hither, saved her from a savage dog?"

"I had that privilege, Monseigneur," answered Ninian, standing stiff and soldierly.

"I think I have not heard your name?" said the Duc courteously. " — —Graeme? Then, Monsieur de Graeme, I pray you to receive this as a small token of the gratitude of my family, and of my father the Duc de Guise in particular." And taking off the flat gold chain, richly worked, and set with jewels, which hung down upon his doublet, he put it round Ninian's neck, and, before the Scot could either refuse it or stammer out his thanks, said quickly: "If ever you need help in your turn, remember that the whole House of Lorraine is in your debt!" and turned away again.

With this valuable gift glittering upon his white surcoat, and the Duc d'Aumale's still more valuable pledge sounding in his ears, Ninian found himself at last mounting the stairs to the little Queen's apartments. His mind was still a medley of exhilaration and regret. He would not wear that surcoat with the royal badge much longer, he who had been in the Scottish Archers since he was four-and-twenty. But he was thinking that if he did meet with Mistress Lindsay, and had not to deliver the veil to an intermediary, he could tell her his news, and see with his own eyes whether it happened to please her, or was a matter of indifference.

As he gained the landing he heard a rapid pitter-patter of small feet, and beheld two little girls running hand in hand through an open door towards him, as fast as their long stiffened skirts would allow. For an instant he wondered if one of them was his sovereign, but soon recognised two of her child companions who, he suspected, were up to some mischief. At this rate they would soon come to the top of the stairs and might tumble down them. He took a few steps towards them and held his arms wide.

"Stop, stop, little mistresses! Are you running away to take ship back to Scotland?"

The sight of the Archer standing there barring their way had already caused the children to pause, looking a little alarmed. But the smile on his face reassured them, and one-it was Mary Livingstone-said gravely in her small, sweet voice:

"We are not running away at all, sir. We were seeking a place to hide —'tis a game we play."

"But does my Lady Fleming——" began Ninian, and broke off as the sound of hurrying footsteps came again to his ears. And along came, to his pleasure, Magdalen Lindsay herself.

"Bairns, bairns, what has taken you? Oh, Master Archer, have you . . . why, it is Master Graham!"

And, a hand of the not too unwillingly recaptured Maries in each of her own, she looked up at him smiling, out of those clear dark-blue eyes under the brows like a blackbird's feather.

Ninian smiled back. "You are wondering, Mistress Lindsay, what I do up in these regions-though perhaps 'tis as well I met these truants of yours. The reason for my presence is my desire to pay my debt to a certain charitable lady. And as I have had the good fortune to come upon her so soon, perhaps she will accept the repayment now." And thrusting a hand into his breast he brought out the little packet and offered it to her.

Magdalen Lindsay undid the wrapping, while the little girls stood on tiptoe to see, and gave an exclamation. Round the edge of the snow-white piece of lawn ran a tiny gossamer-like embroidery of pale heart-shaped leaves. A flush mounted into Magdalen's cheeks as she recognised from what tree they came.

"Oh, Master Graham! . . . but this is much too fine for me. And . . . you had it worked for me . . . you did not buy it thus."

"And how do you know that, pray?" asked Ninian, half-teasingly; it gave him a sudden sharp delight to see that delicate pink on the pale cheek.

"Why . . . are they not the leaves of the linden, the badge of the Lindsays?"

"They are," said Ninian. "I found an embroiderer in Lyons——"

"Let me see, let me see!" clamoured both the Maries at once, and while the childish heads bent over the gift Magdalen said to the giver: "Never have I owned a veil like this! But indeed, Master Graham, this is worth tenfold that poor thing which I took off in the galley."

"Not to me!" said Ninian, and so meaningly that the colour which had been fading rose again in the girl's face. "It is a fair exchange then, if you will accept this veil."

"Indeed I will, and gratefully. I shall wear it at Monseigneur d'Aumale's wedding, and be the envied of all."

Half unconsciously, at the mention of that name, Ninian glanced down for a second at his breast, and Magdalen's eyes followed his.

"You are admiring my fine chain?" he said, half laughing. "The Duc d'Aumale himself put it about my neck, and now I, too, shall have something to wear when he weds Mlle. d'Este. . . . No, Mistress Lindsay, indeed I am not of his intimates. I think it is the first time that one of his house hath ever spoken to me. But it seems that Messeigneurs de Guise are grateful for the small service which I was able to render her Majesty that day on the galley."

"Lord Robert Stuart's dog!" she exclaimed. "Oh, sir, I am indeed glad that they are grateful. They had cause," she added gravely.

"I saw you fight with the great dog, sir," piped up a small voice. Ninian had almost forgotten the presence of the two little girls. "I was not frightened, but Mary Beaton"—she pointed an accusing finger across Magdalen's skirts—"she cried!"

"She was a great deal nearer to the dog than you were," said the maid-of-honour reprovingly. "Yes, her Majesty owes a heavy debt to Master Graham, and we know that she wishes she could repay it."

Ninian glanced down for a moment, surprising the golden-haired Mary Beaton in the act of putting out her tongue at her detractor. Of these small folk he was like to see more in future. Suppressing a smile, he looked up again.

"She has repaid it, Mistress Lindsay. That is to say, King Henry has granted her the request she was gracious enough to make."

The pools of Magdalen's eyes deepened. "You would say, sir, that you are to be attached to the Queen's person?"

"For the present, yes."

"As . . . ?"

"As . . . Master of the Horse-or, it would be more fitting to say, as Master of the Palfreys! For it seems that our little Queen desires to ride. Is that so?"

"We all desire to ride," came up the same childish voice. "Will Master Archer teach us too, Mistress Lindsay?"

Mistress Lindsay must have surprised on the just-appointed Grand Ecuyer's countenance something which he himself did not know was there. "You regret this!" she said quickly, in a low voice. "You are a soldier, and you like it not, this new charge!"

"I am a Scot," answered Ninian promptly, "and, like you, Mistress, proud to serve my Queen in any guise. And because I am a soldier I obey a command-and accept an honour-without question."

The girl looked as though rebuked; then she saw the kindliness of his smile. "Come, children, we must go back," she said. "Give me my beautiful veil." She held out her other hand and said softly, as he raised it to his lips: "You know that all about the Queen's person will welcome you, Monsieur le Grand Ecuyer!"

10

"I canna but feel it's a peety, Maister Ninian," said Sandy Forbes, Ninian's middle-aged body-servant, who had been with him ever since he came to France, looking down at what he was folding up and putting away. "I'm wonderin' when ye'll pit this on again. Ou aye, I ken it's fine to sairve oor ain wee Queen —I ken that!"

His sentiments reflected pretty exactly Ninian's own. It was the first of December, and here he was, habited like any other private gentleman, no longer, save technically, an Archer of the King's Scottish Bodyguard with its record of honourable service of a century and a quarter. What he was chiefly going to regret, he fancied, was the loss of the society of his comrades, fellow-Scots, all of them. The old intimacy, the old communal life, was shattered, even though he could count on seeing Patrick Rutherford and the rest from time to time, when the Court and the royal nursery happened, as now, to be established under the same roof. And the King loved to have his children near him.

But he went towards the apartments of the Queen of Scots and the Princess Elisabeth with none too joyous a heart beneath his grey doublet.

It was a very quiet interior upon which he entered. None of the Queen's little playmates was there for fear of passing on to her the cold which Mary Livingstone had caught from the Dauphin's so constant store, and which was indeed this morning confining him to his bed. A great fire burnt in the room, a fire too large for it. By it on a low stool sat the Princess Elisabeth nursing a doll, with a French maid-of-honour in attendance. In the centre of the room stood an embroidery frame, at which was seated Lady Fleming, working, while the child Queen, standing beside her, a skein of bright silks drooping from her hand, watched the needle go in and out. The only sound was the yapping set up by a litter of puppies in the far corner of the room.

The first person to move was Lady Fleming, who rose with a smile and dropped him a curtsey. "Welcome, sir!" The Queen stood where she was for a moment, overtopped by the great embroidery frame, then letting fall the skein of silk danced a few steps forward as one who sees a friend enter.

"You are verily come, Master Graham? You have left the Archer Guard for my sake?"

Ninian went down on one knee before her. "Yes, Your Majesty. I am come to be your very humble servant."

Child rather than Queen at that instant, she clapped her hands together, so that he was unable to kiss one of them. And she went on almost without drawing breath: "I wish to have a white palfrey with a very long tail . . . and a dapple-grey . . . and I think a black horse. Master Graham, if you can procure me a black horse I shall call it 'Sultan,' or perchance 'Morocco.' "

"Marie," said Lady Fleming, intervening, "Master Graham waits to kiss your hand. Do not keep him longer upon his knee."

"I crave your pardon, Master Graham!" said the child instantly; and next moment, not without a recurrence of the emotion he had felt upon the galley, Ninian was putting a small warm hand to his lips. The last Queen's hand which he had so saluted had been Queen Catherine's, that day at Lyons.

Yet he was still unable to rise from his position, for all at once he perceived at his elbow the still smaller form of the Princess Elisabeth, holding out, in embarrassing proximity to his face, the totally unmeaning countenance of her doll, and uttering some command or request which he was not sufficiently quick to interpret. But the French maid-of-honour had hurried to the scene.

"The Princess wishes you to kiss her doll, Monsieur. If you would have the complaisance to do so, lest she should weep. . . . She is a little fretful to-day."

Ninian hastily complied, the doll's owner meanwhile imparting some completely unintelligible information about it. He was fond of children, and this was, after all, a child of royal blood, but he was not altogether sorry that he was on his feet again when the door opened and there came in, behind Madame d'Humières, the tall, burly, bearded figure of perhaps the greatest man in the realm, Anne de Montmorency, Grand Constable of France.

He was fresh from the barbarities of his repression of the revolt in Guienne, he was at all times rude, overbearing, cruel and grasping, he had immense possessions all over France and the King's ear always, but, father himself of eleven children (whose nests he was busy feathering), he could also concern himself with the Dauphin's insufficient use of his pocket handkerchief, recommend his keeping indoors in cold weather, and write constant letters of advice upon nursery matters to his kinsman d'Humières, the prince's governor, and to Madame d'Humières-whose own offspring numbered eighteen. And directly she saw him the little princess, dropping her doll, ran towards him with outstretched arms, crying: "What have you brought me-what have you brought me?"

The soldier-statesman picked her up and held her high in the air. "Ah, my little mistress, I must have payment before I give it to you! One kiss, that is all!"

And the future bride of Philip II of Spain threw her little arms round his neck and was kissed by the ironic mouth whose rough speech had earned Anne de Montmorency the title of *le grand rabroueur* .

II. THE MAY TREE AT ST. GERMAIN

(June-September, 1549) —(1)

A June day was flaunting over Paris, its blue skies and green foliage vying with the banners and the tapestry-hung windows, for a week of banquets and processions had just passed over that still medieval city constricted within its girdle of walls and towers, with its dark and narrow streets, where even the town dwellings of the nobles had the look of castle keeps. The daughter of the Medici was Queen now-that is to say, she was a crowned Queen, for in other respects her sway was no whit more potent than before. The King's heart was still, as it would be to the end, in the possession of Madame Diane, created last autumn Duchesse de Valentinois.

But the tenth of June, 1549, had seen Catherine crowned in state at St. Denis, and to-day, the eighteenth, she had made her solemn entry into the capital in an open litter whose silver hangings had swept the dusty streets. The King having made his ceremonial entry two days previously, they were both, with the Court, at the Palace of the Tournelles, inconvenient as it was, since the new palace of the Louvre was still in the hands of the builders.

Yet, since it was a public holiday, there was no hammering to come over the still remaining walls of the old Louvre, all towered and crenellated, to the ears of the three men who stood by the moat, on the river side, talking together in the sunshine. Two of them wore the white of the Scottish Archer Guard, the third was habited as any ordinary gentleman.

"And so our little Queen saw neither to-day's junketings nor the Queen's entry!" remarked Patrick Rutherford, who was one of the Archers.

"No," replied her Master of the Horse, "for his Majesty-and the Constable and Madame Diane also-feared some infection from the crowds of Paris for the children. But the Dauphin and her Majesty my mistress were at the Queen's coronation a week ago."

"Aye," put in Heriot, the other Archer, "I saw them there, and right bonny she looked, bless her heart, in her gown of gold damask! But they did well who would not bring our Scots rose-bud into the air of this city."

"It was strange, Ninian, passing strange," said Patrick Rutherford reflectively, "not to have you at my side that day, as at the King's coronation. D'ye mind that we stood together-and were a thought weary, that long day at Rheims?"

"I mind of it well," answered Ninian. He gave a half-checked sigh. "It was strange to me also, two days agone, to be an onlooker here in Paris, and to see the King ride past in his white armour, instead of riding behind him."

"But you are a great man now, Monsieur le Grand Ecuyer!" said Heriot, smiling, "no longer, like our humble selves, one among many. And how heavy are your duties? Doth her Majesty ride much? Faith, I would fain see her in the saddle!"

"Until last month it was not thought well that she should ride at all, but now the summer is come she begins. So you see that although I have held my post seven months and more, my duties have not been heavy. The main has been to see that the palfreys and jennets were kept in good condition. And now indeed it is time I were on my way back to St. Germain. To our next meeting!"

With a wave of the hand he turned away in the direction of the Rue de l'Autruche.

"There goes a good Archer wasted," observed Heriot, looking after him. "I warrant he knows it at heart himself. To keep palfreys in condition for a child!"

"Are you not forgetting who the child is?" asked Patrick Rutherford gravely.

2

With Sandy Forbes behind him, Ninian rode westwards along the banks of the shining river between Bougival and St. Germain. It was good to be out of the city again, to hear the lark overhead, and see the shadows chase each other over the thickly wooded slopes. The first rapture of spring was over, but everything was green and joyous beyond belief. What, he was wondering as he rode, had been Queen Catherine's thoughts to-day. Had she recalled those splendid wedding ceremonies at Marseilles in 1533, which had brought thither to marry her, a bride of fourteen, her kinsman Pope Clement VII, the King of France and more than half a score of cardinals?

And then his thoughts went to another Queen-his own little royal mistress with her enchanting ways, to whom he was now hastening back. Never, surely, had there been a child like her in palace or in cottage! Because of her he was able to smother the regrets which did sometimes assail him for the life and the comradeship which he had given up. . . . At St. Germain there was another attraction, too, though he would hardly admit it to himself. He could not name what it was which drew or seemed to draw Magdalen Lindsay and himself increasingly together, despite the sixteen years or so which lay between them. It was not, he assured himself, that the memory of his lost love was growing fainter; Béatrice was for ever apart. But it could not be his fancy that Magdalen had something of Béatrice in her! . . .

Yet the days in which he could look at Magdalen Lindsay and study that resemblance were numbered, for she was to return to Scotland next month, the year for which her father had lent her to the Queen's service being nearly sped. All Ninian would have for remembrance then would be his own conviction of an unspoken sympathy between them which, as he told himself now, was probably occasioned by nothing more than the natural drawing together of fellow-Scots in a foreign land. For, as King Henri had decreed, nearly all the little Queen's compatriots were by now gone back to their native land. Lady Fleming, of course, remained, but she was assisted as *dame d'atours* by a Frenchwoman, Madame de Curel-whom indeed the Duchesse de Guise would have preferred to see made gouvernante herself, though conceding that the choice of Lady Fleming had the great advantage that the Scotswoman had known the Queen and her constitution from birth. On the male side of her little establishment the Sieur de Curel, her major-domo, Antoine de Layac, one of the two *panetiers* or pantlers, and her *écuyer tranchant* were French. Her cup-bearer indeed was a Scot, Arthur Erskine, Lord Erskine's fifth son, as was her almoner, the Prior of Inchmahome, an Erskine also; but her chaplain Messire Guillaume de Laon, was French, as were not unnaturally her tailor, dancing master and apothecary.

* * * * *

In the gardens at St. Germain the Dauphin and his future bride were playing with a hind which had been given him by the Constable. A page held its leash, and the little prince was trying to make the gentle, unwilling creature eat a handful of daisies; half timid, half trustful, it glanced about with its liquid eyes all the time. But directly the Dauphin became conscious of Ninian's arrival upon the lawn he left his pet, and ran over the sward towards the new-comer, followed at a more sedate pace by the Queen of Scots, a daisy-chain dangling from her head.

"Monsieur de Graeme," he cried, "tell me about the entry! Was it a fine procession; did the people cheer a great deal?"

"Indeed, they did, Monseigneur," answered Ninian, smiling. "And her Majesty was magnificently arrayed, and so was the whole city."

"And the King my father?" asked the little boy eagerly. "What did he wear-how did he look?"

"But, as your Royal Highness knows, the King made his entry two days ago, and as you have already heard, he — —"

"But tell me again!" demanded François.

"Well then," said Ninian good-humouredly, "first you must know, my prince, that over his Majesty's head as he rode the four sheriffs of Paris held a canopy of light blue velvet covered with golden fleur-de-lis, edged with gold and embroidered with his Majesty's arms. Apart from that, all about the King was white; he rode a beautiful white horse caparisoned in cloth of silver; he wore white armour, with a tunic of cloth of silver over it, and a hat of white satin covered with silver lace. I heard that his white plume was sown with pearls, but that I could not see for myself, though I saw rubies and diamonds sparkling on the silver scabbard of his sword."

Still clutching a few dishevelled daisies the little prince hung upon his words. So also did someone of maturer years, and when Ninian finished he heard a little sigh of pleasure behind him.

"Ah, Master Graham," said Lady Fleming meltingly, "would that I had been in your place! Surely his most gracious Majesty is worthy of the name his royal father bore-surely he too is *le roi chevalier*! And his kindness! Do you know that he is striving to bring about the release of my son who is still a captive in England, and that he has deigned to write on the matter to her Majesty the Queen-Mother in Scotland?" Gratitude made her handsomer than ever.

"Indeed I trust, madam, that his Majesty's efforts will be successful," said Ninian courteously. He had observed on one or two occasions in the King's manner towards the attractive Scotswoman a something which, had that monarch's heart not been so securely held by Madame Diane, would have suggested possibilities of an intrigue. But surely, matters standing in that quarter as they did, such a thing was impossible!

By this time the little Queen was intent on fastening about her gouvernante's wrist the daisy chain which she had fashioned, and a dispute had broken out between the Dauphin and his little sister Elisabeth, who had just come up with Madame d'Humières.

"I want to play with the little deer too!" she stammered. "Madame, bid François let me play with the little deer!"

"You shall not play with my hind!" asseverated the Dauphin angrily. "You are too small." And as his sister tried to run past him, he put his arms round her and held her prisoner.

Madame d'Humières detached the two, and the little boy held out his hand to Mary. "Come," he said, and the two ran back. Ninian watched them. What a contrast-the boy so sickly, with his perpetual catarrh and intermittent ear-ache, and the girl-child glowing with health and vitality.

"I want my husband!" said the Princess Elisabeth querulously, referring by this strange pet name to the Constable of France. "He promised me a dog. But I shall ask him to bring me a . . . a little lion!"

3

The sun had gone down in serenity and glory; the Seine, running some two hundred feet below the scarp on which the château so nobly reared its bulk, was no longer coloured by its departing glory. Now that the royal children had supped and were safely in bed some of the members of their household strolled in the coolness up and down the sanded walks near the lawn where they had played.

To the Queen of Scots' Master of the Horse and to her cup-bearer there presently joined himself that young gentleman, Charles de Pontevez, Chevalier de Brion, her esquire trenchant.

"Hé, messieurs, a fine evening! I warrant it will bring out some of the ladies, too. I think I see some already, stealing forth like the bird of night."

"If you mean the owl, Monsieur de Brion," returned Arthur Erskine, "then give me leave to say your image is not of the most gallant."

"By the bird of night, my dear *échanson* , I meant the nightingale, no less. Or, if you like it better, stealing out like stars. Indeed, there is one of your countrywomen here, Messieurs, whom I could well compare, since I am in the vein, to the moon-as beautiful as she, and as pale. What a pity, is it not, that as with the moon we shall soon be deprived of her light, and I fear for ever . . . unless one could take some step to persuade her to remain on this side the sea!"

Ninian involuntarily stiffened. It was clear whom the Chevalier meant. Arthur Erskine gave a laugh.

"Your step of persuasion, I suppose, Monsieur de Brion, would be to propose marriage to the lady?"

"And why not?" retorted the young Frenchman airily.

Ninian slipped behind and detached himself. A sudden bitter jealousy ran through him like fire. Perhaps-though his tone had not sounded exactly like it —M. de Brion with his nightingales and moons was really contemplating something of the sort. Perhaps indeed he had already received sufficient encouragement to warrant such a proposal.

He must have speech with Mistress Magdalen Lindsay at once. But neither of the two ladies pacing arm-in-arm over there was she, he could tell. It was her night for watch, no doubt, in the chamber where slept the little Queen and the Princess Elisabeth, dreaming perhaps of a lion-cub. . . . He turned away.

Could this young Frenchman be wooing Magdalen Lindsay-could she be listening to his wooing? Was he himself to learn that she was unattainable just when he had come to know that he wanted her? But if not to young Charles de Pontevez, then he must lose her to her father . . . unless indeed she would consent to marry *him* if he asked her. But though Ninian was not wont to feel his years nor even think of them, he had nine and thirty of them on his shoulders now, and Magdalen Lindsay, he believed, but three-and-twenty. He saw no reason which would incline her to accept his hand.

Pacing moodily along with bent head, all but unconscious of his surroundings, he perceived that he had come to the end of the high garden, and to the place where its verge was threatened by the lateral terracing down to the river which the King was planning to put in hand. Just there stood a quincunx of hawthorn trees, formally planted and pruned, but yet, last month, as full of blossom as their hedgerow sisters. Ninian had heard Magdalen saying not long ago that they reminded her of Scotland; and so when he found himself approaching them, he would have thought of her even had she not already been filling his mind to the exclusion of any other person. It was therefore-at first-no shock to see in the dimming light a woman's figure standing under the farthest may-tree looking out over the river . . . and to recognise it.

But when he had done so he stopped dead, and that unwonted and cruel flame spired up again in his heart. Why was she here at this hour, alone? To meet her French gallant? There was something white glimmering in her hand —a letter of assignation, perhaps. She was waiting for the Chevalier de Brion!

He would soon make sure. And this time, as he advanced with a quick and almost threatening step, the girl under the hawthorn turned her head.

Ninian doffed his cap. "It is I, Mistress Lindsay-Ninian Graham. I disturb you, perhaps; you were — —" No, now that he was so close to her under the flowerless branches, intuition told him that she was not waiting for anyone, and he substituted rather sadly, "you were taking farewell of this prospect?"

But her voice, to his surprise, was joyous as she answered: "No, no, Master Graham. There is no need now for me to bid farewell to St. Germain. I am not returning to Scotland after all; I am to bide here with her Majesty."

"Not returning-you are to bide here!" stammered Ninian, his heart leaping in a most unaccustomed manner. He took a step nearer; the hawthorn suddenly seemed in flower above him. Then he knew that it was not. "You bide in France to . . . to wed, perhaps?" (And indeed the ice in his tone would have frozen any blossom).

"To wed!" exclaimed Magdalen in astonishment. And then she laughed. "Is that, Master Graham, the only reason which would keep me in France? No, it is another who weds-my father! He is to marry again. I had his letter but to-day. And thus I need not leave the Queen."

Was she not of those whose lightest word is true? Ninian knew that he need have no fear of misinterpreting the joy which thrilled through her voice in that last phrase. The answering joy in his own heart carried him on a surge past those reefs he had thought so formidable, the difference in age, his own comparative poverty. Unmindful that he crumpled the letter which she held, he caught her hands.

"Magdalen! Then I can say it! Surely you have known these many months that I love you! I believe I have loved you since that day at Roscoff-nay, since I first saw you on the Queen's galley. Say that you will be my wife!"

She made no answer in words, but yielded herself with only the most momentary reluctance to his arms, and he did not long have to seek her lips. And afterwards, as she hid her face against his breast, murmuring his name, he fell to kissing the white hand which clutched his doublet. The hawthorn *was* in flower-and sweet with scent.

(4)

And now began for Ninian Graham a second spring, a time of such happiness as he had never thought could be his again. Although it was not passion which he had to offer Magdalen Lindsay, his service and his surroundings seemed lifted for a while into a realm more serene and timeless than that actual world of his experience, which alternated so sharply between pageants and executions, banquets and slaughter. Yet the impacts of that world could not be escaped, for July came in with its sunshine horribly challenged by the fires which only a dozen miles away in Paris-and so soon after the festivities of mid-June —were consuming Huguenots. It was true that the King, who had witnessed the spectacle from a window, was so haunted by it that he vowed never to witness another such; unfortunately he had not vowed that the just-revived Chambre Ardente should not continue its work. . . . Not being of his guard now, Ninian escaped having to watch the holocaust of July 4th, and was thankful for it.

But burnings at the stake were one thing, war quite another, and when in the middle of August the Archer Guard accompanied the King, as was natural, to the camp before Boulogne, which town it had been decided to wrest by a final attempt from the English, it was with some misgiving that Magdalen asked her betrothed whether he did not deeply regret his change of service. He told her that he would have done so, save for a certain compensating circumstance, the nature of which she might be able to guess. Nevertheless, there was really only one hour when his absence from the Guard did not fret him, and that was the hour when the news came that the Constable de Montmorency had treacherously surprised and cut to pieces the garrison of one of the forts while they were actually treating for surrender. Ninian liked not the deed; and then told himself rather bitterly that this was a scruple natural to a man whose mission in life was now to lead a little girl about on a pony.

With September he broached the question of the date of his marriage, which there seemed no reason to delay. Magdalen agreed to sound Lady Fleming on the subject, her kinswoman knowing and approving of the betrothal and having always shown herself gracious to the Master of the Horse. But when, the next day, Ninian came to the ante-chamber of the Queen's apartments to learn the result of her conversation, Magdalen met him with a face very different from yesterday's.

"Alas, Ninian, it seems that our marriage cannot be thought of! My kinswoman says that she will make discreet enquiries, but she is sure that neither Queen Catherine nor Madame de Valentinois would allow it, while I remain a maid of honour, and that His Majesty would be most seriously displeased if he heard but a whisper of it. So that, unless I give up my post about the Queen's person . . ." She broke off and looked at her lover imploringly. "Truly, I think it would almost kill me to do that!"

Ninian took the blow in silence. Then, seeing the tears which had sprung to those clear and candid eyes, he fought down his own feelings. "You shall not give it up," he said, taking her hands. "We must wait awhile-though God knows that is the last thing I desire to do."

"Yes," said the girl more cheerfully, "if we have patience, if we watch for some good opportunity, we shall surely obtain leave to wed."

"Nevertheless, Mistress Lindsay," admonished Ninian, "my stock of patience is not over-large, and I warn you that when it is emptied, permission or no permission, you will marry me!"

For answer his betrothed, disengaging her hands, put a finger to her lips and, beckoning him to follow, tiptoed to one of the doors leading from the ante-room. Very cautiously she then pushed back a sliding panel in the upper half and motioned to him to take her place and look through.

Ninian did so, and saw, framed as in a picture, and outlined clear against the many-paned window of the chamber within, a man in sober attire and a little girl of seven, seated on opposite sides of a table. The tutor was pointing with a pen to some words written upon a sheet of paper which lay between them.

"*Corona* , a crown," he was saying slowly and distinctly, " —nominative case singular —*rosarum* , of roses-genitive case plural —*habet* , has-verb of the second conjugation in the present indicative tense, third person singular —*spinas* , thorns-accusative case plural." He ceased to point. "Observe, Madame, that all these nouns are of the first declension, which we are now considering, ending as to the nominative case singular in *a* , in the genitive in *æ* . To these we will add to-day *puella* , a maiden, *aquila* , an eagle, *columba* , a dove, *mensa* , a table, and-ahem, most appropriate to our studies —*regina* , a queen. I desire your Majesty to repeat these nouns."

Very serious, upright, and a model of attention, she who was Regina Scotorum repeated them.

"And now, could your Majesty frame a sentence with them such as I have just shown you upon this paper, employing the verb *habere* in the present tense, and the cases proper to the occasion?"

Her Majesty considered. Then she glanced down at her lap and Ninian saw a tiny smile lift the corner of her mouth. "What, Maître Olivier," she enquired, "is the Latin for a cat?"

"I fear, Madame, that it is an animal —*feles, felis* —which cannot be dealt with until your Majesty arrives at the third declension."

"Then I must make haste," said Mary, "for the cat is here already. See!" And she suddenly produced a sleepy white kitten from its couch on her lap. "And I wish to feed it-but is milk of the third declension also? Poor Minette!" She held the kitten to her cheek.

And as Maître Olivier, looking for a moment as if he did not know whether he were being made game of or no by that small, smiling intelligence, murmured automatically, "*Lac, lactis* ," Ninian, afraid of being discovered in his eavesdropping, turned away and slid home the panel.

"You could not take me away from *that* , for ever!" urged Magdalen, clinging to him. And he answered: "No, my heart, I could not, and I will not . . . yet."

III. MALISE GRAHAM'S SON

(May, 1550-February, 1551) —(1)

At Anet in Normandy, in the pleasant valley of the Eure, between Evreux, Dreux and Mantes, some forty miles from Paris, the lords of Brézé had since 1444 possessed a medieval castle. To this castle, thirty-six years ago, the last of them, the ugly, middle-aged Louis de Brézé, Sieur de Maulevrier, Grand Seneschal of Normandy, had brought his fourteen-year-old bride, the Demoiselle Diane de Poitiers; and here (and elsewhere) had lived with her for seventeen years in undisturbed wedlock and the company of two daughters until his death in 1531, after which he lay in the magnificent tomb which his widow erected in Rouen Cathedral, under an epitaph breathing that undying affection to which her never-abandoned mourning attire was to testify until the end of her life.

But nowadays, when a man spoke of the Château d'Anet, he meant something very different from that tenth-century fortress. A great Renaissance palace had risen in its place. For its construction and adornment the Grande Sénéschale, having at her command the great sums which her royal lover poured into her lap from the public revenues, was able to command all the skill and taste of the day. So Philibert de l'Orme was its architect and Jean Goujon's hand wrought the sculptures and much of the ornament; the glass was by Cousin and the enamels the work of the two Limosins. Very soon the place became the marvel of the age —"that Paradise of Anet" as du Bellay called it; more splendid, surely, than the golden house of Nero, pronounced an Italian traveller.

Of immense size, the actual building occupied three sides of a square, a majestic gateway and its adjuncts filling the other. Behind it lay a great garden full of rare flowers; there was a vast park, a chapel, an orangery, an infirmary, an aviary, a heronry, all kinds of dependencies. Above the great portal of the main façade, which was seventy feet high, stood the statue of Louis de Brézé; letters of gold proclaimed on the black marble below, without any sense of incongruity, that *Diana pergrata* had placed it there *ut diuturna sui sint monumenta viri*. Similarly the stone balustrade above the moat beyond the outer gateway showed his initials alternating with hers, interspersed with the palms of mourning, and with the Greek capital deltas and the crescents which recalled her name and her attributes as goddess.

But elsewhere-and everywhere-it was either the conjoined H. and D. of Henri and Diane which prevailed, on column and pavement, frieze and ceiling, tapestries, furniture and ware, even on the books in the library, or else the emblems of Artemis, arrows, crescents, javelins, and scenes from her story. For, crowning the façade, Actaeon was torn to pieces by his hounds, and, in the left-hand courtyard, the sun warmed the lovely marble limbs of Goujon's masterpiece, just set in place above the fountain, the seated Diane chasseresse fondling her stag. Even the high roofs of the building bore a crest of gilded half-moons, even the cross on the chapel displayed the same emblem on its arms-and there, too, the weathercock turned its openwork H. and D. to the four winds. Madame de Valentinois had indeed created here an enchanted dwelling which was nothing but a pæan glorifying the mutual relation of herself and the King, twenty years her junior, who could beg her in his letters never to forget him who had known but one God and one "amye," and never to deny him the name of servitor which she had given him. For Henri II, deeply imbued with the false chivalry of the time, inebriated by the atmosphere of the *Amadis de Gaule*, that breviary of the Court, was pleased to regard himself as one of the paladins of old with a lady to whom he was eternally true; and this devotion the lady in question, always practical, nourished in a manner at once business-like and artistic.

Not unnaturally the King loved the magnificent shrine raised to this romantic idyll, and had already several times visited it since its construction began. Indeed he would probably have been at Anet on this May day of 1550, but for the fact that yesterday, the 15th, Ascension Day, he had made his entry into Boulogne, now finally in French hands (for it had been given

54

up by the English for a money compensation, and peace with them had been signed). He had then formally placed the town under the sovereignty of the Blessed Virgin, and given to the Cathedral, in performance of a two-years-old vow, a three-foot high statue of her in solid silver.

His two elder children and the Queen of Scots were visiting Anet in his place-for had not Madame Diane made herself as much a guardian of the royal nursery as the Queen herself? (And, at St. Germain, Catherine, who in any case never came to Anet, was within a few weeks of the birth of that fifth child who should afterwards reign as Charles IX.) The princelings had arrived that afternoon, and while they were reposing after their journey, Madame de Valentinois was taking the opportunity of displaying the glories of her palace to the superior members of their cavalcade of guardians and attendants, of whom M. and Madame d'Humières, Lady Fleming and Madame de Curel were the most important. With the d'Humières she was on intimate terms; they were her liaison officers with the nursery. She had never attempted relations of this sort with Lady Fleming; indeed it had more than once been observed that her manner to her was curiously cold-but then it was never genial to anyone. Nevertheless, it was with the Scotswoman on her right hand and M. d'Humières on her left that, stately in her black and white, she preceded her guests through the long left wing of Anet.

In this cortège the Queen of Scots' Master of the Horse found himself walking, not with the companion whom he would have chosen, but with Mistress Jean Ogilvy, who was full of lively comment on what she saw. Was it true, she had just asked in a prudent whisper, that it was here-or, rather, in the original château-that the marriage contract between his present Majesty and Madame Catherine had been drafted years ago, in the days of King Francis? Ninian nodded; it was a nice point of irony which he had forgotten, never having been at Anet before.

He had indeed been reluctant, he knew not why, to visit it now; but since the little Queen was here he was bound to accompany her. It was not that he felt any private scruples about the child's being entertained by the royal mistress, for the King's children with whom she was brought up accepted quite naturally "ma cousine de Valentinois" —even Queen Catherine gave her this honorific title-and it probably never entered their heads to wonder what exact rôle she played in their father's life. No; it was rather a presentiment which had fastened upon him that the stay at Anet would not be personally pleasant.

He had indeed a grievance against its mistress, but he had it in common with a grievance against the King and Queen also. For his betrothal of last June remained merely a barren betrothal. Consent to his marriage with Magdalen Lindsay was still unobtainable, and for these past eleven months he had had to content himself with nothing but tantalising snatches of her society-just as he could not see her now unless he turned his head, for she was walking some way behind him in the admiring throng. Very soon after the day in September when she had given him that piece of ill news about their union he had sought out Lady Fleming for a fuller explanation. The Queen's gouvernante, always gracious to him, had been quite frank. The reason for the prohibition of their marriage was simple; it was because in the event of Magdalen's having a child —"and you'll not tell me, Master Graham, that that is unlikely!" — she could not attend to her duties about the Queen's person. There was a secondary reason too against the marriage, for it appeared that the post which Magdalen was supposed to be resigning that summer had been promised to a young French lady of rank, and it was only through Lady Fleming's intercession that her young kinswoman had been allowed to keep it. It would give great offence if, after this concession had been made, Magdalen should now throw up her position-as she must if she married. Lady Fleming professed herself grieved, but the lovers must wait.

It was just that indefinite waiting, a sacrifice perhaps of years, which Ninian was finding increasingly irksome. He was no longer in his twenties with all time before him. And yet he had promised that he would not take Magdalen from her royal charge.

* * * * *

The party had arrived now at the splendid guardroom on the first floor of the west wing; here some of the decorations were not quite finished. But above the heads of the visitors, complete in every detail, stretched its ornate ceiling, in an elaborate pattern of interlaced squares of varying sizes, each with a richly carved and gilded device recalling either the royal lovers or the goddess Diana alone. The panelling of this *salle des gardes* was appropriately ornamented with carved trophies of arms, all the work of Goujon, some of which were still in course of being gilded and discreetly picked out in colour by half a score of craftsmen. These, however, respectfully ceased work and stood bowing as the Duchesse and her visitors approached-all but one shabbily-attired young man who, mounted on a short ladder, seemed entirely absorbed in painting, though he could not, unless completely deaf, have been unaware of the advancing throng. A fellow-workman reached up and plucked at his sleeve; upon which the industrious craftsman glanced over his shoulder, came slowly down the ladder and stood beside, almost behind it, his head slightly bent, examining the tip of his brush instead of showing a becoming interest in the visitors from St. Germain.

Whether his action were due to real absorption, desire to avoid notice or to intentional discourtesy, mattered not at all to Madame Diane, who had already gone past, nor did her guests as a whole observe the little episode. But it had drawn Ninian's attention, and as he neared the young painter he glanced at him, idly enough . . . and having done so looked again. He could not, indeed, easily remove his eyes. For the half sullen face bore a striking resemblance, both in features and colouring, to that picture of his father at Garthrose.

"Oh, Master Graham," came the admiring voice of Mistress Jean Ogilvy in his ear, "look, I pray you, at the framework of this door! 'Tis all of the finest marble!"

It might have been of any material for all Ninian saw of it when he obeyed her.

Later that afternoon the Master of the Horse found himself being taken, under the guidance of an officer of the household, over the great stables in the right-hand court of the château, the Cour de Charles le Mauvais. They were vast and excellently appointed, and the grooms who had come with the Queen's two palfreys and those of her little playmates seemed to find them much superior to the accommodation at St. Germain-en-Laye. But as he looked them over Ninian was conscious that the background of his thoughts was not occupied, as hitherto to-day, by Magdalen, nor by the royal mistress, and that hard smile of hers which had showed him afresh that it would be useless to try to enlist her sympathy for their marriage, but by the sulky young workman in the Salle des Gardes.

Directly his inspection was finished he asked where he could find the overseer of the workmen-or rather of the painters, alleging that he believed there was a man working among these in whom he was interested. To Maître Gorron he was forthwith conducted, and in a little wooden hut tucked away in the same courtyard found a middle-aged man brooding over some specimens of gold leaf. He at once put them aside and consulted his registers.

"A young painter just now employed in the Salle des Gardes? But there are half a score there, Monsieur. You would know him again? Shall I have them all sent for?"

But this offer Ninian refused. "He had not somehow the air of an ordinary workman," he volunteered.

"Ah!" exclaimed Maître Gorron with immediate enlightenment, "then it might well be a young man who came here a few weeks ago from I know not where, but with a recommendation from the Sieur de l'Orme himself. It is true that this young man is not as the others; when I first spoke with him it seemed to me that he must be of gentle birth, and after I had engaged him I found that he scarce knew how to handle a brush. But he improved, and showed himself industrious, wherefore I did not discharge him-moreover, the Sieur Philibert's orders are not lightly to be disregarded, he having, as I dare say you have heard, Monsieur le Grand Ecuyer, the quick wrath of the south. The young man's name-yes, I have them all here. It will be —" he ran his finger down the page —"it will be Gaspard Leconty. Your honour will allow me to send for him?"

"On no account, Maître Gorron," said Ninian hastily. "I shall come upon him again, no doubt, during her Majesty's stay here. The matter is of no great importance; but I am obliged to you for your courtesy." And to dismiss the subject he embarked upon praise of what he had seen at Anet.

Three days later he came unexpectedly upon the young man in a small gallery not far from the quarters of the royal children-the only workman there. Kneeling on one knee, he was outlining with a fine brush the carved design on one of the lower panels, a design where the arrow of the divine huntress traversed two intertwined branches of laurel. And Ninian, in as natural a manner as he could, stopped, feigning to study the panel.

Good God, there was no escaping the likeness, even when this Gaspard Leconty was looked down upon from above, as now, and when only his profile was visible! He, too, was clean-shaven —as Malise Graham had been when that portrait was painted; it increased the resemblance while accentuating the points of dissimilarity. To these Ninian suddenly realised that he was clinging. . . .

"You are not painting the laurel branches, I see," he remarked abruptly.

Without rising or indeed moving, his brush going steadily down one side of the arrow, the young man answered: "The laurel branches, no, monsieur. They are to be covered with gold leaf. That is skilled work, not for me."

The opening was good. "You are not of the craft of gilders, then?"

"I am not of any craft," replied the workman, rather indifferently, replenishing his brush with paint. And indeed, unless the craft were a very delicate one, his hands bore out this statement.

"Yet you use that brush well," said Ninian. It was sufficiently curious (though of a piece with his behaviour the other day in the Salles des Gardes) that this man should not cease work and stand respectfully in his presence.

"Needs must," was the reply. "And Madame Diane pays good wages-as well she may, seeing how surpassing great are her own!"

Before Ninian had time to get over the startling rashness of such a speech in these surroundings, one of the little Queen's French pages came hurrying along the gallery, and advanced to him.

"Monsieur de Graeme, Madame de Flamyn begs that you will speak with her. It seems that her Majesty has a desire to ride this afternoon."

Ninian turned at once. His departure had the effect which his presence had not, for at the page's first words the young painter had risen to his feet, and thereafter stood as still as any statue of Jean Goujon's, staring after the receding figures.

It was Wednesday, the twenty-first of May, a date Ninian was never likely to forget. The little Dauphin and the Queen of Scots, each with their separate instructors, had just returned from riding in the park of Anet, and in that great columned inner court Ninian was lifting his small sovereign carefully from the saddle. She still rode in the old-fashioned manner, sitting sideways with her feet upon a support, though she was very anxious to emulate the example of that good and fearless horsewoman Queen Catherine, who had introduced the fashion of the pommelled saddle. Next month was, in fact, to see her promoted to this method.

Bright-eyed and eager, she was talking of this prospect now as she was dismounted. "I could ride much faster so, Master Graham, could I not?"

"But suppose," objected her Master of the Horse, smiling, "that I should find myself unable to keep up with your Majesty! What then?"

"Now you are jesting, sir!" replied the royal child, looking up at him with a laugh, but not at all displeased. She had a naturally sweet temper and was rarely put out, and despite imperious little ways inevitable in one who had been a Queen from the cradle, would take instruction and criticism, Ninian had found, with the utmost good humour. "As if Bravane or La Réale could trot faster than your Lion!"

At that moment the Dauphin came running round from his own mount, Fontaine, one cheek noticeably flushed. "Ah, Monsieur de Graeme, I am too late then! I wished to assist you to dismount the Queen of Scotland."

"Pray accept my regrets, Monseigneur," said Ninian. "Had I but known I would have waited before dismounting her Majesty." In this half pathetic, half ludicrous intention he recognised the desire which the little boy always had to prove himself the perfect knight and squire of dames. "Next time that you ride together I will remember to ask your Highness for assistance."

Mary gave a little smile as she gathered up her habit. It was plain that she thought the assistance would be of little value; but child as she was, she had the tact not to say so.

The heir to the throne went and stood in front of Ninian's bay, which a groom was holding. "I hope that I shall very soon be able to ride a horse like that," he murmured rather wistfully. And then, with more assurance, turning towards the little girl: "When I do I shall wear the fine inlaid suit of armour which M. de Guise has sent me; and then I can prove myself your true knight, Madame my betrothed" (for thus it pleased him to speak of her, though the actual betrothal was not to take place until a few days before their wedding, eight years later). "Already, you know, I gallop on Fontaine, and to-day in the park — —" He broke off with a sudden little scream, and clapped his hand to the side of his head. "Oh, my ear, my ear!"

His attendants came running, and hurried him, moaning, towards the entrance. Mary looked compassionately after him. "It is quite a long time since poor François had the ear-ache," she said reflectively.

"There is no doubt that Monseigneur will grow out of it," observed Ninian. It was the general opinion-or hope. "But I see your ladies awaiting you there, Madam, and I will conduct you to them if you permit."

And doing so, he had one of those tantalising glimpses of his own betrothed, standing there with Jean Ogilvy below the statue of Louis de Brézé, waiting to attend the child to her own apartments, serene in a gown of dark azure which contrasted with her companion's lively flame-colour.

On an impulse, when he went back to the horses, he dismissed the groom, saying that he would return to the park and ride awhile alone. He pretended to himself that Lion needed exercise, but it was much more for his own sake than for his horse's that he rode back into that great pleasance, more forest than park, so green with young life and so full of bird-song. But he was unable to gallop much, for the rides were rough, and some only half made. Yet he felt his spirits lighter when, some three-quarters of an hour later, he returned at a walking pace under a lovely canopy of chestnut leaves, incredibly green, and coming to a branching of the rides pulled up, not knowing which would lead him back more directly to the château. So, on an impulse, he cast the reins on his horse's neck for Fate to take up. And Fate took them up.

The bay gave his head a shake, selected the path which offered the better sustenance, moved along it a little way and then stopped, with intent to graze upon the undergrowth.

"No, no!" said his master, laughing. "That was not my design!" He gathered up the reins again and proceeded at a walk past a brake of hawthorn, shining like silver. Its scented breath came to him-the May in bloom, and he still serving for Rachel!

In his hour's ride he had met nobody save some wood-cutters; now, beneath an unfolding oak-tree, golden-brown against the green, he suddenly saw a man standing-by his garb neither wood-cutter, nor peasant . . . nor gentleman. He seemed to be whittling at a piece of stick. As Ninian advanced he looked up, frowning-for though pose and occupation seemed careless, his face was dark-and made as if to move away. Then he stood quite still, staring at the rider, now within a few feet of him.

And Ninian met his gaze. Slowly his fingers tightened on the reins. He drew up.

"You have a holiday, it seems, my lad?"

Leconty-if that were indeed his name-gave a twist of the mouth. "*In perpetuam.* I am now as free as air-freer indeed than you, Monsieur de Graeme."

"So you know my name?" commented Ninian slowly.

"I heard it the other day, after you had spoken to me in the château."

"But why have you been dismissed? Was not your work sufficiently skilled?"

The young man gave a curious, half triumphant laugh. "The work I did, pardieu, was too skilled! I flatter myself I am better at kissing a woman's lips than at smearing paint on her devices. No, I do not mean that I have kissed Madame Diane's lips —I prefer a younger mouth. But my exploit, coming to the ears of that old pelican, Maître Gorron, has brought about my dismissal. And where I am to turn next for a means of livelihood I know not . . . unless *you* can advise me, Monsieur de Graeme?"

Gone now was all pretence of deference; he was speaking as though to his equal.

"Why should *I* advise you?" asked Ninian, suddenly stiff. The young man detached himself from the support of the oak-tree and came to his saddle-bow.

"I could answer that question more fitly, Monsieur de Graeme, if I had the honour of knowing your Christian as well as your family name . . . and also, by your leave, the quarter of Scotland whence you come." And as Ninian stared at him rather haughtily he went on: "Is your name by chance *Malise* , and your home the château of . . . of Rosegarth?"

It was like the descent of a blow which one had half foreseen yet hoped to evade. Ninian looked down on the face at his saddle-bow.

"No, my name is not Malise," he replied curtly. "And the house you speak of is called Garthrose." His desire, his almost overpowering desire, was to touch his horse's flanks and ride away without further parley. But he could not. He remained gazing down. The eyes-yes, the eyes . . . that dark amber which he so well remembered. . . . And after a moment the words came out of him: "But it was at Garthrose that I was born."

"Then," said Gaspard Leconty gravely, "I must think that Sir Malise Graeme was your father as well as —" he laid his hand on his breast —"mine!"

A bird on the budding oak above them broke into jubilant song; the notes were mere discord in Ninian's ears. And he sat his horse motionless, his eyes still fixed on the speaker in a last desperate effort at disbelief. But, sweet Virgin, that very pose-the hand laid just so on the breast, even the expression, half-defiant, half-amused, which had now come upon the young man's handsome, arrogant features . . . !

"What proof have you, Leconty?" His own voice sounded to him as distant as that far cuckoo's.

"Ah, you have found out *my* name!" The smile became tinged with mockery. Then the Frenchman who claimed to be brother to the Scot drew out from round his neck an object on a cord, and detaching it, held it up to him.

Ninian took it mechanically, and instantly found himself looking with a shock at the facsimile-or perhaps indeed at the original-of that signet ring of his father's which he wore himself. There, bitten into the sardonyx, sharp, unmistakable, was the hand holding a rose-branch, the crest of Graham of Garthrose.

Over and over Ninian turned it, in an unconscious effort to gain time, for he knew that, however acquired, it was Malise Graham's ring. There was no great degree of surprise in coming upon a bastard of his father's; he knew of more than one at home, and suspected others. Yet as he handed back the ring there was more chill even in his heart than in his words as he muttered briefly: "We must speak of this at length another time, and elsewhere."

"But why not now, and what more private place than here?" urged the young man. "At the château we might be interrupted; moreover, I have now no right to enter it. But perhaps, Monsieur le Grand Ecuyer, you do not wish for further talk with me? I have small claim upon you, and my father, I think, is dead."

Better, after all, to get this over at once. Before he made any reply, Ninian swung down from the saddle, threw the reins over his arm and faced the challenge.

"Yes, Sir Malise Graham has been dead these seventeen years," he answered, not conceding the relationship. "Yet tell me one thing. You are at Anet as a workman; yet you are surely of gentle birth on your mother's side . . . also." (The short, significant word cost him a pang.) "And by your speech you are well educated."

"Sang Dieu, but I am both!" exclaimed the young man, throwing back his handsome head, and once more fixing those disconcerting amber eyes upon his hearer. "Let me tell you what my real position was . . . until a year ago. I was Gaspard d'Estoublon, heir to a fine estate here in Normandy, with money, friends, horses, servants, all to my desire. My father, as he believed himself to be, as I believed him, doted upon me. My stepmother-for my mother had died when I was an infant-my stepmother preferred me to her own children. I was a prince there . . . a year ago!"

"And what befell?"

"Sir Malise Graeme's letters to my dead mother and this ring of his were discovered-after all those years. There was no disguising their meaning. And on that my father-my reputed father-made enquiries, and found a servant who had been privy to the intrigue — —"

"But when — —?"

The young man gave him no time to finish his question, but swept on. "It seemed that Sir Malise Graeme had come to France in the year 1522, the year before my birth, upon an embassy with some Scottish nobleman or other. So much was made out from these letters, and then my-Monsieur d'Estoublon-established the fact that there had indeed been such an embassy in that year."

"My Lord Albany's," said Ninian slowly. "And my father *did* accompany him. I remember his absence. I was a boy at the time."

"Would he had stayed in Scotland!" cried Gaspard d'Estoublon passionately. "Would he had never set eyes upon my mother! . . . Is it of no moment to you, his son also, that I was turned out from Estoublon like a serving-man, at an hour's notice, branded and nameless, with the clothes I wore and a paltry sum of money-which lasted me less than a month —I who was (I believed) the apple of my father's eye, who had held my head so high in Rouen and Paris, who had such fair prospects, who was on the eve of betrothal . . ." The fierce, bitter voice faltered and broke; the disinherited speaker turned away a moment towards the oak-trunk, then swung round again with an accusing gesture. "And all this wreckage, all this misery lies at your father's door!"

Even as he made it there came from not so very far away the sound of voices and laughter and of the trampling of horses. Some cavalcade from the château was riding through the park. Galvanised into activity Ninian seized his horse by the bridle, his young bastard brother by the wrist, and began to drag him away.

"Come, we must finish this now!" he said, in a tone almost as fierce, and they plunged together through the thickets like two fugitives in search of shelter.

They came out after a while upon a small clearing strewn with felled tree-trunks, but empty of woodmen, and silent save for the ecstatic bird-song of May. Ninian gave a quick glance round, and then tethered his horse to a sapling.

"I must think for a while," he muttered, and sank down upon a log lying close to another, with green shoots of dog-mercury pushing between them. But almost instantly he started up again, at a rustle and the momentary glimpse of an arrow-branded head, a writhing, gliding body. A viper had been basking between the logs.

"Only a snake," he said indifferently. He did not, however, return to his seat, but began to walk up and down, his arms crossed on his breast, while the young man watched his every movement.

Why should he, a Scot, go out of his way to help a young Frenchman who might well be lying to him about his broken prospects, his sudden undeserved penury? Lying about his origin he did not think this Gaspard was; ring and looks bore him out too securely. But, thought Ninian, the wrong my father did eight-and-twenty years ago is no affair of mine! Let his bastard go to some patron of his own nation who can better afford to play the part than I, who have little money and no influence-though the young man may well think otherwise. . . . And yet-he is not only my half-brother, but I cannot look at him without recalling the father whom I loved! Surely if I can but bring him to the notice of someone about the Court he will be able to make his way, and I shall be rid of him. And then I shall not feel that I have refused a helping hand to my father's blood.

He had come to a halt just where two green tunnelled alleys, mere rough pathways, over-grown, channelled with ruts, and a little mysterious, left the clearing-curiously, too, from a mere arrowpoint of an angle, so acute that it was strange that there should be two paths at all. Fitly enough, it was standing here-for the second time in an hour at the parting of the ways in this wood-that Ninian made up his mind. He turned and went back to the outcast.

"Since there is small doubt, Monsieur . . . d'Estoublon, that you are my father's son, I cannot leave you to want or to an occupation unworthy of your upbringing. But the help I can give will not be great, and in money, indeed, very little, for I am not rich. As, however, I hold a position about the person of the Queen of Scots, it is possible that if you were attached to me in some way I might be able to procure you some small post either there or among the Dauphin's retinue."

"Monsieur — —" began the other warmly, but Ninian went on: "If you will consent to take service with me, as a page of gentle birth, something might be done. Sooner or later some chance might come your way — —"

He broke off as the young man seized his hands in a feverish grip. "Brother . . . I'll not name you so, never fear, in public . . . brother, I am yours till death for this! A pittance will suffice me, and you can treat me as you will-if I have but the chance of regaining the life to which I was born." He made as if to kiss the hands which he had captured, but Ninian, none too gently, pulled them away.

"There's no call for gratitude. I have a duty towards you, and you have, on your own showing, been most harshly used. I shall do all I can for you; but once more, remember that my influence is very small. And now first, let me know by what name you would choose to be known, for surely that of Leconty had best be abandoned."

"Although I have no greater right to any other!" exclaimed his protégé with a return of bitterness. "Nay, that's not true. In my own heart, since I am no longer Estoublon, I am my mother's son, Gaspard de Vernay. That was her name. Perchance with the help of my true father's son I may make it better known than Estoublon. No, you shall not stay me-brother!" And flinging himself suddenly on his knee among the wood anemones he succeeded, this time, in kissing his benefactor's reluctant hand.

* * * * *

They parted at the edge of the clearing. Before they met again it was imperative that Gaspard de Vernay should be as much metamorphosed as the one presentable doublet which he still possessed would permit. Appearing at the château of Anet-even if no one knew whence-as the Grand Ecuyer's page, his identity with the dismissed workman was not likely to be guessed. Afterwards, if there were time before the royal nursery returned to St. Germain, he could pay a visit to some tailor at Mantes or Evreux.

These details settled, the unwilling Good Samaritan turned his horse towards the château once more, while the mocking note of the cuckoo made the wood ring behind him. His own heart was far from singing. He was not elated by the consciousness of a good action, nor even at having performed an act of piety towards his father's memory. The salary of this post of his which had so fine a name matched rather its slender duties than its title, and he was putting by every crown he could spare against the day, however long delayed, of his marriage. The pay of a page of good birth would put a stop to that process. Moreover, he would have to acquaint Sandy Forbes with an arrangement which he knew would be highly distasteful to him, and at which he would undoubtedly take offence.

What a strange, unpredictable encounter! and a distasteful one to boot! Had he not known a foreboding that this visit to Anet would not be pleasant? Fate had evidently been determined to throw him and this fruit of his father's French amour together, even to bringing them three times face to face within so short a space and in a great dwelling so populated as Anet. It appeared from what he said that Gaspard de Vernay owed his employment as a workman here to a recommendation from its architect, the great Philibert de l'Orme himself, even as the overseer had told Ninian, but Ninian had not received from the young adventurer himself a very clear impression of the manner in which he had obtained this recommendation. However, that was of no importance now. What mattered to Ninian Graham was that he had attached to himself, against his own desire, an unknown half-brother of gentle birth to whom he was not personally attracted.

(3)

The weathercock on the chapel, with its ubiquitous monogram, was swinging to and fro rather fitfully when a few days later the royal children in their horse litters, and their cavalcade of mounted attendants, passed over the drawbridge which crossed the steep moat of Anet. High above the many roofs of the château the clouds seemed to be holding steeplechases in the blue. It was a day of April rather than of May; nevertheless, in spite of the prospect of showers, the cortège would dine *en route* in the open air.

Behind the litter which contained the little Queen and some of her Maries rode her Master of the Horse, and behind him again his new gentleman page, already a model of tact, self-effacement and (very nearly) of efficiency. It seemed clear that he did not intend to presume upon his kinship, by which attitude he made matters easier for Ninian-though nothing would ease the situation created by his advent as far as Alexander Forbes was concerned.

At noon they all halted by a thicket where nightingales were making a daylight essay of their roulades, and the repast was spread upon grass sprinkled with violets. Amidst laughter and chatter the royal children were served first, and then put back into their litters under proper surveillance to rest while the household ate.

When the meal was over Ninian (not without Lady Fleming's connivance, for she continued partial to him) contrived to snatch a few moments alone with his betrothed, and drew her to walk with him under the trees. After trying in vain to get a glimpse of the nightingale whom they could hear practising above them, they were speaking of the glories of Anet when Magdalen suddenly asked: "Who was that handsome young man who waited upon you just now, Ninian? I have not seen him before."

Her lover had made up his mind what to reply, for the present, to any questions upon this score, even though the questioner were Magdalen herself, so he answered with an air of un-concern: "Merely a young gentleman desirous of advancing himself at Court, who has taken service with me-though God knows I am not like to advance him much. Yet some day I may be able to bring him to the notice of one of the great lords-of the Constable, perhaps, when next he pays a visit to the nursery."

"Taken service with you —a Frenchman? For by his looks he is no Scot-and yet . . . yes, in some respects he might be."

"No, he is a Frenchman. See, my dear, it begins to rain; let me put your cloak about your shoulders."

"But why then should a Frenchman seek service with you rather than with one of his own countrymen?" asked Magdalen, looking up at him as he folded the cloak about her. And seeing a curious expression about his mouth she added quickly: "Especially as I think you would have preferred that he should not!"

She could hear the drops pattering on the hazel leaves near her as she waited for a reply. Then Ninian said quietly: "A man must do a kindness sometimes, *m'amye*. And perhaps the less he is able to be a patron the more he is pleased to fancy himself one. Yet I confess to a hope that my patronage may be brief, a mere stepping-stone for Monsieur Gaspard de Vernay . . . since you know well to what end I am become a miser! Oh, Magdalen, cannot there soon be an end of this waiting? You indeed are young, but the years go apace with me. Cannot we be wed before the summer ends? It is May already; nearly a year is gone!"

She caught his hand between her own, and there was pain in her beautiful eyes. "Ninian, Ninian, I also long for our marriage day. But have patience a little longer-till the Queen is somewhat older. She has so few of our country about her now, and she has, I know, some affection for me. And I, I love the sweet child dearly. Leave me with her a while longer!"

"You speak as though I asked you to quit her service!" said Ninian with indignation in his tone. "I do not think to quit it myself yet awhile, for I, too, love her, and she is my sovereign as she is yours. I do not wish to separate you."

The girl beat her hands together. "But that is what you would do," she said in distress. "Have we not discussed this difficulty many a time? No one can bear me better will than my kinswoman Lady Fleming, yet she swears 'tis impossible to get me leave to marry and yet remain about her Majesty's person. Queen Catherine would not hear of it, it seems, and Madame Diane is adamant."

"Queen Catherine-Madame Diane!" said Ninian half scornfully, his brows dark. "Is there no will but theirs? I know of a higher."

"You mean the King! But I dare not petition him upon such a subject."

Her lover looked at her significantly. "You have no need, Magdalen. Is not that kinswoman of yours an ambassador ready to your hand, well enough accredited? Or at least, so rumour begins to whisper."

Over Magdalen Lindsay's clear skin rushed a flood of colour, and she cast a glance of alarm about her. But there was no one within earshot.

"Is it true?" asked Ninian, bending closer. "Is the King her lover?"

"I fear there is no doubt of it," said Magdalen, very low. "And, Ninian, I fear, too, all manner of things if it should be discovered! Madame Diane's wrath-her vengeance . . . can you not picture it? And I, the kinswoman, perhaps supposed privy to it, though indeed I am not. I might well be sent out of France."

"That affrights me not at all," answered Ninian promptly. "I should resign and follow you; we could be wed in our own country. Nevertheless, I see that it would be unwise to use the channel of Lady Fleming in this matter."

"And distasteful," added the girl. "I was not bred to ask favours through any man's mistress, even a king's. —Oh, forgive me. I meant not that you had ever done so . . . or would do so, despite what you said."

"And although, like all the Archer Guard, I was accustomed to wear the mistress's device," completed Ninian, with a certain cynical good humour. "Nay, you have not wounded me, Magdalen. Madame de Valentinois has stood so long in that relation that, my faith, one forgets she is not a wife. But since I was of the Archers, and am indeed still borne on their muster-roll, I will petition the King myself if I can but find the chance. When I was ever about his person I had naught to ask; now that I have a boon to crave I have lost my access. —Here comes the sun again-and my new page."

The sun indeed might have re-emerged in order to strike, as it did, bright glints from Gaspard de Vernay's dark auburn hair as he advanced bare-headed through the wet hazels. He wore his clothes with such an air that one could hardly observe that they were far from new, and, bowing, said with just the right shade of deference:

"Preparations are being made, Monsieur de Graeme, for moving on. Your horse and that of the Demoiselle de Lindsay are here, at the edge of the wood."

"Thank you, Gaspard," said his master. Then he beckoned him to come nearer. "Mistress Lindsay, let me present to you Monsieur Gaspard de Vernay."

He thought he detected surprise and pleasure on the young man's face, but it was with complete and respectful composure that the latter kissed Magdalen's hand, thereafter following them at a due distance as they went out of the little wood to find Sandy Forbes gloomily holding the horses.

"I thocht it best tae bring the beasts here," he said, thus repudiating the idea that he had done so by the orders of a young jackanapes from whom he would never submit to receive any.

" —*qui m'est le plus grand heur que je pourroy souhaiter en ce monde, et m'en resjouy de telle sorte que ne pense plus qu'à faire mon plein devoir* — —"

The small hand gripping the quill with such resolution came to a stop, and the other hand was put up to hide a yawn.

"Yes, Marie, go on," said Lady Fleming, stooping over the royal scribe for a moment. Back once more at St. Germain, the little Queen was writing, on this day of early June, a letter to her grandmother, the now widowed Duchesse de Guise, on the subject of her own mother's visit to France, for which plans were already being discussed.

She looked down now at the draft which had been prepared for her. "I cannot read what should come next," she said sleepily. "Mistress Lindsay, pray read it aloud to me."

"Aye, do so, Magdalen," said the gouvernante, and the girl, laying down her work and coming to the table, took up the draft.

"What have you writ already, your Grace? Ah, I see, 'my whole duty.' You have that? After '*mon plein devoir*' comes '*et d'estudier à estre bien sage .*' "

The pen resumed its travels, and after a while reached the end of the sentence, '*pour lui donner contentement au bon désir qu'elle a de me veoir telle que vous et elle me désirez .*' Then it came to a standstill once more. Mary looked up.

"It is nearly two years since I saw the Queen, my mother," she said reflectively.

"Two years next month, yes, your Majesty."

Yes, and two years since she herself had said good-bye to Scotland-two years since she had had her first sight of Ninian Graham, between whom and herself there still stood, all unconscious, this little Queen of Hearts. Biting her lip suddenly, Magdalen came away from the table, said to Lady Fleming, "I will go see why the children are so boisterous in there," and without waiting for permission went into the adjoining room.

It was merely an excuse which she had given, but when she entered she found that it was justified. The four little Maries, who should have been at their lessons under the temporary supervision of Jean Ogilvy, were engaged in a romping circle round a chair empty indeed of that young lady, but occupied by a swaddled-up doll belonging to Mary Livingstone. And it was eagerly explained to Magdalen that they were pretending that this object was the new little brother or sister which Monseigneur le Dauphin, the princesses and little Prince Louis were soon to have.

Quieting them, and finding out why Jean Ogilvy had deserted her post, seemed to smother that sudden heartache and the memory of her lover pleading angrily in the rain, while the nightingale sang above them.

It was quite true that the end of this month of June would see Queen Catherine delivered of another child, and at St. Germain. It was on this event that Ninian Graham was basing his hopes of an audience of the King, since the latter, though now absent, would certainly come to the château for the Queen's lying-in.

Meanwhile Ninian's private life had suffered a certain transformation. In his own chamber the ministrations of Sandy Forbes, to which he had been so long accustomed, had given place to those of Gaspard de Vernay. Ninian himself had not explicitly ordered it thus, but the deep offence which his old servant had taken at the introduction of the new-comer had never grown less, and Sandy had withdrawn himself to less personal duties. He was evidently, he burst out one day, fit only to have the care of horses and baggage. If Maister Ninian preferred a fine French popinjay who spent his spare time dangling after women he could have him! In vain Ninian tried to mollify him, telling him that the young man had only entered his service until he should find his feet at court. But when Sandy roughly asked him why he should put himself to all this trouble and cost for a stranger and a Frenchman, Ninian was faced with either telling him the real reason or intimating that it was none of his business. Against his will he took the latter course, and the breach between master and man was widened.

For the acknowledgment that Gaspard was his bastard brother had become increasingly distasteful to him. Fortunately they were so unlike in personal appearance that no one was likely to guess their relationship. It was only to his dying mother's vision that the dark-haired and grey-eyed Ninian resembled his auburn-haired father. There were days when he told himself that he was keeping silence on the point of Gaspard's illegitimacy purely for the sake of the young man himself, charming, discreet, gay and attentive as he was proving himself. For something indefinable which had repelled Ninian on the day of their fateful interview at Anet affected him in this manner no longer, or only occasionally. To Magdalen, on the rare occasions of their encountering each other, Gaspard showed a becoming respect and courtesy, steering very adroitly a dexterous course between the demeanour of an inferior and that of an equal. No idea of any kinship with her betrothed had obviously occurred to her, but Ninian had found himself obliged to promise that some day he would tell her what had really induced him to take the young Frenchman into his service.

At last, on the morning of the 27th of June, the news ran round the little world of St. Germain that in the early hours the Queen had been safely delivered of a son, who was to be called Charles.

After this Ninian began to look for a favourable opportunity of approaching the King. He knew that he must be careful how he set about this, for though Henri II was, in spite of his melancholy and heavy temperament, usually genial and easy of access-even sometimes inclined to strange fits of horse-play—he was also liable to sudden accesses of rage. But there was time enough; the King would not depart yet.

But about a week after the child's birth Henri, probably considering that he had done his duty by the mother of the new prince, suddenly left St. Germain for Anet.

Ninian heard this news from no less a person than his own royal charge as she rode by his side on her grey jennet Bravane in the forest of St. Germain with a small train behind, including three of her little playmates. It was a hot afternoon, the successor of several such, for the past month had been remarkably dry, occasioning prayers for rain on the part of the peasants. The promise of a pommelled saddle had now been carried out, to the royal child's great satisfaction, for she had never been timid, and was soon accustomed to the loss of the support for both feet. Indeed when they pulled up after a short canter, she said, her face all rosy: "I am sure that I have made much better progress in this new manner, Master Graham, though you have not told me so, for this afternoon I feel that I could ride many miles without fatigue-even as far as Anet! Would not his Majesty be surprised to see me ride into the court-yard!"

Ninian on his tall bay smiled down at her. Every line of that little figure in its green riding costume was instinct with natural grace, and the face she turned up to him alive with intelligence and charm. She was only seven and a half years old; what would she be when she was seventeen?

"His Majesty would indeed be surprised-if he were there to see."

"But he is there!" returned the child. "That is, he will be there by night, for he departed early this morning. He came to take farewell of Madame Elisabeth and me at six o clock. —Did you not know that he had left St. Germain, Master Graham?"

Ninian's smile had vanished. Used though he was to suppressing any sign of personal feeling in the presence of royalty, an exclamation of annoyance had escaped him which did not go unnoticed by the little girl riding beside him.

"What ails you, sir? You are displeased because his Majesty has gone to Anet? But he is so happy there with Madame Diane!"

Great heavens, she must not be allowed to think that he was criticising the King's action, especially as in her innocence she accepted his going there as a perfectly natural proceeding.

"I only regret his Majesty's departure," he said lightly, "because I had hoped to make a request to him while he was at St. Germain."

"And what was the request, Master Graham?"

"One of no moment, your Grace," lied Ninian. " —See, you must not let your reins loose in that manner when you ride in the forest! Bravane, indeed, is full sure-footed, but Madame la Réale might stumble over a root or the like."

The child Queen tightened the reins obediently, but was not diverted from her enquiry. "Good Master Graham, cannot you make your request to me? Am I not" —her little figure seemed to grow taller in the saddle —"am I not the person to whom a Scot should first bring his petition?"

Unable to tell her that she herself was for something in that request, Ninian was considering how to answer, when he heard a commotion behind. Not the Queen's, but Mary Seton's palfrey had stumbled, and though pulled up by the groom who held the leading-rein —for the child was little of a horsewoman yet-its rider had been frightened and was proclaiming the fact. The Queen instantly pulled up her mount, and Ninian, turning Lion, rode back.

The coming of July brought a notable change to the household of the royal children in the death, after a short illness, of the Dauphin's governor, M. d'Humières. It affected the little boy more than his sisters, for while Madame d'Humières, that mother of many children, was confirmed in her post with the princesses, M. d'Urfé, a former ambassador to Rome was appointed to succeed her husband. And after a little life in the nurseries went on as before.

Magdalen Lindsay, like others, was looking forward to the coming of the Queen Dowager of Scotland and the breath of home which the train of Scots accompanying her would bring with them. Jean Ogilvy, who pretended to be weary of France (though no one believed her), announced her intention of returning to her native land when Mary of Lorraine went back. She made this statement whenever she encountered the Chevalier de Brion, who had now transferred his admiration from Magdalen to her, and whom she protested so stoutly that she would never consider in the light of a suitor as to make it very probable that she would.

All the same, it was remarkable what interest she showed in the books of divination then so popular, to which the Princess Elisabeth's maid of honour had introduced her. But the consultation of these volumes was no easy business. For that called the *Dodecahedron* dice had to be used, and for the most popular of all, the *Giardino de' Pensieri* , cards were necessary, after which the enquirer was led through many pages and a labyrinth of figures to some vague prediction. And ever since the Chevalier de Brion had discovered Mistress Ogilvy busy with the *Giardino* in a corner, he had possessed a weapon against her which he did not scruple to use, as on the August afternoon when he craved admission to the chamber assigned to the maids of honour when not on duty, and told Magdalen and Jean that, since the latter was so much interested in the question of her future husband, he could tell her of a much simpler method of learning his identity than the last she had employed.

"I have no wish to know his name yet awhile," retorted Jean loftily.

"What a pity, because it seems that Madame Cathérine's new astrologer — —"

"Madame Cathérine has a new astrologer?"

"Fresh come from Italy, and does not keep his knowledge of the future for her Majesty alone, but will impart it to any enquirer-for a fee. You have but to ask Pini, the dwarf, if you can find him (which can most easily be done through your unworthy servant here), and he will take you to Signor Giacomo, who is lodged, I believe, in a little room not far from Madame Cathérine's apartments. Thus, Mesdemoiselles, you may have at small cost a glimpse into the future . . . and I can see that Mademoiselle Ogilvy at least is resolved to look through that window."

"If I thought that I should see you through it, Monsieur de Brion, I should never look! Otherwise —I own I am tempted. But what would Madame Cathérine say? This Signor Giacomo is not brought hither for all the world to consult!"

"Madame Cathérine is not to know . . . I perceive that I am to go and find Pini for you?"

"Not for me, monsieur," said Magdalen, with a smile that seemed to say she knew her future, and wanted no other.

"But I cannot go alone!" protested Jean. "Surely, Magdalen, you will not be so cruel as to deprive me of this chance of learning for what good Scots name I am to change my own?"

In the end, Magdalen had to give way; Pini, the Queen's dwarf, was found, and, following his misshapen and gaudily clad figure with a rather delicious sense of misdoing and of apprehension, they found themselves in the presence, not of a reverend greybeard surrounded by skulls and stuffed crocodiles, but of a little smooth, round-faced man of forty speaking French with the disfiguring Italian accent. At first he shook his head, saying that he should have cast the ladies' horoscopes first, but subsequently relented, and after making some preparations involving incense and mutterings, which they watched in awed silence, he bade the Signorina Ogilvy sit opposite him at a table and gazed intently into a crystal mounted upon the back of a dragon. As a result of this scrutiny he prophesied that she would have several children, whom he described in some detail; but when pressed as to the appearance of her husband, replied that he could see no such person. Jean, affecting at first to be much scandalised, consoled herself by declaring that the man she married would obviously be of small account in her life; and that she should make a point of telling M. de Brion so. But since this essay was inconclusive, Magdalen must relent, and ask for her fortune.

"No, I'll not do that," said her companion, "but, if he permits, there is one question which I will ask Signor Giacomo . . . Signor, I am betrothed, but my marriage is delayed . . . there are difficulties. Is it possible for you to tell me when it will take place?" And then in a very low voice, as though the words were forced from her: "Or whether it will take place at all?"

Signor Giacomo motioned to her to take Jean's seat. This time he pushed away the crystal-bearing dragon, took her hands between his own plump ones, gazed hard into her eyes for a long moment, and then shut his own.

"He looks like a lizard, so," thought Magdalen. "If he says that I shall never-oh no, he cannot say that! If he does, I shall not believe him." Yet she feared that she might. So she thought hard of Ninian, of his infrequent but transfiguring smile, of how she loved him. . . . And at last Signor Giacomo, still with his eyes shut, spoke.

"You will be married, signorina, not long after Hercules shall have slain the hydra-the seven-headed hydra. Yes, within —— —" he paused, and seemed to shut his eyes tighter, "within four months afterwards."

"Hercules . . . the hydra . . ." stammered Magdalen, bewildered. "But, signor —— —"

Two sharp knocks sounded at the door, outside which the Queen's dwarf was stationed. Opening his eyes the astrologer instantly loosed Magdalen's hands.

"*Scusi*, I am summoned. Farewell, *bellissime donne*! I have told you both the truth as it was revealed to me. Payment? Signor Pini will tell you the sum." And he was gone, leaving the girls for the moment alone in his little chamber.

"It must surely be some matter of astronomy-of the zodiac, perhaps?" hazarded Magdalen. Her eyes were bright; she must now assiduously watch the stars. "But is not Hercules a constellation?"

"You must ask the Master of the Horse," answered Jean Ogilvy, laughing. "For, of course, you will tell him this news, which will mightily rejoice him if he can put a meaning to it."

"Not I," replied Magdalen. "I should be ashamed to confess a visit to a sooth-sayer."

But September, the month of Mary of Lorraine's arrival, so eagerly awaited by all in the little Queen's entourage, began in deep gloom at St. Germain, for on its very first day the royal child had fallen ill of the flux which was prevalent there at the time. Four days went by in increasing anxiety, and she grew no better, but rather worse, in spite of all the King's physicians and her own.

On the fifth, a day of dull, lazy rainfall, Gaspard de Vernay, charged by the Dauphin's governor with a message for his master, and seeking for him in the neighbourhood of the Queen of Scots' apartments, came suddenly upon a girl sobbing in a passage. Seeing who it was, he stopped and softly uttered her name.

"Mademoiselle de Lindsay!" And then: "The Queen of Scotland-is the news then worse?"

Still sobbing, she moved her head in assent, and murmured: "Oh, God, if we should lose her!"

"You would break your heart, would you not, Mademoiselle? But take courage! Has she not every care and devotion-and so many prayers?"

Magdalen put down her handkerchief and stood, her hands fallen before, gazing at him with swimming eyes. Somehow there was comfort in this voice; save that it spoke in French it might almost have been Ninian's. She had never observed the resemblance before, and indeed was too greatly overwrought to be entirely conscious of it now.

"Ah, that is better, Mademoiselle; you should not weep so!" Very respectfully Gaspard took a hand and raised it to his lips. "Reflect, Mademoiselle, that her little Majesty has youth upon her side. Whoever heard of a Queen dying at so tender an age?"

At that Magdalen, trying to smile, murmured that she must go back, and slipped through a neighbouring door.

Only a few seconds later Gaspard encountered the Master of the Horse, also making from the opposite direction towards the Queen's chamber. The young man delivered his message, adding that he had just seen Mlle. de Lindsay and had speech with her.

"And what said she of the child?" asked Ninian abruptly. "Better or worse?"

"She thought-worse," Gaspard told him. "She was weeping. But may it not be that a crisis — —"

"Then I will not trouble them with enquiries at the chamber door," broke in his half-brother, his face grown still graver. And he added, half to himself: "Great God, if the Queen should die, what would become of us in Scotland?"

"The young King of England would then claim the crown, I suppose," hazarded the young Frenchman, sympathetically, if inexactly. "So her Majesty's death-which the saints avert! — would not precisely cause grief in England?"

"There could be no more joyful news to some in that realm," answered Ninian in a hard voice. "Not that the King of England has a claim upon Scotland, but that the Queen of Scots stands so near the throne of England. . . . You can go, Gaspard; give M. d'Urfé my service, and tell him that I will wait upon him at noon as he desires."

His page and kinsman made his usual graceful salute and went away, leaving Ninian standing there with a sombre face. But, once out of sight, M. de Vernay's pace slackened, and he appeared to forget that he was charged with a message, for he finally came to a standstill near a window, and remained there for a few minutes gazing out through the rain with a reflective expression. Then shrugging his shoulders, he came out of his reverie and went on his way.

And the very next day the tide of the little Queen's illness turned, and flowed hereafter so rapidly towards the quick recovery of childhood that two days later again she was out of danger. When her mother entered Rouen on the 25th of September, she was completely well again, able to go with King Henri to meet her, full of excitement at the prospect, and at that of seeing the great and costly entertainment by which the good citizens of Rouen hoped to outshine those of Lyons.

Mud-coloured and majestic, the six elephants advanced with unhurried gait. Hung about with trappings, they bore also on their backs, one an assemblage of lighted lamps, one a church, one a house, another a castle, another a miniature town, and the last a ship. And at the sight of these marvellous beasts, of which they had often heard, the children almost screamed with rapture. Mary Fleming especially was quite red in the face with excitement, in that bedecked Rouen balcony. The men carrying live sheep who had preceded the elephants were already forgotten.

The great procession had begun with less of marvel to childish eyes, though it was imposing enough. First after the clergy had come the city guilds on horseback, very fine in white satin doublets if they were drapers, in red satin if they were fishmongers, in grey taffeta with white feathers if they were of the corporation of the salt merchants. And after the riders had come companies of men on foot in white and green, or in white and red; then triumphal cars full of nymphs and goddesses.

But those had gone by before the elephants, and their passing was not regretted by the little Maries as were the disappearing hind-quarters of the last of those wonderful and mountainous creatures. But now the murmur came up: "The King! the King!" And, preceded by the Constable de Montmorency, a magnificent figure in gilded armour bearing the great state sword upright, rode Henri II in white velvet and cloth of silver on a chestnut horse. Behind him came the cohort of his Archers, the sun glinting on their white and gold. And Mary of Lorraine, tall, queenly and still young, smiled down at the little Queen, her daughter, seated in state beside her in the balcony, who, she saw, had much ado not to clap her hands with pleasure at the sight of them. No doubt there was equal satisfaction in the hearts of the Scottish nobles who had accompanied the Queen Mother, where they stood ranged farther back along the balcony-the Earls of Cassilis and Sutherland, the Earl Marischal, Lord Hume and Lord Maxwell, and the Bishops of Caithness and Galloway to boot.

But none of those who had witnessed the procession from balconies had been able to see the marvels which preceded it-shows designed for the entertainment of the King and his suite as they rode into Rouen. It transpired that evening that the enterprising Charles de Brion had somehow contrived to join himself for the nonce to the King's household, and, sitting at supper with the rest of the Queen of Scots' little train, he gave them an account of what he had seen.

"First of all," he said, addressing his remarks more particularly to the ladies, "you must know that there was a huge whale floating about in the Seine-no, not a live whale, but a counterfeit creature. Then we witnessed a battle between two ships, one of which was manned by fifty Indians-it was said from Brazil. These captured and burnt the other vessel; a very fine sight, though not over flattering to our own mariners. Then, lest even a King should forget that he is mortal, near one of the bridges, there was a sort of Elysian field, with two figures reposing therein, one representing his late Majesty François Premier, and one our present king, with a goddess watching over their slumbers and two Latin inscriptions. One of these signified, 'That they may rest from their labours,' the other I have forgotten. Pardie, I should think the inhabitants of Rouen will need some rest after theirs!"

The company agreed, laughing, and supper had proceeded some way farther when the Chevalier broke in: "Ah, one notable device I have forgotten to mention. Near another bridge was constructed a great cave, with Orpheus within upon a throne, and nymphs discoursing music around him. And there came out from it Hercules with a great club, and the Hydra itself-seven heads it had, all complete; I counted them. It was a fine sight to see him slay it with his club. —Did you say something, Mademoiselle de Lindsay?"

The leaves were dropping from the trees and floating down the Loire; the days were shortening rapidly, for it was November. But at Blois the galleried palace high above the town blazed with the lights of perpetual dancing and feasting. There were three Queens there now, as indeed there had been at Rouen when Queen Catherine in cloth of silver had made her entry the day after the King, with Madame de Valentinois, all black velvet and ermine, in nominal attendance upon her. And through all the coming winter Blois was to be very gay, for much was made of Mary of Lorraine, reunited now to her little daughter and to her six Guise brothers; she was treated, as it was said, like a goddess.

Much also was made at first of the Scots nobles and gentlemen who had come over with her, although Sir John Mason, the English envoy, had written home from Rouen, with no honey-dipped pen, of their brawling and fighting over their accommodation there. Ninian, too, when he encountered his compatriots, had not been edified by their lordly and boastful attitude. They seemed to consider that they (and the Queen Mother) had deserved great things at the hands of France for having preserved the little Queen of Scots from an English match, and were determined to receive their deserts. Nor was this attitude left behind at Rouen.

Neither the prevalent gaiety nor the presence of the less arrogantly behaved of his countrymen did much to uplift the spirit of Ninian Graham just now. A little seed of doubt and mistrust which, against his will, had obtained lodging in his mind was not dormant; it had vitality and a possibility of growth. Magdalen, he was beginning to fear, did not share his eagerness for their union, and if she still put the service of the royal child above their marriage she plainly did not love him as he had thought. He tried hard to convince himself that her manner to him had not changed in any way-and could not entirely succeed. Not that he thought her heart was turning towards any other man; at least, he could see no sign of it-but then, how much of her life was there not in which he could have no part, how many hours were there when she was lost to him! If they were but married! . . . Then the continual contact with his half-brother fretted him, for as yet no opportunity had presented itself which that young fortune-seeker could seize. No person of importance had taken notice of him, though several of Queen Catherine's maids of honour seemed sensible of his charm. The only hours of real happiness for Ninian in those autumn days were the hours which he spent with those miniature horsewomen, his royal charge, and her playmates.

The Feast of the Conception in early December brought her eighth birthday to his little sovereign, and a shower of gifts. In the two and a half years since she had said farewell to the towers of Dumbarton she had developed both physically and mentally, but she had not changed. Remarkably intelligent for her years, knowing her own mind very clearly (as how should she not, being a queen, though still under tutelage), high-spirited and yet sweet-tempered, she charmed everyone who approached her, not least her future husband who, of equally tender years, considered himself more than ever her knight, and loved to talk secrets with her in a corner. Poor boy, thought Ninian sometimes when he saw them together; the physical contrast between the two children was not greater than the contrast between the Dauphin's spirit and his weakly, disease-ridden body. Yet, though he was almost always in the grip of some indisposition or other, he longed for the day when he should be old enough to go to war; his miniature suit of armour must always be kept mirror-bright, and in one of the galleries at Blois he had caused to be set up, not very conveniently for other persons, a target at which he might practise archery.

(11)

Dear sister, wrote Ninian, in the dark, cramped little room assigned to him in a building which had to house so many persons of more importance than himself, *dear sister, I am rejoiced to hear of the birth of your first-born, and that you purpose to name him after me. You know how fain I was to have been at your wedding last year, but it was not possible* .

Weddings indeed do not seem to come my way, he reflected rather bitterly, though he did not pen the words. The thought had brought him back from visions of Agnes, of Garthrose-even from a fleeting picture of the future of Magdalen and Agnes embracing on the banks of the dear river of his childhood-to the château of Blois. And there, before he had added another word to his letter, came a quick knock at his door. Without rising he called out to enter.

There came in Gaspard-but a transformed Gaspard, animated as Ninian had never seen him. He had always at command, not unjustifiably, two manners towards his half-brother and master, a public and a private. There was something about him now, as he stood hand on hip, which suggested that the latter, now in the ascendant, was likely to be permanent. And before Ninian could ask him the reason for his presence, he began cheerfully:

"Brother Ninian, I am come to say that I need trouble you no more. I ask leave to resign from your service-which I know you will grant me without the ghost of a regret!"

Betraying no emotion of any kind at this request, Ninian laid down his pen, and merely asked: "For what reason, pray?"

"Because I need now depend upon no man's charity! My fortune has turned at last. I told you some weeks ago that my-that M. d'Estoublon had died. I have not, naturally, inherited a penny from him, but my step-mother, who has always shown me much kindness, has sent me a sum of money sufficient to set me upon my own feet again. Moreover, she proposes (blessings light upon her) to renew the gift at stated times. I can at once — —"

"Is Madame d'Estoublon then diverting this money from the inheritance of her own children, your reputed step-brothers and sisters?" demanded Ninian, rather sternly.

"No, no," answered Gaspard, smiling. "Do not make me a cuckoo in the nest from which *I* was thrown out! She has a fortune of her own-did I not say that she was rich? She writes that she would willingly have given me the money earlier-at my expulsion, even-but while M. d'Estoublon lived she dared not, lest he should discover it. Now she is free to do what she pleases, the good lady. And so, my dear brother, I am at last assured of sufficient means to enable me to make a modest figure at court. That is the first step. Afterwards — —"

"A figure at court-if you are willing to have those things said of you which were said of M. de Jarnac and *his* step-mother," commented Ninian, referring to the aspersions which at the beginning of the reign had led to the famous judicial duel before the King and Court at St. Germain between that gentleman and his slanderer, La Chataignerie.

For a moment his half-brother coloured. "Those things were said falsely-as the combat proved," he retorted indignantly. "You surely do not propose to spread such a report about me!"

"Certainly not. Nor is it any person's business to ask who supplies you with money, my dear Gaspard. I am glad to hear your news, and release you willingly, wishing you a further speedy rise in your fortunes. I regret that I have done so little to better them."

At that Gaspard threw his cap upon the table with a gesture of what looked like exasperation. "Ninian, my brother, why are you so harsh to me . . . and to yourself? You have done for me more than I can ever requite, although if ever I can bethink me of a way of repaying a part of my debt, be assured I shall pay it. But for you I should be a beggar in rags by now, perhaps-whereas through you I am at least upon the outskirts of the King's Court, and have made acquaintances in it. You like me not —I know not why! For that reason I have all the greater cause to be grateful for what you have done. Perhaps when I trouble you no more with my presence, you will think of me more kindly. Will you give me your hand?" And he held out his own over the table.

He had spoken with real dignity, his air was no longer full of that jaunty assurance, and Ninian, uncomfortably aware how he had penetrated his own feelings towards him, clasped the hand.

"It seems I am becoming a curmudgeon before my time," he said with an effort. "Forgive me, Gaspard; and when the turn of the wheel comes for you, do not fail to give me word of it."

"That I will!" returned Gaspard, with almost Malise Graham's smile, as their hands fell apart. "And you will bid me, will you not, to dance at your wedding? My attire shall not disgrace you."

The somber look came over his brother's face again. "I fear me your fine clothes will be worn out ere that day comes."

"Why, is your marriage so far off then? When is it to take place?"

"Not before the Greek calends, methinks," answered Ninian, turning away and picking up his pen, which Gaspard's cap had brushed to the floor. And then, fearing jealously that the young man might imagine matters not well between him and his love, he added: "It is only that Mistress Lindsay and I still cannot obtain leave to marry. But when we do, Gaspard, be assured that we shall expect your presence at the feast-unless indeed we should chance to be wed very privately. —Farewell then, and good luck go with you!"

Well, that was the end of the strange and-to him-uneasy interlude which had begun last May. There was no disguising the relief which its conclusion brought him. But at any rate, he had paid his debt to his father's memory. Ninian sat down again and resumed his letter to Agnes.

* * * * *

It was a surprise to the Grand Ecuyer, in the week that followed, to find himself once or twice near to missing his late "page." Gaspard at least had never been surly, as the now reinstated Sandy was; nor, with him, had Ninian ever needed to express a want twice. And yet . . .

About a week later again Arthur Erskine, overtaking him in the street as he was returning from a leather-worker on the quay, whither he had been to supervise an alteration in the Queen's saddle, walked back with him up to the château, and in the course of conversation observed: "What a transformation has overtaken that young Frenchman you had as page, Graham! If I mistake not, I saw him a day or two ago in the company of M. de St. André-and not only in his company, but with St. André's hand resting upon his shoulder as they walked. The young man seemed, as we should say at home, very chief with the Maréchal."

Ninian stopped in amazement. "Chief with the Maréchal de St. André!" he exclaimed. "Then he has indeed made his mark! I did not know he flew so high."

"As to be favourite of the favourite," commented Erskine dryly. "Aye, as long as St. André's favour lasts, your late protégé is like to feather his nest. I have been told since that all this came to pass through the Maréchal slipping on the stairs and this young gentleman catching him."

"I had heard nothing of it," answered Ninian. Nor would he probably hear any more of Gaspard now, though the latter had promised to acquaint him with the course of his fortunes. He was a fool to have thought that his half-brother would keep his word. And he told himself that he had looked for nothing else, for he had never felt that he could trust Malise Graham's French son farther than he could see him. If they happened to meet, his former page would probably only toss him a careless nod of the head, if so much. . . . Saints, how petty-minded he was becoming! Surely at his age he had learnt never to expect gratitude! And he was inconsistent to boot, since he had from the outset looked forward to the day when his own path and Gaspard's should diverge again.

* * * * *

For once court gossip had been well informed. It had been exactly four days after leaving Ninian's service-just time to procure himself a new wardrobe-that Gaspard de Vernay had been coming up one of the staircases leading to the Galerie de Louis XII when the Maréchal de St.

André, the King's favourite, was starting to come down it. The other factors were that the staircase had been over-polished and that Jacques d'Albon de St. André, Grand Chamberlain and Marshal of France, arrogant, young, debauched and rapacious, had been drinking rather more wine than he could carry. Nevertheless, he came carelessly down the stairs with a throng of friends and hangers-on behind him, seeing which Gaspard flattened himself against the tapestry to let the group pass. St. André, still descending, but intent on a last interchange with a friend above, waved a jewelled hand up to this latter, missed a step in consequence, half toppled, half slid . . . and found salvation by clutching and being clutched by a handsome young gentleman of his own age who happened to be in precisely the right spot for saving so important a personage from a humiliating, perhaps even a dangerous fall.

"Mort de ma vie, monsieur, I am greatly obliged to you!" said the Maréchal, half laughing, half annoyed. "I think I have not the pleasure of knowing your name? . . . Monsieur de Vernay, I might well have toppled you down this accursed staircase-or, by St. Calais, I might have crippled myself. Tell me how I can serve you?"

One afternoon, in the lull between the festivities of Christmas and those of the New Year, the Master of the Horse to the Queen of Scots came into his little chamber to find a letter lying on the table. The reinstated but still aggrieved Sandy Forbes, brushing a cloak in the corner, observed: "Yon was brocht from that braw callant ye had a while syne, Maister Ninian. It seems he has servitors o' his ain the noo!"

Out of the letter fell a slip of parchment, signed with a single name. Ninian read it with incredulous eyes.

"Learn all by these that our trusty and well-beloved Sieur de Graeme, formerly of our Archer Guard and now by our royal appointment Master of the Horse to our dear daughter the Queen of Scotland, has our full permission to take in marriage the Demoiselle de Lindsay, one of the said Queen's maids of honour, so soon after the Feast of the Circumcision as may be convenient to the said parties. And the said Demoiselle is thereafter to remain if she so wish about the person of the Queen of Scots as heretofore. Given at our château of Blois on the Feast of the Holy Innocents in the year of our Lord MDL. Henri."

Ninian read this through twice, three times; and only at the third time did he believe what it seemed to convey. Then he took up the letter itself.

You see, Monsieur le Grand Ecuyer , it began, *that I do not forget my debts. M. de St. André was good enough to procure this for me yesterday from his Majesty. If I might offer a counsel to my elder* (there was a word erased here, but Ninian easily guessed what it was) *it would be that he should take advantage of this permission as soon as may be, lest an influence even stronger than M. de St. André's should persuade his Majesty to withdraw it* .

There was no signature to this missive; it was not necessary.

His heart's desire at last! And he owed it to-of all people-the bastard brother whom he disliked and distrusted and was already secretly accusing of ingratitude! A wave of compunction surged over Ninian. Gaspard had more than repaid; he was himself Gaspard's debtor now.

As soon after New Year's Day as was convenient. Yes, Gaspard was right; the sooner the better. Madame de Valentinois could easily induce the King to revoke his permission if she thought fit. She must therefore, if possible, be kept in ignorance of its having been given. With spring in his heart, Ninian folded up the precious parchment and put it in his breast.

"Ye'll hae had guid news, I'm thinkin'?" hazarded Sandy Forbes, who had evidently been watching him.

"The best," answered his master, smiling. "You shall know it, too, before long." And with that he left the room to find Magdalen.

But on the other side of the door the glow suddenly began to fade. Ninian paused; then he threw back his head and said to himself: "*That* I shall know by her face when I tell her."

* * * * *

"Are those jewels her Majesty wore yesterday not replaced yet?" asked Lady Fleming. "I thought I had told Jean Ogilvy . . . Magdalen, my girl, take them and lock them up in the little strong-room. Here are the keys."

Magdalen came forward and took from her kinswoman the velvet-lined casket and the little bunch of keys. The proximity of Lady Fleming perturbed her nowadays. That the Queen's *gouvernante* was five months pregnant was not in itself very obvious to the unwarned eye, her carriage was so good and her skirts so wide. What dismayed Magdalen was the extraordinary indiscretion she displayed about the cause of her condition, for she was so elated to be with child by the King of France that she rather proclaimed the fact than otherwise. Magdalen was terrified by this rashness, since her boast must certainly come to the ears of Madame de Valentinois, who had never known a rival and would never tolerate one now, and to the knowledge of Queen Catherine also. What made Lady Fleming's conduct the more incomprehensible was that the

King, as always in his exceedingly rare lapses from his devotion to Madame Diane, had acted in this matter with the greatest discretion.

"Why are you looking at me in that manner, child?" asked Lady Fleming, smiling. "Is there aught amiss with my looks? You cannot be about to tell me that I have a sickly air, for I never felt better in my life! There is virtue in the royal blood of France. —Now speed away, and remember to lock everything after you."

Magdalen went out with the casket. Was it because Janet Stuart was herself a King's bastard that she was so imprudent, even shameless? And it could not but strike Magdalen as ironical that the chief reason why her own marriage was forbidden was that if she found herself with child she would be unable to fulfil her duties properly.

Magdalen Lindsay, at four and twenty, though she often fretted against this postponement, had not the same sense of the too-rapid passage of time and opportunity as her betrothed. And Ninian was never far away, a staff to lean upon, even though some days might pass without a sight of him. And meanwhile there was her little Queen, her "Reinette," daily more captivating and more dear to her. Magdalen believed that it would break her heart to be separated from her. That she was sacrificing Ninian to the royal child did not occur to her, because it was Madame Cathérine and Madame Diane who were responsible for the decree against their marriage. It was not in her power to hasten it.

Nor, it appeared, in Ninian's either, since he had failed to gain access to the King, surrounded always now by a ring-fence of courtiers, each intent upon furthering his own prospects. It was no doubt on account of this failure that her lover had become a little moody in the last few months. For weeks he had not spoken of their marriage. It had always been a tacit agreement between them that the little Queen, at least, should never be the avenue of approach to King Henri, and that even though Mary had once or twice lately asked when Mistress Lindsay and the Master of the Horse were to be married. But when Magdalen had replied, more placidly than her own feelings warranted, "Some day, your Grace," the child had not probed farther into the matter.

The eight-year-old Queen had now so many jewels that three brass coffers scarcely sufficed to hold them all. At Blois these valuables were kept in a little slice of a strongroom which had been constructed, in the time of François I, by running a stout trellis of painted iron-work across one end of a room of moderate size, and making in the wall behind these bars and scrolls of metal a series of cavities with iron doors. Inserting the largest key into the screen Magdalen let herself through and locked it behind her, unlocked the first of the panels in the wall, then the brass coffer within, threw back its lid, on which was fastened the list of its contents, and began to study this. She had to make sure that each piece of jewellery was put back in its proper chest.

The first thing she took out of the casket she had brought with her was a little golden girdle enamelled in white and red. She smiled as she held it across her palms-the span was so small. She looked next into the brass coffer for a piece of soft leather in which to wrap it, and while she had her back turned she heard a man's hasty step coming across the outer room. Thinking that someone had come to summon her she turned round again, and saw her betrothed with an unfamiliar radiance in his face, standing on the other side of the barrier.

"Ninian!" she exclaimed. "Are you sent to fetch me?"

"What are you about there?" he asked. "I must speak with you at once!"

"Then," said Magdalen, smiling at him through the bars, "speak!" Evidently he had come upon a private matter, not a summons.

"Not with this between us," answered he, tapping impatiently upon the painted metal. "Lock away those gew-gaws and come forth!"

A desire to tease him came upon the girl. "Come forth indeed! The Master of the Horse must think that I am Bravane or La Réale! But will even they leave their stalls at his command without so much as a handful of oats to tempt them?"

"Even that I have here!" Ninian laid a hand on his doublet. "Lock away the Queen's jewels, my dear, and I will show you what it is."

There was something so urgent yet so happy in his tone that she knew he was not in the mood for jesting. "I will come," she answered, and turning once more to the casket began to transfer its contents to the larger receptacles.

And Ninian stood outside, gripping in his impatience the red and gold foliation of the trellis work so hard that his palm was indented by the iron rose-petals. He watched her carefully and quickly bestowing the shining things in their places. In a moment or two she would be through the barrier to learn that the other barrier between them was down now, fallen before the King's word as the walls of the city fell before Joshua. Everything then would turn for him on how she took the news of the fall. The precious paper was valueless to him unless the light came into her eyes at the sight of it. . . .

At last every coffer was shut, the panels locked, and she was unfastening the iron door, where salamander and porcupine were enmeshed in the tendrils of a frozen rose-tree. Now she was through, and swept him a curtsey.

"And now, Master Graham, for my handful of oats!"

He pulled out the King's rescript, opened it and put it into her hands. "Read that!"

He hardly dared watch her face as she read. And yet he did, and saw, after the first instant of surprise, such a dawn of joy upon it that his head almost whirled.

"Magdalen, my heart, my darling, are you glad?"

"Glad? Oh Ninian, Ninian, what else should I be?" Letting even the precious paper fall to the floor she came into his arms with a readiness which shamed his recent self tormentings.

And, the first joy over, she beset him with questions. How had the permission been procured? When had he contrived to see the King?

Ninian shook his head as he smiled down upon her happy face. "I have not seen him. This permission was obtained, unknown to me, through the good offices of two persons. The one was the Maréchal de St. André. The other you will not easily guess."

"Who ever it was I shall bless him!"

"The other was the Maréchal's new favourite-my late page, Gaspard de Vernay."

She showed her astonishment. "M. de Vernay!"

"No other. I admit I was never more surprised in my life."

"He must indeed have more credit with the Maréchal than one knew."

"That was not what surprised me," said Ninian, half to himself.

She made no comment, but said: "Then he has indeed repaid you for your kindness to him-that kindness which I know you did somewhat unwillingly."

Ninian looked down. "Yes, I did do it unwillingly . . . and now I am ashamed that I was so grudging."

Magdalen slipped her hand inside his arm. "No, all the more honour to you for befriending him. Is not what a man does of more importance than what he feels? But you promised me one day that you would tell me the true reason for your taking him into your service."

Outside the strong room, moved with his own change of heart towards Gaspard, he told her. At the end she said thoughtfully: "Then, Ninian, if you acted the part of a good brother to him he has acted the same to you. . . . Your brother! . . . Then that is why it once seemed to me —'twas when the Queen was so ill last September-that his voice sounded strangely like yours. But in no other way do you resemble one another."

"No, fortunately," said her betrothed. "Our kinship must be kept secret, for his sake if not for mine. I know not what tale he has told St. André of his origin and parentage. But that concerns us not. There is only one concern now, Magdalen; we must be wed as soon as possible."

And, well knowing how wise were haste and secrecy, she agreed to this, willing, also, for the sake of the necessary privacy, to forego the display of a Court wedding. He thanked and praised her for that, as they walked slowly together back towards the Queen's apartments. Not far from the door Magdalen observed thoughtfully: "Then the astrologer was right. Within four months, he said, of the slaying of the hydra by Hercules."

"What hydra-what astrologer?" asked the puzzled Ninian.

A lovely mischievous sparkle came into Magdalen's eyes. "I must keep nothing from you now, I know!" And she finished the confession of her visit to Signor Giacomo just as Jean Ogilvy came hastily out of the Queen's door.

"Magdalen, what has taken you? We began to think a thief had entered the — —Good day, Monsieur le Grand Ecuyer!" Smiling, she made a reverence.

"No, I was not admitted within the strong-room," said Ninian, smiling also.

That night, that happy night, Ninian had a curious and disconcerting dream, fruit no doubt, as he told himself afterwards, of Magdalen's confidence about her visit to Queen Catherine's astrologer. For he dreamt that he himself was a soothsayer, an old man in a long black gown with a high conical cap covered with cabalistic designs. He was sitting in some vague place which seemed to be a wood, when he discerned through the trees a woman coming towards him. When she was near he saw to his surprise that it was Magdalen-for, as so often in dreams, beneath the identity of the soothsayer lay his own, so that he knew that he was merely Ninian Graham feigning to be an astrologer.

What he did then he could not remember, but one phrase of what he had presumably predicted was echoing in his ears as he woke: "Beware of the rose-branch, for it will undo us both."

He could make no sense of this fragment from the world of dreams, yet it disturbed him by its implication that even in that fantastic region he could have done a thing so extraordinary as to warn his future wife against himself-for was not the hand with the rose his own crest!

The morning broke frosty and bright, but the January sun was not fully up when Ninian, with Sandy Forbes behind him, left the château of Blois by one of its discreeter exits. He was half picturing his beloved stealing down into the great courtyard by that marvel of a spiral staircase, but in his heart he knew that she and Jean Ogilvy would never slip out by that way to the secret bridal.

His other witness, Patrick Rutherford, would await them at the church in the town where they were to be married. Ninian had wished to ask Gaspard to be present, as seemed fitting-though there was no question of dancing at this wedding-but in the few days which had intervened since receiving the King's permission he had never been able to meet him in person, and he was afraid to commit the secret to writing. In the end, too, as he reflected, it was very probable that a young man so bent upon making his fortune at Court, and already so successful, would prefer not to risk incurring the displeasure of either the crowned or the uncrowned queen by his presence at the ceremony. Magdalen's squire, who would also represent her father, was Arthur Erskine, who with Lady Fleming, had been admitted to the secret. Magdalen's "Reinette" had somehow found out about the wedding, said she longed to attend it, which of course was impossible in the circumstances, wished it to be performed by her own chaplain Messire Guillaume de Laon (which likewise was vetoed) but had succeeded in giving her dear Mistress Lindsay as a bridal gift a gown of carnation brocade which Magdalen considered much too fine for her. And fastening the plume in Ninian's hat at this moment was the Queen's gift to him —a golden brooch fashioned like a stag, with antlers of crystal.

Down the steep lane from the château, its steps slippery with rime, went the two; and just inside the porch of the old abbey church of St. Nicolas found Patrick Rutherford waiting. They went together up the cold, shadowy aisle till they came to the appointed altar, where the candles burnt before a picture, reft from some Lombard church during the Italian wars, in which the Child upon his Mother's knee seemed more attentive to the bullfinch on his small finger than to any worshippers. The priest and his boy came in; presently there were other steps approaching; Magdalen was by Ninian's side, and but a little time elapsed ere her hand was in his and he was slipping on the ring.

* * * * *

The sun was up when they came out man and wife, the blue wood-smoke rising from the hearths of Blois, the townspeople awaking to a domesticity to which the newly married pair could not look forward-although both their lives centred round a child. But it was just on that account that they could have no hearth of their own-for the child was royal.

But to contrive some shadow of a home, Ninian had succeeded in exchanging his tiny chamber for two larger ones opening out of each other, nearer the little Queen's quarters. He would have liked to replace the hangings and furniture, both of the reign before last and rather shabby, by something more modern, but this he could not afford to do. But out of the remaining links of François de Guise's chain he had had fashioned for Magdalen in the Rue des Orfèvres a lighter chain, ending in a boss of hawthorn flower with petals of the mother of pearl. And when, as his first act on entering, he hung it round Magdalen Graham's neck, the little place that chill January morning seemed bright as a June midday.

Try as he might, it was fully a week before Ninian succeeded in finding and thanking his half-brother for his intervention. At last he presented himself as a spectator at a ball which M. de Saint-André was giving, feeling sure that Gaspard would be present, and hoping to snatch a few words with him.

But the difficulty, when he got there, was to pick out that young man. Ninian had forgotten the mania for things Eastern, or supposedly Eastern, which had arisen in the Court of Henri II. The guests at the Maréchal's ball were all arrayed according to the current ideas of the costumes of the half-fabulous Orient, and the effect was gorgeous enough, if bizarre. But the dances were the dances of the west, tourdion, galliard, allemande or branle; and in one variety of the last, the *branle des lavandières*, the Master of the Horse did at last perceive M. Gaspard de Vernay in a flowing garb of embroidered yellow silk and a green turban, partnering a lady dressed (as he conjectured) in Persian costume —a lady whom to his surprise he recognised as the much-courted Madame de Saint-Cernin, of Queen Catherine's household. His ex-page seemed certainly to be making his way with wonderful rapidity!

He contrived to waylay him a little later as he passed, and plucked at his draperies to attract his attention.

"What the — —" began Gaspard, turning; and then saw who it was. "Oh, my dear Grand Ecuyer, it is you! You are not dancing? Oh, you wish to speak to me perhaps?"

"Indeed I do!" returned Ninian. "I have been trying to come at you these seven days and more! Give me a moment! —Gaspard, now that I have found you I have not words to thank you withal!"

Gaspard laid his hand upon his yellow silk breast and made him a bow. A little flushed from dancing, very sure of himself now, he looked more like their father than ever. "I am delighted to have been of service, my dear brother. My debt to you was heavy. Did you not pluck me from servitude to set me among princes! If I have partly repaid it — —"

"Partly? You have more than repaid!"

"Then I am happy. Present my duty, pray, to Madame de Graeme, the pearl of the Scottish Queen's ladies."

"She would wish to thank you herself."

"Then I will wait upon her some day," answered Gaspard, courteously but vaguely.

"The dance begins, and I'll not keep you further," said Ninian, "but tell me first-though indeed since what he did at your request I have no need to ask-you are as firmly set as ever in M. de Saint-André's good graces?"

"More firmly, I believe," answered the young man, fingering the jewel at his ear, and smiling with closed eyes-their father's trick.

"And," added his elder, "from what I saw a while ago I think you must be well advanced in the good graces of a certain very fair lady also."

"Not so far as I hope to go! Wish me luck, Ninian, for I am desperately enslaved in that quarter!"

But the violins had indeed struck up the music for an allemande, and with a swirl of his yellow draperies Gaspard was lost once more among the dancers.

And, whether his heart were genuinely engaged or no, Ninian knew that for Gaspard to become Mme. de Saint-Cernin's avowed lover —a rare privilege-would be to set the seal on his social ambitions. He was indeed aiming high.

One morning in February, when Magdalen, a month-old bride, was sewing in an inner chamber in the Queen's apartments, Jean Ogilvy slipped in, put a finger on her lips and said mysteriously: "Our Reinette has a visitor-though I think it is not she but another whom the visitor has come to see. I would not enter, were I you-unless you are summoned."

"Who is it?"

"Madame Diane!"

Magdalen's needle slipped. Since the advent of the Queen Mother of Scotland Madame de Valentinois had naturally concerned herself less with the welfare of the Queen of Scots, and Magdalen had been glad of it. She had never ceased to fear Madame Diane's possible displeasure on account of her own marriage.

But something told her instantly that this visit had no connection with anyone of so little importance as herself. "She has come to see . . . Lady Fleming," she faltered, turning pale. "What has passed?"

"First, Madame Diane looked her up and down, then she bade the Queen go away to the end of the room-and Marie, who is fond of her, as you know, obeyed-and then in a quiet voice, but a terrible one, she told her that she appeared to be suffering from the dropsy, that she must find her duties impossible to perform, and that she would arrange with her Majesty Queen Catherine to have her sent away into the country to some skilled physician. Then she swept out. She had never raised her voice, but she terrified me. Is she going to the King?"

"He is away hunting."

"To the Queen, then. —I would I could be present," added Jean irrepressibly. "If I could but change places with one of her ladies for an hour!"

Next moment Lady Fleming herself came in, two vivid patches of colour burning fiercely in a face paler than its wont. She showed her condition now.

"You have heard, Magdalen, the affronts put upon me by that woman? But she will find that she has met her match. She dare not send me away, nor the Queen either. Only one person can dismiss me-and he will not. Come, both of you, I need you." And, her head high, she left the room again.

Before they followed her the perturbed Magdalen whispered to her companion, "Madame Catherine . . . some Italian poison . . . or my poor kinswoman may be cast into a prison, or worse!"

"No," said Jean Ogilvy. "She is safe at least till the child is born in April. Is it not the King's?"

* * * * *

"The Duchesse de Valentinois craves an audience with your Majesty," said the gentleman usher.

"Admit her instantly," said Queen Catherine, taking up a book. "Mademoiselle de Raimbault, set a chair."

The great, if they dined or danced in vast apartments, were often content with exceedingly small private rooms. At Blois, Queen Catherine's own chamber was tiny, and space was precious; therefore chairs did not stand about indiscriminately.

Regal herself in her black and white, the royal mistress appeared in the doorway, advanced a step or two, then sank in a deep and reverential curtsey. The decencies were always observed in this strange ménage à trois. Indeed, they were about to be still further honoured.

"Be seated, cousin," said the Queen equably, and she closed the book over her finger.

"Your Majesty is very good," murmured Diane as she obeyed. Her lips appeared more pursed together even than usual. "I should not have disturbed your Majesty at this hour for any but a serious matter-one indeed which concerns your Majesty's honour."

This time Catherine slipped her finger from the book and laid the volume down. "I am much beholden to you for your care, Madame. —You can go, Raimbault. —My honour, I am aware, is as dear to you as to his Majesty or myself."

It was impossible to tell whether the words were instinct with a deadly irony or were uttered in good faith. In any case Madame de Valentinois bowed her head as if accepting this meed of praise.

"It is precisely my knowledge of his Majesty's fervent affection and respect which emboldens me to tell your Majesty of a certain woman, now in the château of Blois, who is spreading a calumny against his Majesty's name and yours."

Catherine's prominent and expressionless eyes opened wider. "I cannot conceive, cousin, to whom you are referring."

"Your Majesty has heard no rumour?"

The Queen looked still more blank. "But a rumour of what, Madame?"

It burst from the mistress then, despite her self-control, in a tone of cold fury. "That Madame de Flamyn, the gouvernante of the Queen of Scots, publicly declares herself to be with child by his Majesty!"

"Madame de Flamyn-with child by the King! But the poor lady must be deranged in her intellect. She must be put under proper care at once!"

"She must be sent away!" rapped out the Duchesse.

"She must certainly be removed from her post about the Queen of Scots, and disposed in some religious house until her senses are restored to her. I had not observed any distraction in her manner. It is true that I have not seen her of late."

"If your Majesty had but seen her," said Madame Diane savagely, "as I have-no later than an hour ago-you would know that it is not a matter of the mind but of the body. Madame de Flamyn is far gone with child; it cannot now be disguised, nor indeed does she seek to disguise it, alleging what she does."

"Far gone!" said Catherine. "Then indeed she must be removed."

"She must be sent out of France!"

The Queen raised her faint eyebrows. "Although I tolerate no light behaviour in my own ladies" (and this was true) "I think that course too severe, since the unfortunate woman is plainly out of her wits." She lowered her eyes for a moment. "As if his Majesty could possibly stoop. . . . The notion is ludicrous, is it not?"

With the question she glanced up quickly, fixing upon her visitor a look which said, plainly and triumphantly: "It *is* so, then, —he has slipped your hold for once?" Madame de Valentinois met her gaze boldly, but the faintest flush crept up on her marvellously-preserved white skin, and Catherine, having learnt what she wanted to know, said with an air of indifference: "It is true that she is not, as I should suppose, more than ten years or so older than his Majesty."

There was biting emphasis on the numeral, and Diane's hands clenched themselves suddenly on the arms of her chair. "Yet certainly, cousin," went on the Queen after a glance at them, "Madame de Flamyn must be sent away directly occasion offers. It would perhaps be best, would it not, to wait until his Majesty is again absent hunting-for he returns to-day, as you know. . . . Though, indeed, since there can be no truth in what the poor lady says, it will be a matter of no moment to the King whether she is gone from Blois or not. He will not observe her absence." Again there was a question in her look, and again she read the unwilling answer.

Diane was pale enough again now, and mistress of herself. "I certainly think, your Majesty," she replied, "that it would be compassionate to send away a woman so crazed as quietly as possible; therefore it would be as well to do as your Majesty suggests." She rose. "Have I your Majesty's leave to withdraw?" Forgetting or omitting her reverence, she added, drawn up to her full height at the door-and the words came out like a thrown spear—"But she must be sent soon-at the first opportunity!"

Quite motionless, Catherine de'Medici sat looking at the closed door. The mask which had already slipped for a moment was off altogether now, when there was no one to see. On her face shone all the hatred of the neglected wife who almost worshipped her husband, yet owed her very pregnancies, so essential to the throne, to the mistress's orders . . . the mistress who was twenty years older than she.

"*Soon!*" she repeated under her breath, and her own hands clenched themselves for a moment. " 'Soon' shall be, for once, when *I* choose!"

IV. PAR HEUR ET MALHEUR (1)

(May-June, 1551) —(1)

It was spring once more, spring in Touraine, and in Magdalen Graham's heart high summer. As she stood this May morning on the terrace at Amboise, whither the Court had arrived some weeks ago, and looked down on the Loire, the little town strung out along its bank and the green countryside spread before her, she tasted that rare vintage, a perfect happiness. Her life with Ninian was all and more than she had hoped for; their marriage had brought upon them no measure of vengeance either from Queen Catherine or from Madame de Valentinois; their own Queen grew daily in charm and intelligence. And the thundercloud which had lately hung over them all had broken now. Lady Fleming was gone-sent away from this very place in mid-April, about ten days before a son was born to her. To the last she had held her head high, and when she took farewell of the rest of the little household it was, "His Majesty has graciously made arrangements for my lying-in elsewhere." None knew what had taken place behind the scenes, but whatever the King's infatuation (which rumour said had now cooled or been cooled) Lady Fleming obviously could not fulfil her duties up to the very moment of being brought to bed. Magdalen missed her kinswoman's presence, and so did Jean Ogilvy, yet they both realised that when there is a large and very keen sword of Damocles most plainly hanging over the head of one person in a group, life is easier for the rest when the weapon has fallen. The little Queen preserved a rather unchildish reticence on the matter, but it was plain-and only natural-that she was not likely to feel towards her new gouvernante, Madame de Paroy, as she had done towards the old.

The episode was over; yet its consequences remained. Because of her royal lover's amour with the Scotswoman, Madame Diane, so it was whispered, had finally thrown over her former ally the Constable whom she suspected (with how much reason was never likely to be known) of favouring the liaison with a view to the setting up of a rival mistress to herself. Henceforward she would throw her immense influence on the side of the Guises; and, faithful as the King always remained personally to his old friend Montmorency-so that it was often said it was impossible to come at him save through the Constable's good graces-in any difference of opinion Diane would always carry the King with her.

Magdalen had recently heard talk about this; but the only way in which it could concern her insignificant self, she felt, was perhaps to render Madame de Valentinois slightly more hostile to her as Lady Fleming's kinswoman. But she need not think of that possibility to-day, for Madame Diane was not at Amboise, any more than the royal nursery, which, with the exception of the Queen of Scots, had remained at Blois. And this morning the Reinette was in her mother's apartments, with Jean Ogilvy nominally in attendance, so that Magdalen was free to enjoy the sun, the breeze, the view, and her own new gown. Sheer down went the containing wall of the terrace; away to her right was the line of the château, the ornate stalactiting of the pinnacles over its topmost windows foreshortened into the appearance of one great cluster; out beyond it jutted the great round mass of the Tour Charles VIII. And down below in the narrow street bordering the river a little pig had escaped from a butcher, and in its efforts to avoid capture had already upset two women. She was smiling at this when she heard a voice at her elbow.

"And what, Madame de Graeme, has the good fortune to amuse you down there?"

Gaspard de Vernay was beside her on the terrace, the very model of a young and fashionable gallant, in pearl-coloured satin with a short cloak of orange velvet hanging from one shoulder. His little pointed beard of nowadays was of a darker auburn than his hair; he wore an ear-ring in one ear, a small ruff of the latest mode, and he was scented with *eau de nèfle* .

"Charming belle-sœur," he went on, leaning beside her on the sun-warmed stone, "is it the river that you smile at? A pity you are not a trifle nearer, and the Loire could then mirror your attractions and be the brighter for them!"

"Yours would be better reflected, mon frère," retorted Magdalen gaily. "You are very fine to-day!"

"Because I go to wait upon M. de Saint-André, and some of the clothes which I have bought me to wear in London I shall wear first in Touraine, since by all account the Thames is not so good a mirror as the Loire."

"You accompany the Maréchal on his embassy, I suppose?" For Magdalen knew that in a few weeks' time M. de Saint-André, with a great train, would go to England to bear the collar of Saint-Michel to the young King Edward VI, while at the same time there would land in France a twin embassy conveying to King Henri II the Order of the Garter. The nominal peace between the two countries which had reigned since the cession of Boulogne by England more than a year ago having now been rendered more actual by the composition of some outstanding difficulties, this interchange of courtesies was intended to mark an era of entire harmony and friendship.

"But naturally I accompany him," said the young man. "Am I not honoured with his especial friendship? And since my apprenticeship with the good Ninian has so perfected my English, I hope to be constantly of service to the Maréchal in his dealings with the islanders-even, perhaps, when the islanders come to France, for it is believed that the two embassies are first to meet on French soil, before M. de Saint André sets out."

"Indeed? They would doubtless meet somewhere near the coast?"

"No, M. de Saint André tells me that it will probably be at the little town of Châteaubriant, in Brittany, where the Constable has a great mansion. At any rate that is where the Maréchal expects to assemble his train before his departure next month. —But enough of plans! The great question for me is, how much my belle-sœur is like to miss me? Do not play the prude, Madeleine, but avow that there will be a small, a very small ache in your heart!" And, laughing, but looking at her with those captivating amber eyes, he took her hand.

Magdalen let him take it, for she knew that the demonstration meant nothing. "You do not need *me* to miss you, Gaspard," she said lightly. "There are too many others."

"Too many! There is only one whose regret means anything to me. This is her hand, her cruel, unfeeling hand!"

"Why hold it then?" asked the girl, and she gently took it away. "For I know that the lady whose regret you covet is not I —and you know that I know it! I am not your dupe, I'll have you know, Monsieur de Vernay. But no doubt you will be able to persuade the English ladies of anything!"

But she smiled at him very kindly, for she was sorry for the great misfortune of his birth, and she had always liked without admiring him.

(2)

As Gaspard de Vernay went away towards the château his heart too was light. All his past was blotted out now by the marvel of his successful present, alike the five and twenty years of fair weather as the heir of Estoublon, and the short and bitter episode of his casting out, his servitude at Anet and the semi-servitude with the Scottish half-brother who had pitied and helped him-against his will, as the young man very well knew. It was, in fact, indisputable that, were he still Gaspard d'Estoublon, he would not have the Maréchal de Saint-André's arm constantly about his neck, Saint-André's Christian name upon his tongue, Saint-André's gold in his pocket. Nor could he have aspired (as yet without success) to the favours of the brilliant Eléonore de Saint-Cernin. Indeed, he would not have been at Court at all, and he would cer-tainly not have exercised for one hour that most intoxicating of all gifts-power over the lives of others. For it was he and none other who had brought about Ninian Graham's marriage, and transformed his benefactor into his debtor. Without his own favourite's influence Saint-André would not have used his influence with the King; and if Ninian were happy, as Gaspard believed he was, with that fair but unfashionable Madeleine of his, he had his father's bastard to thank for it. It was the man without a right to a name who had defeated the wish-the decree-both of the King's mistress and of the Queen —a deed to hug one's self over.

From so auspicious a beginning as Saint-André's friendship to what enviable heights might he not rise! As it was, he was already greatly to be envied, accompanying the young Maréchal on this important embassy to England. Gaspard had, when he chose to exert it, a power of attraction which rarely failed. It had served him well in his former limited sphere, and was not failing him now at Blois or Amboise. Behind him, too, was all the training of a gentleman, if only of a country gentleman. That he was poor mattered little, since Saint-André's coffers were open to him-the only drawback to this source of supply being the fact that a good many others had access to it also, for the Maréchal had a host of indigent relatives. Yes, Gaspard was well contented with the world this morning. He almost wished that M. d'Estoublon's ghost could appear at Court, to see the success of the reputed son whom he had so brutally driven out, the son of the man who had cuckolded him more than a quarter of a century before.

Towards that unknown Scottish father of his Gaspard's own feelings had undergone a change. It was from him-so his half-brother had let fall-that he had inherited the warm colouring and amber eyes which, somewhat unusual in France, were beginning to mark him out for especial notice among the ladies of the Court. Malise Graham, he had gathered from the same source, had also been dowered with much physical charm. A very useful asset; witness one of its fruits, his "step-mother's" monetary contributions which, sent punctually every month, constituted his only regular source of revenue, since Saint-André's gifts, though generous, were apt to be spasmodic. At this very hour, indeed, having just received the last consignment from Estoublon, he was about to write a letter to his "bien-aimée Madame Clémence," as he always called her, to make sure that her next was in time to reach him before he left for England next month, which reminder he would despatch by the returning messenger.

There were a quantity of pleasurable things to be done before that departure took place, more fine clothes to be laid in, further siege to be laid to the divine Eléonore de Saint-Cernin (had she really a shadowy husband in Auvergne who never came to Court?). Even his sister-in-law Madeleine was not, on some days, without charm. And always there was the dazzling and kaleidoscopic life of the Court-the feasts, the hunting-parties, the dances, the little rivalries in which a trivial triumph counted for so much-and he won these triumphs now. Truly that dull Scots half-brother of his had done him an excellent turn. But it had been more than repaid-which in itself was a triumph.

Gaspard de Vernay had not long disappeared from Magdalen's sight when there came into it a group of gentlemen very conversational among themselves-all, as she recognised, kinsmen of the Constable de Montmorency. They were his eldest son, who was but one and twenty, a younger brother, and two of those three Coligny-Châtillon nephews whose advancement the Constable always pushed with that of his own family. Intelligent and singularly united, the three Coligny brothers passed for some of the ablest men at Court. Magdalen Graham was idly wondering what they and their young cousins were discussing, when she saw the group suddenly come to a standstill and step aside, bowing low.

For from the opposite direction, with her little daughter at her side, and her eldest brother, the Duc de Guise, on the other, tall and stately in a gown of shot cherry-colour decked with crystal, came the Queen-Mother of Scotland. The little Queen of Scots herself was looking up and talking with vivacity to another Guise uncle, her favourite, the twenty-six year old Charles de Guise, Cardinal-Archbishop of Rheims-the Cardinal of Lorraine, as he was called since the death of his uncle, the Cardinal Jean, last year. His complexion rivalled his child-niece's in its purity; he smiled down upon her with sparkling blue-grey eyes, one delicate hand caressing his little fair beard; the scarlet of his robe outshone his sister's. Between them, the soldier-Duke and he (the lion and the fox, as some termed them-for the Cardinal was the cleverest of the six brothers) could rally a good part of the nobility of France, and the bulk of the clergy. But they had not the Constable de Montmorency's great wealth.

Behind them came the remaining members of that band of Scottish nobles who had arrived with Mary of Lorraine last autumn. It was always pleasant, thought Magdalen, to see one's fellow countrymen; but not so pleasant to remember that they were not nearly so popular in France as they had been, and that the Queen-Mother herself was considered by some to be outstaying her welcome. For Magdalen's part, had she been in her place, she could never, she thought, have borne to part yet again with that marvellous and bewitching child.

And then, as she made ready to curtsey when the two Queens should have approached nearer, it suddenly occurred to the girl, there on the terrace at Amboise, what a dramatic coincidence was this chance encounter-perfectly decorous and courteous-between these persons of the Guise blood and the Montmorency. Happily her own obscurity protected her from being affected by a rivalry so high placed.

For what was there, on such a jewelled morning, to warn her that in a few weeks' time everything of value in her existence and Ninian's was, in the ultimate issue, to depend upon that rivalry, mere pebbles though he and she might be in the path of two warring mountain streams?

June had come; and none had better right to know it than the inhabitants of the little walled town of Châteaubriant, set by its river in the well-watered, rolling country, plentiful in game, about forty miles north of Nantes —a town invaded by an outgoing embassy and expecting the arrival, not only of an incoming one, but of the entire French Court.

The name of Châteaubriant covered in reality more than a *ville close* and a splendid new château; it comprised also the species of feudal estate, stretching from Angers to Rennes, which was one of the innumerable possessions of Anne de Montmorency, who owned in various parts of France more than a hundred and thirty châteaux, properties and seigneuries, more than six hundred fiefs. Yet it was not but Châteaubriant's former lord, Jean de Montmorency-Laval, who had begun in 1524 to build, side by side with the ruins of the old mediæval castle, a spacious and beautiful dwelling instinct with the best feeling of the Renaissance. Fourteen years had its construction occupied; now, under its new owner, it waited with its mullioned windows, its tourelles, its spiral staircase, its great interior gardens and its cloister-like arcade of blue stone, to receive the Court of France and the English envoys. For, having regard to the space all these would occupy, the Constable de Montmorency had given orders for the lodging of M. de Saint-André and his train under silk and canvas in a meadow without the walls.

And this encampment, this little town of brightly-coloured tents and pavilions, where the setting sun shone on rippling pennons and banners, seemed to the dispirited and bewildered groom from Estoublon a strange sight this evening, and he wondered dully why the nobles and great people of this embassy going to England were thus accommodated, and not in Châteaubriant itself. It was there that he had searched for Monsieur Gaspard. But Monsieur Gaspard's body-servant, whom he had at last succeeded in finding, and whom he was following now, stumbling occasionally over a tent-rope, answered his unspoken question.

"All this, my good fellow, is because room was being reserved in the town itself for the Lord Marquis of Northampton, a nobleman of England, and the great train he will bring with him. Yet now it appears that M. le Maréchal will not after all await their coming, as was at first thought, for he sets forth to-morrow or the next day upon his journey. You have but just come in time to find my master."

"The saints be thanked," muttered the messenger, yet not as one thankful. "God knows I have ridden hard enough."

Gaspard, when his man found him, was in the horse-lines, wondering whether he could afford to take a second horse to England. Even with his step-mother's bounty this expedition was going to try his resources pretty high. The rich attire which he had bought (and only partly paid for) had proved alarmingly costly; yet the Maréchal had openly said that he expected the gentlemen of his suite to dazzle the English both by their splendid appearance and by their lavish spending. The young man had been on tenterhooks for the last day or two lest Madame d'Estoublon's messenger would not arrive in time. Now that anxiety was relieved-and it was even possible that Madame Clémence had responded to the hint conveyed in his last letter and had sent a rather larger sum than usual. Anyhow, there was always Saint-André's purse open to him if his need became too pressing.

He slapped his mare on her glossy flank and came away humming a song. What glorious weather! Heaven send it continued thus for the journey to the coast and the voyage to England.

Standing by the centre-pole in the empty tent (which was shared by several members of the Maréchal's suite) was the man whom Gaspard expected to find there, his stepmother's own groom, whom she had employed as messenger before.

"Good morrow, Didier!" he said cheerfully. "You are come in the nick of time, since we set out for England to-morrow. —Bon Dieu, what is amiss? Have you met with mischance on the road hither?"

For now that he saw the man's face more clearly the thought ran like poison through his brain—"He has been robbed of what he was bringing me!" And his own expression in that moment almost matched the messenger's.

But the man shook his head. "No mischance has come to me, Monsieur Gaspard." His voice came out in jerks. "But my mistress-that good and charitable lady . . ."

Gaspard took a step towards him. "Out with it, man! She is ill?"

Again the groom shook his head. "No, not ill. Oh, Monsieur Gaspard, how can I tell you? She . . . she is with the saints."

The young man stood stockstill, staring at him as if he had not heard aright, so stupefied that the man Didier prepared to repeat his heavy tidings. But Gaspard opened his lips and after a second or two the word "Dead?" came from them. He said it again, still dazedly, and then, "How long was she ill . . . she was strong . . . and not old. It is not possible!"

"She was not ill, Monsieur Gaspard. She did not die in her bed. It was in the forest . . . riding . . . the mare took fright . . . the branch of a tree. She was . . . killed outright. And I was with her and could not save her. . . ."

He put his shaking hands over his face, while Gaspard, shaking, too, clenched his at his sides.

"Did she leave no . . . no message for me?" he asked after a moment's silence.

"There was no time, Monsieur Gaspard. She was dead when we reached her."

"And nothing was found . . . among her papers, her possessions?"

"Nothing that could be brought to you, Monsieur. Feu M. le Vicomte's brother took possession of them. The money she would have given me to bring this month was not prepared . . . there wanted still three days. . . ." His voice died away.

Gaspard groped his way to a stool and sank down on it with his head in his hands. The man Didier resumed:

"If I could have begged some memento of her from one of her women I would have brought it for you, Monsieur Gaspard, but all was under lock and key. I could only get permission to leave from M. François d'Estoublon by feigning to be summoned to my father's death-bed. He does not know that I have come to you."

And you will come no more, thought Gaspard. . . . Oh, why had Madame Clémence chosen to ride in the forest . . . why had this wretched Didier allowed her to ride a horse which took fright . . . why, at least, if the tragedy had to be, could it not have taken place a little later, after her envoy had started out, not thus . . . empty-handed?

He sprang up as laughter and voices outside warned him that privacy was at an end, and beckoning the bearer of this shattering news to follow him, rushed out of the tent into the mocking sunshine.

It was absolutely essential to speak to his patron without delay. But the Maréchal was exceedingly busy with last preparations for departure. Dusk came down on the encampment, and still Gaspard could not get a word with him, and at supper in the great centre pavilion no private conversation was possible. The talk was all of England, of the fine show to be made there, of the hunting to be got, of the five hundred horses to be taken as far as Boulogne, of the musicians . . . and then the musicians must show their skill here, which they did, thus delaying still longer the moment when St. André should rise from table. It was not indeed until the heat in the pavilion became insufferable that he did so, and Gaspard, who had been watching his opportunity for long enough, contrived to detach him from the rest of his gentlemen.

"For God's sake give me a moment, Jacques!" he pleaded, slipping an arm into his. "I have something of particular moment to say to you."

"I marked you at supper, mon beau Gaspard," said St. André. "You had a face more befitting a funeral than a banquet."

"I had just received news of a funeral."

"My poor friend! And you mourn the defunct?"

"More than I can say. This death leaves me dependent on my own wits and-the generosity of a very noble heart."

"Ah, whose is that?" asked the young Maréchal, detaching his arm and throwing the end of his cloak over his shoulder, for under the week-old moon the June night was fresh after the heated tent. "There are not many such nowadays. If I were you, my dear Gaspard, I should rely on my wits rather than upon that other commodity you mention."

In the silence that followed between them the hum of the surrounding camp beat loud upon Gaspard's ears; the June night took on a winter coldness.

"Who is it that you mourn with so much reason?" asked St. André. "The rich uncle whose heir you hoped to be?" (For by this fable had Gaspard been wont to bolster up his status, since he could not assign himself father or estate.)

"No," said the young man with difficulty, reduced to the truth. "My step-mother, who has hitherto. . . assisted me. With her untimely death that assistance has . . . come to an end. And the sojourn in England promises to be a costly one."

"Yes, it will be costly, dear friend. As his Majesty's representative I must not keep up less state in England than my Lord Northampton is like to keep up over here. And, as I have said, I do not wish my gentlemen to be niggardly with their private moneys."

Gaspard essayed a laugh. "Parbleu, my dear Jacques, one cannot be lavish with what one has not got!"

The Maréchal de St. André turned his head towards him, his eyes glittering in the camp lights, a sardonic little smile on his mouth. "In that case, Gaspard, one does not cross the sea to England. One stays in France and-uses one's wits!" Then he laid a hand on his companion's arm. "Listen, my friend, and spare a thought to my position. I am not King Midas, but a man with a great many poor relations always begging from me. And though his Majesty is very generous to me, there are others whom he has to satisfy-Madame de Valentinois first of all, and the Constable, not to speak of MM. de Guise. Now the gifts you have had from me were gladly given, not only because you saved me from a broken nose or worse, but for your own sake. But I cannot now proceed to undertake your sole support. You must find another . . . step-mother!"

He turned and left Gaspard standing there in the moonlight. But it was not the moon which blanched his face, so that youth and vitality seemed drained from it. He felt as a man may feel who, scaling a precipitous peak and nearing the summit, has twice known a good foothold give way beneath him. The two persons who had sponsored his rapid ascent to fortune had both failed him, and he had learnt of both catastrophes in the space of a few hours. Grinding his teeth, Gaspard went back to his own tent.

Before he slept his companions had commiserated with him on the death of a near relative which, at this eleventh hour, would prevent his accompanying the Maréchal to England.

Next morning one of Saint-André's pages brought to him in the tent, where the serving-men were packing up their various masters' baggage, a letter in the Maréchal's own handwriting.

I fear I may have sounded harsh last night, my dear Gaspard, but I had no choice save to be frank. That I may not be too long deprived of your society which, believe me, I shall miss in England, pay heed to what follows :

His Majesty has promised me the reversion of the revenues of the priory of Lincennes when the Prior dies-and he is near his deathbed. But I have already promised them in my turn to my kinsman the Baron de Marillier-needy and nearly as old as the Prior. If you could contrive to compound with the old gentleman for a lesser sum, to be paid immediately (which I think you might find it possible to do) the revenues of Lincennes are yours as soon as it shall please God to call the venerable Prior to Himself. And this I promise you on the faith of a gentleman. Only-you must raise somehow the sum which will induce my kinsman to relinquish his claim upon them. You will find him living at the Manoir de la Sillerie near Etampes.

With the letter clenched in his hand, Gaspard de Vernay stood in the doorway of the tent between relief and bitter laughter. His patron had not cast him off entirely; there was a chance that he would not fall back into the quagmire of poverty and insignificance. The steps across it had been pointed out to him-but how slippery and difficult of foothold! Raise a sum of money sufficient to buy off this old Baron-how could he, when he soon would have barely enough for his own needs? On what could he raise it?

Gaspard went out gloomily into the hurly-burly of the encampment, a place of excited turmoil, where half the tents were struck already. Not very far away he could see the keep of the old eleventh-century château and two of the graceful tourelles of its neighbour, the new. Over the latter the lilied banner of France was not yet floating, but when it did, the château would be housing (besides the English envoys) the King, the Court, the two Queens of Scotland-and Ninian Graham. But he knew enough of Ninian's financial position to be aware that there was not much further assistance to be had in that quarter. He had had from his half-brother all that was available . . . and had paid him for it by smoothing his way to that pale Scottish girl. Now he who had, indirectly, exercised enough influence to do that stood here poor and powerless again.

No, pardieu, he was not yet either! He would dismiss grooms, sell his horses, all save one, and without a servant, to save expense, he would set out at once for Etampes and the Manoir de la Sillerie, persuade this old Baron de Marillier to be accommodating, go on to Paris, raise money somehow there to satisfy him, and be back at Châteaubriant in time for-or soon after-the arrival of the King and the English embassy. For to disappear from Court (unless one were on a diplomatic mission or had some high charge in the provinces) was in his estimation to disappear from life altogether. He would not risk severing the thread which bound him to his appointed place in the arras.

(5)

Straight as lances, the poplars of the avenue barred the sunset sky as Gaspard, hot, dusty, and not a little weary, rode between them on a weary horse. But the poplars were untended and the avenue grassgrown. The Manoir de la Sillerie, which, after nearly four days in the saddle, he had reached at last, was plainly not the home of a man who had prospered.

The Baron de Marillier proved to be frail, white-bearded and shabbily attired; but he was also a veteran of the Italian wars and downright in speech. At first he imagined that this young gentleman, who represented himself as sent by his kinsman Saint-André, had come to announce to him the decease of the Prior of Lincennes and his own consequent enrichment. When he was told the truth his manner became frosty and his language vehement.

Since he appeared to have no family, there was nothing to prevent the ensuing meal, and indeed the whole of the evening, being spent in argument. When Gaspard stressed the vigour and good health of the Prior (since to repeat what St. André had said in his letter about his imminent death was not politic) the old gentleman, suddenly manifesting Huguenot leanings, replied that no doubt the fat monk took good care of himself, having every means at his disposal to make life easy-very different from the case of an impoverished old soldier like himself. Yet as the evening wore on he did show some signs of considering a compromise; and when Gaspard went to bed in the sparsely-furnished room with its worm-eaten furniture, he was not without hopes of inducing his host to compound for his claim.

And in fact next morning the old man announced his arrival at the conclusion that, at his age, it was not wise to sacrifice the substance for the shadow. He was willing to sell the reversion of the revenues of Lincennes for ready money. But the sum he named was a great deal more than Gaspard had anticipated. The whole of the forenoon was consequently spent in warfare, and when the young man left for Paris in the afternoon, the amount was still much larger than he had hopes of raising there.

Next day, indeed, he had the greatest difficulty in obtaining the half of it, but did so by going to three different moneylenders. His only security for borrowing was the very reversion which he was trying to buy. He was not heir to Estoublon and its revenues now. Back again at his hostelry in the Rue de l'Homme Armé, the money he had scraped together hidden under the planking of the floor, he walked up and down above it for more than an hour, while the idea which had never been wholly absent from his mind for the last few days took entire possession of him. If Fate were so perverse and old Marillier so grasping and obstinate, then the old man must predecease the Prior of Lincennes. It was quite simple; indeed, Gaspard had realised from the first that it would be the best solution of the difficulty.

But the Baron must not die by violence. It would have given the exasperated young man great pleasure to feel his dagger hilt check against those lean ribs, but that method was quite out of the question. Yet here in Paris, if anywhere out of Italy, there were other and subtler means of death, could one find the right source of them. He sought the innkeeper, made discreet enquiries about a "love potion," and was advised to go under cover of nightfall to an apothecary in the Rue des Chardonnerets, a little street leading down to the river, and went.

The street was steep, and at the end a gleam of light showed the quayless Seine, flowing dark and menacing. It must have been long since any goldfinch sang here. There were no roisterers about, nor could one hear a single drunken laugh or cry of a man assailed; the only sound was the gurgle of the runnel in the middle carrying filth to the river. This should be the door of the man who sold love philtres, for above it hung, as he had been told, the sign of two hearts conjoined above a goblet. There was a light somewhere within; Gaspard went down the worn steps, knocked, and when the door opened was drawn by a cautious hand into a little low room, very ill lit, and asked his pleasure, in a man's voice which added banteringly, "Surely you, *mon beau seigneur*, have no need to buy a love potion!"

A kind of stupor descended upon the young man during the colloquy which followed. He was not sure what his own actual words had been, but he could guess, when he saw a little bottle being held out to him. The same voice said:

"Now this, young sir, is the very thing for you—a most gentle, natural-seeming medicament. For an old man-or indeed for a youth not come to his full strength-there is none more efficacious, especially if he be already failing. You will comprehend that there is the less risk of suspicion because it is not violent or sudden in its effects. Empty this phial in the old gentleman's wine cup or his posset drink-and you can be gone before he dies."

And now for the first time Gaspard seemed to see clearly the face of the speaker, and he was no old wrinkled wizard, but youngish, benevolent-looking and trim-bearded. It was he himself whose cheeks were pale as he looked on the tiny phial with its mortal contents. Death in that little measure of colourless liquid-death and a fortune!

"I will buy your . . . love philtre," he said.

* * * * *

He left Paris next day with the money heavy in his saddlebags, the phial a featherweight in his breast. And all the way back to La Sillerie he debated the method of its administration; wondering whether the Baron took a cordial upon retiring, or whether he could give him the poison at supper, when they were likely to be alone, save when the dishes were brought in. He had learnt that Madame de Marillier was long dead, the Baron's children too-which was lucky. What servants Gaspard had seen at the Manoir were old and foolish-seeming. It ought not to be too difficult.

The poplar avenue once more, the entrance, and M. de Marillier chilly by the fire in the hooded chimney, June though it was. Clearly he was ailing as well as old, thought the returned guest, with satisfaction; his sudden decease would be all the more natural.

But first, more bargaining. No, said the Baron, it must be the whole sum he had named or none! A little time to find the rest? "Eh bien, as a concession, if the remainder of the sum be forthcoming within a month-within a month, mind you! —I might consent to sign a deed relinquishing my claim. But if it be not forthcoming in a month, I shall maintain it . . . and not return the sum you have brought either, I warn you!"

"And much good will this money do you!" thought Gaspard, watching him count over the gold which he had brought from Paris. Yet leave it behind with the doomed man he must, in self-protection. Suspicion might fall upon him otherwise. His eyes followed the Baron as he rose with the bag, to deposit it in some safe place, no doubt.

But no; M. de Marillier went to the door and called "Nicolas! Nicolas!" on which there appeared, so quickly as to make it seem probable that he had been just outside, a large and muscular serving-man of forty or so who looked far from foolish.

"Put this gold away for me, Nicolas," said his master, "and bring me back the key. It is the money I told you of, that is to say, a portion of it. After that you can serve supper."

This was disconcerting enough. But something far more disconcerting occurred at supper, where they were waited upon throughout by this unexpected, powerful henchman who seemed so trusted. For about half-way through the meal the Baron, without any warning, observed, chuckling:

"You had not seen my watchdog before, Monsieur de Vernay! I call Nicolas my watchdog because he looks after me with such care. He was a little indisposed when you were last here-but that happens very seldom. Some more of this hare? —No? —Nicolas knows all my affairs, too, even why I have the pleasure of entertaining you now. So if" —and here he looked hard at his young guest under his white brows —"if it should have crossed your mind how greatly it would benefit your pocket if I should die before the month is out-he! he! he! . . ."

"Monsieur," broke in Gaspard quickly, "such a jest ——"

"You must bear with it, young man, you must bear with it! Fill M. de Vernay's glass, Nicolas!" The Baron laughed shrilly. "No, no, I am not afraid to stand with you at the top of my half-ruined tourelle or to walk with you along the river-bank, because, you see, my good Nicolas would know what it meant if I turned giddy in either of those — —"

Gaspard sprang up in his place, white and furious. "Monsieur de Marillier, who gave you the right to insult so grossly a guest at your own table! I shall leave your house at once!"

The old gentleman rose also, more slowly. "No, no, I pray you not to do that, Monsieur de Vernay-lest I should think my foolish arrow had found its mark. —Come, forgive an old man, for I confess that it was a jest of an exceeding ill savour, and that I ought not to have made it. Ah, that is right!" as Gaspard, not knowing what else to do, sat down again. "But do not tell my young kinsman the Maréchal of my ill-conduct —though I think he would have liked to see the fire of you when you are angry!"

'Fire' when there was a cold hand laid suddenly on his heart like that! Gaspard could not be sure, he felt he never would be sure, whether his host had been merely jesting, as he said, or . . . conveying a warning. But one thing was clear: that he himself was the veriest simpleton ever to have been blind to the suspicion that must have fastened itself upon him if he had used that phial in his breast . . . if indeed it was still there! All at once he had a terrible fear that he had dropped it, and that it had been found, here in the manoir, and recognised for what it was. Only strength of will kept him from thrusting a betraying hand into his doublet there and then.

However, the only course was to pass the matter off, accept the apology, such as it was, and leave La Sillerie next day, all of which he did, seething with wrath and chagrin. The morrow found his horse's head turned for Brittany once more; Châteaubriant drew him like a magnet. Once there he could also discover whether the moneylenders of Nantes, only forty miles farther away, were more amenable than those of Paris.

And meanwhile, there being no lack of water this summer, so that the sandbanks were less of a danger, the Loire was bearing three Queens and their attendants to Nantes, where they would disembark for Châteaubriant. The King and his nobles were going by land; the royal children remained at Blois and Madame de Valentinois at Anet.

It was the day on which, later, the Queens would reach Nantes —a hot, sultry day with more than a threat of thunder. The string of gilded, silk-canopied barges, which earlier in the week had slid past Langeais and Candes and Saumur, and had made Gennes and St. Maur echo to the sound of lutes and laughter, was approaching Ancenis and Champtoceaux, where the wide river seemed almost to be split into different arms by the long wooded islets in its course. Beneath the awning in the stern of the last of the royal barges, that of the Queen of Scots, a laughing group composed of three of her child companions and Mistress Jean Ogilvy were watching a contest between Arthur Erskine and the Chevalier de Brion at cup-and-ball, in which the grave young Scot appeared to be scoring highest. Mary herself, sitting rather sedately in her little crowned chair, divided her amused attention between this rivalry and the half-frightened manner in which Mary Livingstone, kneeling on the carpet at her feet, was playing with the little monkey on a silver chain which the Constable had recently presented to the nursery. And that irreproachable middle-aged French lady, Françoise d'Estamville, Madame de Paroy, who had been appointed to the place of the erring Lady Fleming, sat with an unopened book upon her knee and her eyes on her royal charge. A greater contrast to the late royal light-of-love could scarcely be imagined. Last of all, near the superstructure of the cabin sat Magdalen Graham, fashioning a close-fitting head-dress for her Reinette which was to have as a border a design of silver strawberries with tiny pearls for seeds.

Leaning against the superstructure itself her husband smiled down at those skilful fingers. Some day they would be sewing a small garment for a child of his and hers-but not yet.

"You are a skilful gardener, Mistress Graham," he remarked, watching the needle pick up a pearl and fix it in place. "But it is as well that this barge is not a galley off the coast of Scotland; your pearls would scarce have come easy to your needle there!"

Magdalen smiled with down-bent head. "Certainly this is a happier voyage." The tone said much more than the words; and next moment she flashed up a look at Ninian which showed quite clearly why she thought it so.

He stooped towards her. "So you do not regret the chance-for it was nothing else-which brought a poor middle-aged Archer back in one of M. de Villegaignon's ships?"

He saw the corner of Magdalen's mouth curl up in the rare way he loved. "It is not the middle-aged, but the old who keep on asking foolish questions! —Sit you down, for pity's sake; you are too tall up there, and I cannot keep my eyes upon my design."

So the Master of the Horse sat down by her side, and together they fell to talking-in a discreetly hushed tone-of Madame de Paroy and her suitability for her post. Ninian thought that she seemed all that could be wished. Magdalen was more critical.

"There is one respect," she murmured, " —nay, two-in which methinks she could be bettered. The first is, that I fear our Reinette has taken a dislike to her."

"Lady Fleming is indeed hard to succeed, the Queen having been accustomed to her from her infancy. If only she had not proved so . . . attractive!"

"If only she had not proved so foolish!" said her young relative severely. "To parade her condition like that! Yet I would she were still here, for she was always good to me, and I sometimes have a fear-and this, Ninian, is my second objection-that Madame de Paroy does not understand her Majesty's constitution as my kinswoman did."

She looked tenderly towards the little girl who was so much to both of them.

"That sounded like thunder," said Ninian a moment later. "It is hot enough."

"I hope we shall not have a storm when we arrive at Nantes," said his wife. "It will be so difficult to keep the children from getting wet as we disembark."

Ninian rose and lifted the edge of the awning. "The sky has a very black look beyond Champ-toceaux," he reported. "But there is no need to fret yourself, my dear: there will be litters at the quay and cloaks in plenty."

"But the Queen takes cold so easily. There it is again!"

The little Queen heard it too, and was delighted. "A storm. Will there be lightning? I would have the awning put by so that I can see it." She turned round in her chair. "Master Graham, will you give an order?"

Ninian moved forward. "With respect, your Majesty, I shall ask to be excused. It is likely that there will be rain."

"And at the first drop of rain," said Madame de Paroy firmly, "your Majesty will enter the cabin."

* * * * *

In Mary of Lorraine's cabin her ladies had been dismissed in order that she might dictate letters into Scotland to her elderly secretary. He had now started to write them out in a fair hand, while the Queen herself, with a furrowed brow, paced slowly to and fro. The first fervency of her reception at the French Court, nine months ago, had long since faded; she had heard it whispered more than once that her Scottish train were now considered in France as mere fortune-hunters, anxious to swallow all that she could procure for them. It was true that, aiming as she was at the regency of Scotland, she had striven to bind the nobles in question to herself by every means in her power. But, instead of the large gifts of money for which she was always hoping from King Henri, she had latterly received nothing but promises.

For some weeks now she had been saying openly that she would be glad to be gone; but would she? Her position in Scotland was no easy one; even if she succeeded in wresting the regency from Arran, God knew it was no land for a woman to govern! Yet she was resolved to do her best for her daughter's heritage, weary to death as she sometimes was of an intriguing and self-seeking nobility and alarmed at the spread of heretical ideas in religion. . . . Oh, to be going to Joinville to her widowed mother, not to be facing a return, widowed herself, to those cold Northern shores, leaving behind that little daughter, so rich in promise, so admired and beloved. . . . But it was the lot of queens to part from their daughters. Why had she not caused that dear child to be with her in this barge to-day, as she had done yesterday? She would not then have felt so lonely.

How hot it was! Mary of Lorraine made a gesture to the page at the cabin entrance, and he drew aside the curtain for her. She passed out to the sound of a long roll of thunder in the distance.

* * * * *

While one of her ladies read aloud to Queen Catherine, reclining on a day-bed, the rest chatted in low tones or worked at their embroidery-all, that is, save the fair Madame de Saint-Cernin. Sitting negligently by one of the cabin windows, she was looking out, but it was probable that she did not really see the islands or the heights of Champtoceaux gliding past. She had a letter in her lap, under her long, slender hand —a short letter, of which she knew the phrases by heart, for it was some days since she had received it.

> *Most cruel beauty* , it said, *most cruel beauty in the world, what can I do to win you; what feat can I perform, what great thing renounce for your sake? But I waste paper, as I waste my sighs, for I am going to an unfortunate land which has never beheld you. And when I return you will have forgotten both me and the hope which you held out of late to your poor captive. —G. de V.*

At last, with a slow smile, her indolent dark eyes veiled, she took up the letter and slipped it into her bosom. For some time no one among her score of admirers had stirred Eléonore de Saint-Cernin to quite the same extent as this gentleman of M. de Saint-André's, who had the bearing of a prince, but of whom no one seemed to know the antecedents, so that it was beginning to be whispered at Court that he was some prince's bastard. After all, perhaps, when he returned from England Gaspard de Vernay might find that she had not forgotten him . . . or might find that she had.

Now Queen Catherine had recently acquired a female dwarf, an unhappy, ageless little creature whom she dressed in all the colours of the rainbow and called La Gioja. This deformity, half child, half old woman, had been crouching at the open door of the cabin gazing out with lacklustre eyes. Now she suddenly sprang up with a shriek, ran in, and crying blindly "*Temporale, temporale!*" fell on her knees at Madame de Saint-Cernin's feet and hid her face in her skirts. A breath of hot air blew in after her, and on it the first mutterings of the distant storm.

(7)

At four o'clock in the afternoon of Friday, the nineteenth of June, eight days after Saint-André's departure and a day after the arrival of the King and Court from one direction, of the three Queens from another, a concourse of more than a hundred mounted gentlemen accompanied the two Bourbon princes, the Comte d'Enghien and the Due de Montpensier, half a mile out of Châteaubriant, for the purpose of receiving the English envoys and their train. Since in numbers and display the embassy was somewhat overpowering these indeed required some reception and housing, for in addition to the Marquis of Northampton, the Bishop of Ely and the other gentlemen who actually composed it, there had come also three earls, five lords, fourteen or fifteen gentlemen, Garter King of arms, a herald, a pursuivant, and servants to the number of nearly two hundred and fifty. Lord Northampton alone had sixty-two. The château was soon crammed to its utmost capacity, and all lesser, and even some important members of the various royal households had to find accommodation as best they could in the tiny villages round Châteaubriant, for the available space in the town itself was occupied by the bulk of the English arrivals.

But, before all this quartering took place, the envoys were straightway borne, booted and spurred as they were, to the King's presence; and immediately it went about how gracious had been their reception and how much satisfaction it had given to these emissaries of an erstwhile enemy.

And in the evening there was dancing in Queen Catherine's great apartment; and here the English nobles and gentlemen saw not one Queen but three, and Magdalen Graham danced with a young gentleman who was ravished to find that he need not address her in French. The sound of his speech was not quite what she had been accustomed to hear north of Tweed; nevertheless, it carried her thoughts oversea to her father and her Selkirkshire home.

Her Reinette, stepping with a childish stateliness through a pavane, looked enchanting, all the more so that she was flushed with what Magdalen sadly feared was the beginning of a cold caught in the thunderstorm at Nantes after all.

Next afternoon an auburn-haired young gentleman, travel-stained, close-lipped and pale, rode into the overcrowded little town and set about the almost hopeless task of finding himself a lodging. Told at first that it was out of the question, every available foot of space being taken up by the English invaders, he yet had the luck to obtain a corner. His serving-man Blaise, left behind when Gaspard had set out for La Sillerie, apologetically put at his disposal the tiny garret which he had by some means contrived to secure for himself and the greater part of his master's baggage, at the top of a house crammed with English. Miserable though the little place was, Gaspard preferred it to betaking himself to some outlying village, as he learnt that most of his compatriots had been obliged to do.

Blaise carried his master's saddle-bags up into the garret and began to remove his own small effects. He could sleep anywhere, he said, under a tree or in a dry ditch, the nights were so warm.

"Or in the hostess's own bed, I dare wager, you rascal!" commented his master. "I saw you making eyes at each other just now, and guessed how you contrived to keep this nook in the teeth of the English. —Leave that new suit I gave you behind, instead of spoiling it by cramming it into that bundle!"

When he had gone Gaspard threw himself down upon the pallet bed. It did not do to be too fastidious; Blaise, however, had just begged a pair of sheets for it. Moreover, as matters were going at present, this unworthy lodging was like soon to be all that he, despite his fine feathers, could afford. . . . Curse the unruly horse which had thrown Madame Clémence! Curse the Baron de Marillier and his grasping temperament! Curse the wave of destiny which had lifted him himself thus high, only to plunge him deep in the trough of the sea once more!

The house itself was strangely quiet, for all the foreign gentry whom it harboured were gone, so Blaise had told him, to watch the King playing tennis at the château. In the crowd of applauding onlookers in the tennis-court, he, Gaspard de Vernay, should have been one . . . no, he should be in England with the King's envoy, sharing in the magnificent entertainments which would be offered to Saint-André there. And it was Saint-André's own doing that he was not!

The sunlight began to move round the hot, sloping-walled little room, over the white face and the chestnut hair on the pillow, over the costly clothes bought for the English adventure which Blaise had unpacked and hung from nails in the lath and plaster walls. And lying there Gaspard asked himself why he had come back to Châteaubriant after all. It was quite true that to drop out from that jostling throng of rivalries which was the Court was to risk being unable to shoulder one's way in again. But did he want to show himself there to be asked with a sneer why he had not gone to England with the Maréchal, his patron? His half-brother, who was presumably here in attendance on the little Queen of Scots, would certainly ask him the reason-though he would not sneer. He could easily keep out of Ninian's way, however. But what of Madame de Saint-Cernin, so nearly won? He had meant to bring her some rich gift from England-but now, unless fortune should befriend him again, he had not the money to buy her the merest trinket.

But he could not keep away entirely. After he had rested a little he would go to the Château. There would probably be some evening entertainment in the open air at which he could more easily avoid being recognised against his will, particularly as none of his acquaintance would expect to see him, believing him to be over sea. There was even a mask amongst his effects made ready for England. He turned over and fell asleep.

It was an aristocratic and polished athleticism which had been displayed this afternoon in the tennis-court, when the English nobles and gentlemen could admire King Henri's vigour and prowess at his favourite game. But, in the long, light June evening which followed, a more rustic and popular amusement was offered to them, for in the fields beyond the château wrestling matches had been staged between their own English serving-men and attendants and the local Bretons, while all the court stood round and the Queen and ladies watched from their litters.

Nothing was easier, as Gaspard soon found, than to walk the outskirts of that applauding throng without attracting attention. The wrestling, of which he caught occasional glimpses, did not greatly interest him, but it was different with the English visitors, for whenever he passed a group of them he overheard wagers being offered and taken and exclamations of "Well thrown, well thrown!" "He has the Breton down!" "Whose man is he?" and the like. And presently he found himself near two middle-aged Englishmen standing under a tree apart from their compatriots. In one of these he recognised Sir John Mason, the resident English ambassador, and passing behind the tree halted there, with some idle purpose of hearing what were Sir John's views on the entertainment offered. The Ambassador was reported to be as crafty, cold and subtle as any Italian, and was suspected of having a mordant pen and, on occasion, a tongue to match.

The two were not, however, speaking of the wrestling. Sir John seemed to be pointing out to his companion, whom he presently addressed as my Lord Rutland, various personages of the French court over on the other side of the meadow.

"I perceive," said the Earl, after a moment, "that her little Majesty of Scotland is not present this evening. The sport, perhaps, was not deemed fitting for her tender years, being somewhat boisterous."

Sir John shook his head. "The reason is more like to be that the child suffers these two days from a cough which it seems grows hourly more troublesome."

"Yet she is a healthy child enough, is she not-unlike the Dauphin, who appears in his nature sickly?"

The Ambassador nodded. "Natheless, she was very ill last September of the flux; indeed, 'twas thought that she could not recover, as I writ to the Council at the time." He paused, and then added in a lowered and highly significant tone: "But God was pleased to order otherwise."

Gaspard, at the side of the tree-trunk, saw the scandalised and startled face of Lord Rutland, as he glanced hastily round to see if his companion had been overheard. "Sir John, Sir John," he stammered, "have a care! These Frenchmen may understand our tongue. . . . You cannot mean . . . I like not to take your meaning!"

"No need, my dear lord, to take it!" said Sir John, smiling into his beard. "I have ever too great a love, I fear, for an unfitting jest. Moreover . . ." here the words were lost to Gaspard . . . "when my Lord of Northampton brings a demand for her hand. Though indeed the chance of King Henri agreeing to the said demand is as slender as the thread of a spider. Do we not all know that?"

"I think my Lord Bishop of Ely — —" began the Earl; and then so great a shout went up from the meadow that the remainder of Lord Rutland's sentence was drowned. There was, moreover, a sudden jostling by spectators striving to get a view of the cause of the acclamation, and Gaspard was by them cut off from the two Englishmen.

But he had heard enough. Throwing his cloak round the lower part of his face he walked slowly away with bent head to the outskirts of the meadow, and there, among the closing buttercups and the scent of meadowsweet came to a stop underneath an elm and stayed wrenching at the little leafy twigs on its bole.

If Sir John Mason had written what he said-or hinted-he had to the English Council of State about the Queen of Scots' illness last autumn, it showed that he had small doubt of what their feelings would have been had she died of it. This English earl had repudiated the idea, it was true, but that was only English duplicity or hypocrisy, and the fear of being overheard. Yes, there could be no doubt that the English Government, whatever they might pretend, would be only too glad to learn that God had been pleased to remove the child from the steps of the English throne (unless, indeed, her hand could be secured for its present occupant).

Why, had not Ninian himself admitted that very thing at the time of her illness last September?

But, as Sir John Mason had admitted, she was a healthy child. And if the flux had not carried her off a cough was hardly likely to do so. Yet with one of tender years it was impossible to tell. So many children died in infancy. . . .

Suddenly Gaspard started away from the elm-tree as though his fingers had encountered a scorpion upon its trunk, and began to stride through the long grass and flowers of the untouched meadows as though he were trying to escape from something. But all the time he was going to meet it . . . and he knew it.

Was not the first move to get into discreet touch either with Sir John Mason or one of the members of the embassy from England? There had been a Bishop of Ely mentioned just now; he knew nothing of him. . . . Oh no, no! That was the very last step that should be taken! Whatever the secret desires of the English envoys, those envoys could not risk having the slightest traceable connection with him, Gaspard de Vernay, and the thought which was driving him at such a rate away from the laughter and applause which still came faintly on the breeze. Though the envoys were so conveniently here at Châteaubriant, he could not open communication with them, for they would not dare to entertain such a proposal. Nor must there be any traceable connection between himself and his . . . thought. And as presently the translucent green sky darkened and a bat or two flickered by, he began to see how that possibility could very smoothly be avoided.

He stopped and turned back then. The grass was heavy with dew, and a few stars had come out timidly to look at him. And as he slowly returned towards Châteaubriant, Gaspard was reflecting on his best procedure . . . afterwards. He would have to go and find the English Council of State, at Greenwich or elsewhere to receive the tangible expression of their gratitude. This could not possibly fail to be great, very great, for he would have changed the whole political outlook of a kingdom.

But meantime there was a delay which must make him pause for a little. From what he had heard, it seemed clear that the Marquis of Northampton was charged to demand the hand of the Queen of Scots for his own young sovereign. But the demand would certainly be refused. It was maddening that he had to wait until it was made, because meanwhile this cough, this indisposition, which was to pave his way for him, might pass. —Patience, patience! Overhaste might ruin all.

A breeze, hardly more than a sigh, swept over the elms and an owl called. But in the château, the wrestling-match long over, they were dancing, and the sound of the violins carried far into the summer night.

Sunday, the twenty-first of June, dawned flawless and bright, of good augury for the day which was to see the Garter bestowed on the King of France. The large room where the Court had danced the night before, after the wrestling match, having been made ready, Lord Northampton was conducted thither betimes, and there he and the Constable de Montmorency, who was already a Knight of the Garter, put on the robes of the Order. Thence they proceeded into the King's private chamber, where, the Bishop of Ely having made a Latin oration to his Majesty, and the Cardinal of Lorraine having expounded it, the Marquis, with the assistance of the Constable, invested King Henri with the Garter, and all in his Garter robes the King went to hear Mass.

In these robes, too, he and Lord Northampton and the Constable subsequently dined at noon, with the Cardinal of Lorraine a fourth at the table. Monsieur de Châtillon-Gaspard de Coligny, the Constable's nephew-entertained the rest of the commissioners, the Earls of Rutland and Worcester, his brother the Cardinal de Châtillon, the Duc de Guise and his younger brother the Comte d'Aumale at his table. But afterwards the Marquis of Northampton, oppressed with the heat of the day and the trappings of the Garter, and with the repletion following a large meal, was by no means sorry to follow the King's advice and retire for a while into his own chamber, where he was thankfully divested of his glories and was able to take his ease. Yet scarcely were his robes off when there came a gentleman of the King's privy chamber to beg the loan of a smaller badge of the Garter for the day; on which the Marquis sent him "the prettiest little George" he had with him. His repose was, in fact, brief, for in an hour's time came M. de Châtillon to convey him to an interview with the King in his bedchamber, where once again the English envoy found himself in the company of the Constable and the Cardinal of Lorraine, augmented this time by the latter's two brothers, Guise and Aumale. Here, unimpeded by his robes, the Marquis made the King a speech about his young sovereign's friendly sentiments towards him, and broached the question of his marriage with the Queen of Scots.

But this was referred to a commission to sit next day, consisting of the English envoys on the one hand and on the other of the Constable, his nephew Châtillon, the Duc de Guise and his brother the Cardinal, the Bishop of Soissons, the Chancellor Bertrandi and one other.

* * * * *

If it was hot in the royal apartments in the château that afternoon, it was stifling in that garret in the town where Gaspard de Vernay sat writing at a rickety table in his doublet and hose, the sweat standing on his forehead. He was writing very slowly indeed, his eyes continually seeking a piece of paper which seemed to be set as an exemplar before him, while his pen painstakingly formed the same words over and over again. . . .

Down below sounded the twanging of a lute, together with a man's voice upraised in some English song. And after a while the words of the constantly recurring refrain beat their way into the writer's consciousness, and despite the muffling effect of distance and the foreign tongue, he took in their purport:

> *Beauty melteth like the snow.*
> *Fairest rose must fall, mu . . . u . . . ust fa . . . all.*

He paused at last and lifted his head, listening.

"Yes," he said to himself in a low voice, "yes, I know English not so ill now. . . ."

Said Madame de Paroy about four o'clock that afternoon to Magdalen Graham and Jean Ogilvy: "It is out of the question for her Majesty to sup with the Court in the park this evening. Her cold is not better and her cough gains upon her."

The three were standing in the small octagonal ante-room leading to the little Queen's apartments-and leading also in other directions, for it had no less than four doors.

"You are not anxious on her Majesty's behalf, I hope, Madame?" enquired Jean quickly. "It is surely nothing more than a fever of cold that afflicts her?"

"No, not precisely anxious," answered the Frenchwoman. "I suggest precaution, that is all. But it concerns me that her Majesty resents my prohibition. For so young a child I find her obstinate, and unwilling to recognise the wisdom of her elders."

The tone of criticism in the new gouvernante displeased Magdalen. "Her Majesty certainly knows her own mind, Madame," she observed. "But do you not find her always ready to see reason?" And to herself she thought, I must try to make her see reason in this case.

And when, a little later, she was with the Queen, and Madame de Paroy's place temporarily taken by Madame de Curel, she set about this laudable task. Madame de Curel, who was skilled at the embroidery frame, had been giving the little girl lessons in the art in which she was afterwards to become so proficient and to find so much solace, and Magdalen watched the small fingers thrusting the needle in and out. Now and again, however, the needle came to a standstill as the child paused to cough.

"Oh, cette quinte!" exclaimed Madame de Curel distressfully from the other side of the room.

"It is nothing," said Mary, recovering her breath. "And not to sup in the park with the Queens —'tis absurd. Her Majesty my mother ——"

"Her Majesty your mother does not wish you to do it," said Madame de Curel firmly. "She has told Madame de Paroy so."

"It is not absurd, your Grace," said Magdalen gently. "We who love you so cannot allow you to run risks."

The Queen put out her hand and laid it on hers. "What risk should I run on so warm a night?" Childishly she stroked the hand under hers. "Dear Mistress Graham, I am sure that if you had been in Madame de Paroy's place ——"

But Magdalen shook her head, laughing. "No, no, ma Reinette! Madame de Paroy is quite right!"

"She may be right, but" —here a little regal air descended quite naturally upon the small speaker —"she does not please me."

"Yet she desires nothing but your Majesty's good, you know that," said Magdalen, after an uneasy glance across the room in the direction of Madame de Curel. "And with that cough of yours ——" She gazed not altogether happily at the flush on that pearl-like skin. "But to-morrow you may perhaps be able to go out, for her Majesty, Queen Catherine, has sent a new remedy for you to take upon retiring."

The child made a face. "The last remedy of Queen Catherine's which I took made me sick-do you not remember? Yet I suppose that since she descends from some leech or apothecary-hath not the name Medici to do with such?"

This time Magdalen laid a finger hastily on her lips, and her glance across the room was almost agonized. "Your Majesty, be careful, I entreat of you! Queen Catherine comes of the great house of Florence ——"

"And the great house of Florence were but merchants not so long ago," said the daughter of kings rather contemptuously. "When I am Queen of France ——"

"Do not be so sure that you *will* be Queen of France!" interrupted another childish voice teasingly. Mary Seton and Mary Livingstone had come over from the other side of the room. "I heard Master Erskine say that my Lord Northampton is to ask for your hand for the King of England! How will you like that?"

"I care not," retorted the royal child, with as much resolution as though her hand were her own to dispose of. "I am to wed Monseigneur le Dauphin, that is well known."

"And wed him you will, Madame, rest assured," said Madame de Curel, who had followed the children. "His Majesty will not give up the daughter who is so dear to him."

"If the Queen is not to sup in the park this evening," said Mary Seton disconsolately, voicing the apprehension of the whole nursery, "then we shall none of us —— —" She broke off with a scream as the Queen's new pet, the little monkey, making a flying leap from the back of a chair, alighted on her shoulder and gave a tweak to her close-fitting headdress.

Magdalen seized his silver chain and pulled him off. "Naughty Gris-gris!" admonished his mistress, laughing. "You are verily more trouble than the Dauphin's bear-cub!"

"I hate Gris-gris!" exclaimed Mary Seton, red in the face, and with tears in her eyes. "I wish he were dead!"

"Hush, hush!" said Magdalen, bringing out her pocket handkerchief.

"But you need not feign to like Gris-gris, Mistress Graham," retorted the child, "for I believe that in your heart you hate him, too!"

12

The supper in the park that evening-banquet, rather, with nothing of impromptu about it-took place in daylight, for afterwards there was to be coursing of snared deer on a neighbouring heath. So it was the declining sun, not candles or torches, which shone upon the rich costumes and the rich food, the roast peacocks and swans, the innumerable pâtés of quails and the gilded sweetmeats, and brought out from the fine table linen the clover perfume with which it was faintly scented.

Queen Catherine, magnificently attired, sat among her ladies at table, smiling and free with her tongue as she could be when she pleased, for she loved a jest, and a broad one at times. And at this feast she had no rival to outshine her, since Madame Diane had not come to Châteaubriant.

Nor among her ladies was there one to outshine Madame de Saint-Cernin, moonlight beauty though she was, a flower of that tree as yet unknown to France, the magnolia, in her pale green gown bedewed with pearls. She was surrounded, directly the Queen had risen from table, by a bevy of gentlemen, some of them English, craving presentation. Two of these-their names were Mr. Carey and Mr. Knolles, but she never grasped them-were fortunate enough to be permitted to walk either side of her along a sanded path between two hedges of clipped and battlemented yew. Each hedge was double also, though this was not apparent, owing to their height. And so neither the lady nor her foreign cavaliers were aware that between the green walls on their left a young man in a mask walked with them unseen.

By the time that Madame de Saint-Cernin and her two English gallants had reached the stone Faun eternally fingering his pipes at the end of the walk, she was tired of them and their halting French. The prospect of returning with them up the vista was suddenly distasteful to her. So she simulated a shiver, folding her hands over the low square-cut aperture of her green gown-sea-water green, the Englishmen would have called it. As she intended, both gentlemen expressed concern: might one of them fetch her cloak-unless she would accept one of theirs? That Madame de Saint-Cernin would not do; but perceiving that she would be no better off if she were left with one of her tongue-tied admirers, and also that neither of them wished to depart and leave the other en tête-à-tête with her, intimated that her cloak might equally well be found in either of two places which she named, and that time would consequently be saved if one of them went to each spot. And as, the short cloaks on their own shoulders swinging with haste, Mr. Carey and Mr. Knolles sped away from her up the alley, she breathed a sigh of relief, and perceiving a sort of doorway in the green wall on her left, made towards it as a refuge.

But she had not quite reached it when a voice which she knew fell upon her ears, apparently from some other sphere. "Is my cloak also unworthy to be laid upon those divine shoulders?" it asked.

Astonished, she addressed the hedge. "But, Monsieur de Vernay, you are in England!"

"For your service," replied the voice, "I can cross the seas in the twinkling of an eye and appear to you!"

"Cross them then," said she smiling, "and appear to me!"

"I may not appear in daylight," said the voice. "You must deign to enter this kingdom of twilight before you can see me."

So she went through the living archway, and found herself in a green dusk (though the sky was overhead) facing a young man in pearl-coloured satin who tore off a mask and held it in his hand. There was nothing therefore to dim the ardour of his gaze. And though Madame de Saint-Cernin had recognised his voice without hesitation, it seemed that she found the actual presence of its owner more puzzling to accept, for she exclaimed: "But, Monsieur de Vernay, how came you here?"

"Why, even as iron follows the lodestone, so was I drawn down this hollow green place side by side with you, Madame, and your English satellites."

"But you should be in England! And-since I believe not in this miracle of transport —I must conclude that you did not accompany Monsieur de Saint-André thither after all!"

Gaspard came nearer and looked her in the eyes. "No," he said in a low voice, "I did not. Do you know why, Madame? After I had nigh beggared myself over my preparations I let the Maréchal and all his company go without me . . . for I found that I could not quit the place to which you were coming, O more beautiful than the stars and moon-and as cold!"

His voice and gesture were those of a man suddenly near desperation, a lover who had abandoned hope. But in truth Eléonore de Saint-Cernin found him in this moment, and in this strange, dimly-lit place, even more attractive than she had remembered. And-had he really made that sacrifice on her account?

"Was Diane so cold?" she asked in that slow, sleepy voice of hers, but with kindling eyes. "What had Messire Endymion to say to that charge?"

Even in that green gloom she saw his colour ebb. "Do you . . . give me that name?" he asked hoarsely, coming nearer still.

"Some moonlit night I may give it to you-perhaps."

"Some night? To-night, to-night!" And he caught her suddenly, strongly in his arms, crushing her beautiful dress. "Your lips, at least, I will have now!"

She returned his kiss almost as passionately, but she was the first to recover herself. "No, not to-night. You must wait until to-morrow."

"I cannot wait until to-morrow."

"You must, Gaspard-or wait for ever!"

At her tone he loosed her instantly, and fell on one knee upon the carpet of yew needles. "If you say that," he answered, his amber eyes burning up at her, "my dagger shall find a living sheath-here!" And he struck his breast. "Give me your commands, and I shall follow the least of them."

"Listen, then," said she quickly, for she thought that she heard her name being cried down the alley without. "My chamber —I have but the one, so close pressed are we in the château-is in the western wing. I know not at what hour Madame Catherine is like to dismiss me to-morrow evening. Be there at eleven o'clock, and if I am not come wait for me within. If you tap four times thus (and her finger beat out the rhythm on the back of his hand) my waiting-woman will admit you-Never fear, she is of great discretion. —When she has admitted you she will leave, according to the orders which I shall give her, for the garret or wherever it may be that she sleeps with half a score of her kind. Then wait until I come . . . Endymion!"

And now the sound of her name in a page's voice was nearer and insistent. A wonderful smile, a rustle of green silk and she was gone.

(13)

By the afternoon of Monday it was all over Châteaubriant that the English demand for the Queens of Scots' hand had been made and summarily refused, on which, so it was said, the English envoys, undismayed, had turned to their real business of asking for the hand of the Princess Elisabeth of France and bargaining about the immense dowry which they considered should accompany it.

Gaspard heard this expected news as soon as any. He went back with a light step to his garret, where the dispossessed but still attentive Blaise was brushing and shaking his master's clothes. Him Gaspard ordered to go to the quarters of the Queen of Scots at the château and ascertain privately at what hour her Master of the Horse was accustomed to return to lodging in the village of Coray.

"And ascertain also," added Gaspard, "what news there is of the indisposition of the little Queen whom, God be thanked, we are to keep among us as the bride of M. le Dauphin."

"Very good, Monsieur."

"Since she is unable to go out," pursued the young man thoughtfully, "it is likely that M. de Graeme merely presents himself at the château and returns at once to his lodging. I wish to know exactly at what hour he comes and goes. But on no account, Blaise, mention my name in all this. I may desire to pay a private and unexpected visit."

He did not say to whom; if the man chose to assume that the visit was to Madame de Graeme at the château after her husband's withdrawal so much the better. And that this in fact was what Blaise assumed was clear from the manner in which he remarked:

"Should I not also, sir, make some enquiries as to the hours of service of Madame de Graeme, the Queen of Scotland's lady?"

"Glean anything you can," answered his master with an unbetraying face. "But beware of uttering my name."

And when the man was gone he locked the door, brought out a paper, and once more settled down to his slow penmanship. But this time he wrote on more steadily.

14

Magdalen Graham and, indeed, the whole of Queen Mary's little suite, Scottish and French alike, had passed the first half of that day in a condition of disquiet. There was first their apprehension-though this was not indeed a very lively one-that their child mistress might be reft away from them to become the bride of the English king and, secondly, the feverish cough which was still afflicting her.

But by evening that first fear at least was laid to rest, and Ninian, going, before returning to his lodging at Coray, into the ante-chamber where, if her service permitted, he met his wife at an agreed time for a few minutes, asked her if she had heard the good news about the refusal of the English demand.

"Indeed I have," said Magdalen cheerfully. "We have known it for some hours. I wonder indeed that the English thought it worth while to make a demand which they must have known would not be accepted."

Ninian dismissed the English with an almost French shrug of the shoulders. "Give my duty to her Majesty, Magdalen, and say that La Réale is stamping with impatience to have her on her back again, especially after the river journey, which the poor beast liked not at all."

But Magdalen shook his head. "I'll not give the child that message yet, Ninian. It is difficult enough to induce her to submit to staying within doors. I like not this cough at all, and it grows no better. You remember how much I feared a thunderstorm that last day on the Loire!"

"Aye, I remember, but indeed, sweetheart, I think you fash yourself overmuch about her. 'Tis but a childish ailment that she has; a few days more in this healthy air and sunshine, and 'twill be gone. Give me a kiss, and return you to your Reinette."

Magdalen gave him the kiss he asked and watched him go, admiring his carriage. Turned forty though he was now, she would not have changed her man for any young gallant at the Court, however splendid.

At the door her husband turned. "By the way, but that one knows him gone to England in Saint-André's train, I could have sworn I saw the back of Master Gaspard yester evening in the park-hair and figure were so nearly his. But I must have been mistaken. Good night, my heart."

* * * * *

Some three and a half hours later Magdalen was once more in the ante-room, waiting to take Madame de Curel's place in the Queen's bedchamber. It was nearly eleven o'clock, and Gris-gris the monkey shivered and chattered in his fur-lined basket, warm night though it was. But the heat of Brittany was not that of Africa.

The Queen's door opened, and Madame de Curel came out.

"Her Majesty is sleeping," said she in a low voice. "Madame de Paroy is so much better content with her state that she is about to retire for the night. Mademoiselle Ogilvy relieves you at three o'clock, Madame, does she not?"

Magdalen inclined her head, and as the Frenchwoman, stifling a yawn, disappeared through the door leading to her own apartment and to that of the Queen's gouvernante, she crossed the ante-chamber. On the way she passed the monkey in his basket. It was quite true that she did not like him, yet she was sorry for him, so she stooped and drew his covering of green velvet over him. Out of the little wizened face the anxious eyes with their human expression looked up at her, and for a moment the creature's tiny fingers fastened upon one of hers. Magdalen drew away her hand with a slight feeling of repulsion.

Just as she did so there came a gentle knock at the main door of the ante-room. The girl crossed the floor once more and opened it. There stood one of the Archers of the Guard, the candlelight catching the golden crescents on his breast.

"Mistress Graham herself, is it not?" he asked, in a tone of satisfaction. "Here is somewhat for you, Mistress." And he held out a little packet. "It was left with me a short while ago at the entry where I was on guard, and since the serving-man who brought it was insistent that it should be given to you in person, I feared to entrust it to one of those careless pages, and have kept it to bring to you myself, since I was shortly coming off guard. But I must crave your pardon for the slight delay, for I see by the seal that the packet is from your husband."

Magdalen answered his friendly smile with one to match, as she received the little parcel from him. Though this particular Archer was not personally known to her, it was always a pleasure to speak with a fellow-Scot. "How did you know my husband's seal, sir?" she asked.

"Were we not comrades for ten years, Mistress Graham?"

He saluted her, the door closed behind him, and Magdalen was left turning over what he had brought. It was true, the packet was sealed with her husband's crest, as well as being addressed in his handwriting. Seeing that she had only parted from him at seven o'clock, it was surprising to have a communication from him.

She opened it; it contained a letter wrapped round a small phial which held some liquid resembling water. The letter began without preamble:

> *By good fortune I find here in my baggage what remaineth of my grandmother Hepburn's remedy against a cough, which I myself used this winter past when I was troubled with one. Chastain himself compounded it for me, wherefore you may employ it without fear to bring our Reinette relief. This phial contains the fitting dose for a child; give it in a milk posset or the like. —Thine, N. G.*
>
> *Postscriptum-Pardon me that I write thus clumsily, for I chanced a short while since to cut my thumb whilst mending my quill.*

More than a little puzzled, Magdalen stood looking from the letter to the phial. It was true-though she had forgotten it by now-that in the winter, before their marriage, Ninian had suffered from a troublesome cough. But when she had urged him to be careful of his health he had laughed at her, just as a few hours ago he had made little, or affected to make little, of the Queen's cough. Yet all the time then-but how unlike him! —he must secretly have been taking a remedy for it . . . and was carrying this about with him too, at midsummer, when he was in perfect health! And since leaving her this evening he had, apparently, thought better of his light-hearted attitude towards children's ailments-so much so that he had written this letter and despatched the remedy soon after arrival at his quarters. And how careless of him to cut himself with his pen-knife! There was even a tiny smear of blood visible at the bottom of the letter. Magdalen remembered that her father was constantly suffering that same mishap. In this case it had certainly altered the character of Ninian's writing, a fact of which he himself seemed to be aware.

These reflections had hardly passed through her mind when a door opened, and Madame de Paroy's voice came sharply, though lowered:

"Madame de Graeme, what are you doing out here?"

Magdalen, startled, turned round quickly, and as she did so the little bottle which Ninian had sent slipped from her grasp and tinkled away on the polished floor.

"Do you not know," went on the gouvernante severely, "that Madame de Curel has retired? Your place is within, with her Majesty!"

"I was just going to her, Madame," replied Magdalen, annoyed at having given cause for a reprimand. She looked round for the phial, hoping that it was not broken, but she could not see it.

"What are you looking for?" enquired the Frenchwoman. "Waste no further time, pray, but go to your post." Then her face changed. "My God, what ails the beast there?"

She was pointing over the girl's shoulder. Magdalen turned quickly. There in the centre of the floor, writhing and twisting in silent agony, was the Queen's monkey.

"The creature is ill-dying!" exclaimed Madame de Paroy in dismay. "Yet why, in God's name?" She hastened to the spot.

But already Gris-gris, victim of his own curiosity, lay on his back, only feebly twitching now. Both his pathetic little hands were clasped round the empty phial which had been his so incredibly swift undoing. For one second the startled gouvernante bent over him, looking at what he held; the next, she had rushed at Magdalen. "You have poisoned the poor beast, you wicked girl!" Then, seeing the fixed and ghastly horror in her face, she added, her voice rising to a shriek: "Or was it —*what is that paper in your hand?* "

And waiting for no answer, but catching both Magdalen's wrists in a frenzied grasp, she thrust her back against the panelling, screaming meanwhile at the top of her voice. "*À moi, à moi!* Call the guard! The guard! Treason! Murder! Call the guard!"

Doors burst open, there was the sound of running feet. From the chamber within could be faintly heard the voice of the little Queen, calling in alarm for Madame de Curel and Madame de Graeme. But Madame de Graeme could not answer that summons now. Pale as her ruff, with her husband's damning letter in her hand, she was pinned against the wall by the elderly, shrieking Frenchwoman, suddenly become stronger than a man, while in the middle of the floor of the ante-room the monkey stiffened into a last agonised immobility.

15

The tiring-woman, moving slowly about the bed-chamber, was putting all in order against the entry of her mistress and of a gentleman who would presently seek admission, she had been informed, perhaps even before Madame de Saint-Cernin was herself released from her service about the Queen. She was middle-aged and of a grim countenance, but the disapproving glance which she cast about her was due merely to the fact that she considered her mistress, as one of her Majesty's chief ladies, very inadequately housed in this small and single apartment. Yet, cramped though the chamber might be, its furnishings were costly enough; golden pomegranates with rose-red seeds twined in the hangings of the pillared bed, and a curtain of gold damask hung over the little recess which served as a tiring-room.

Jeanne Potier was lighting a couple more candles upon a high, richly-carved ebony chest, and the second had hardly trembled into flame, when there came four discreet taps upon the door. Without hurrying she went and opened.

Dimly seen-for there was little light without —a young man in grey and silver with the edge of his black cloak thrown half over his face stood there. As he slipped in she made him a reverence; and a second afterwards he had given her a piece of money. The hand which gave it was so noticeably unsteady that ere leaving the room Jeanne Potier stole a glance at the handsome young seigneur (now that his cloak was dropped she saw him clearly) to whom her mistress was granting so signal a favour, and thought that he looked as though he had come from some encounter of a very different nature. Well, it was none of her business. She closed the door behind her.

Gaspard drew a long breath and passed his hand over his eyes. He had come, not from any mere disquieting encounter, but as it were from one planet to another. This chamber, where the candles shone in a scented air, was not only the shrine of love but a sanctuary. Here Lethe flowed between him and what he had just done; here he was safe, and not only safe, but would soon be blest beyond his hopes; here he was Endymion, not a forger, a poisoner . . . and a monster of ingratitude.

Yet his heart was still throbbing violently. But that was only the effect, he told himself, of the great haste he had made back from the entry of the château to his garret in order to rid himself of the serving-man's clothes-Blaise's spare suit-which he had worn to carry out his errand. He could still see the face of the Archer on guard who had promised to deliver the packet very shortly. By this time the little phial was in Magdalen's hands; the prologue to the play was over. Next would come . . . Oh, forget, forget! He laid hold of one of the curtains of the bed, where the wreathed pomegranates disclosed the glowing seeds within, and stood looking down at the silken coverlet edged with miniver, and the white, faintly-scented linen. When would his Diana come?

There was a silver posset-cup standing upon a table by the bedside. Gaspard hardly knew that he had put out his hand to it, yet he found that he had removed its ornate cover, topped by a dolphin, and had looked into its silver-gilt emptiness. He knew quite well that the cup held nothing . . . yet for a second there seemed to be milk in it, milk for a child. It looked no different from ordinary milk, because the liquid which had been added was colourless . . . and imperceptible in its action, though potent. He had wondered how that could be. . . . The cup was empty again, quite empty, and he replaced the cover. When would she come?

He walked slowly to the foot of the bed. The candles wavered for a moment, but the mirror on the wall showed him the face of the man whom all circumstances had conspired so marvellously to help. The poison itself he would never have dared to try to purchase so near as Nantes-but he had it already in his possession. Then there was his six months' service with his half-brother, which had given him such invaluable knowledge-of Ninian's mother's maiden name, for instance, and of the cough from which he had suffered last year; the good fortune which had caused him to preserve a scrap of Ninian's writing to copy; the fact that he could express himself easily in English, because, at his own desire, they had always spoken English together; most of all, his possession, equally with Ninian, of their father's crest. The ring with the rose was still on Ninian's finger, for all he knew-certainly in Ninian's possession-to identify the letter as his. But *his* ring was securely hidden, and to-morrow should be committed to the river.

And Madame Madeleine? Poor tool, it would be a pity if she were sacrificed too! The letter, if she had the sense to keep it, should prove her own innocence of intention. Had she really been in collusion with her husband the latter would never have written to her in that strain-never written at all. But she would undoubtedly have had a better chance of escape if she were not the wife of the criminal. Gaspard was disposed almost to regret that he had helped on their marriage. Had not someone truly said that a man's deeds of kindness were those which, in the end, he had most cause to lament? Stay, though-and here was another circumstance which fought for him-Ninian's supposed recommendation of the potion would have had much less weight with Mademoiselle de Lindsay than with Madame de Graeme-in fact the Grand Ecuyer would scarcely have ventured to make it. Poor Madame Madeleine . . . poor catspaw . . . and she had a pretty turn of the head, too!

But there was a sound; the door was softly opening; Eléonore de Saint-Cernin was here at last! Gaspard went forward without a word and knelt humbly at her feet, pressing the jewelled hand she gave him so passionately to his lips that her rings almost bruised them. She was wearing peach-colour this evening; a cluster of garnets gleamed on her stomacher. Her eyes were very luminous as she said, looking down on him:

"Must I ask you what you do here in my chamber, Monsieur de Vernay?"

And for a moment as he gazed up at her, he could not answer. His speechlessness did not seem at all to displease her, however. She moved past him and glancing at herself in the mirror murmured: "And so I have no tire-woman to-night."

"Let me supply her place?" whispered her lover, close behind her now.

She shook her head, and began slowly to take off some of her rings, laying them in an ivory box which stood on the chest below the mirror, while Gaspard watched her in silence, overpowered by her nearness, and wondering when he would be able to make her a gift of some bright jewel, some curiously set ring? When to-night's work was paid for?

He came closer still. "That is a beautiful amethyst you have there," he said.

"I always wear it. It is sovereign against what is most to be dreaded in life-melancholy."

"And this is a strange ring," said the young man, taking out of the box another with a large dull green stone in a thick setting of tiny silver leaves. The stone was oddly opaque, and the whole effect rather clumsy.

"It has a strange history," said Madame de Saint-Cernin. "There was poison in it once-oh, 'tis empty enough now. But it was used — —"

Gaspard put the ring hastily back.

"Let us not speak of poison to-night, most beautiful! So you did not take it I care not how it was used!" And his arm stole round her.

"Sir, you are very peremptory! And let me tell you that the subject of poison is much in men's mouths to-night! The talk this evening in her Majesty's apartment was all of that, because news has just come from England that a Scot who, it seems, has plotted to poison the little Queen of Scotland — —What ails you, my friend?"

For with an uncontrollable exclamation her lover had loosed his clasp of her, retreated a step or two, and was staring at her as he might have done at a spectre.

"A Scot . . . poison . . . the Queen of Scotland. . . . What is this?"

So surprised was Eléonore de Saint-Cernin at his white-lipped dismay that she too stared at him, speechless for a second or two.

"Are you ill, Gaspard? —you have the look of it!"

His head turning, he managed to answer her coherently. "No, no-only horrified. A Scot, you say-in *England* !"

"Yes, a Scot with a grievance, or I know not what. . . . Who can follow the politics of that country? He went to the English Council of State, it appears, and acquainted them with his design, hoping for some great reward-for as you know the little Queen stands so near that throne — —"

"Yes, yes! And the English Government agreed?" It was hard, when one felt so breathless, to frame even a short question.

"On the contrary," said Madame de Saint-Cernin as she closed the ivory casket, "the English have acted most properly in the matter. They have not only made known this treacherous design to his Majesty, but are sending the wretch over to this country for trial and punishment. That is the 'reward' he will get! . . . But this seems to discompose you very highly, Endymion. Yet I do not wonder at it-that pretty child!" She thrust her hand into a drawer. "Smell this pomander; it will revive you!"

Forcing a smile, Gaspard waved aside the scented orange. "I am not a woman, Diana-as I shall show you presently. But your news . . . shocked me. One must indeed thank God that — —" But the false phrase turned in his mouth; try as he would he could not finish it, but went on hastily: "As I said, let us not talk of so ugly a thing to-night, when there is but one subject for the tongue."

"And that is?" asked Eléonore provocatively.

"You and your loveliness," answered Gaspard, and catching her hungrily to him, kissed her full on the lips.

The kiss seemed to intoxicate her as well as the giver (whose own mouth was so dry) for she returned it, clinging to him. Then, freeing herself gently from his arms, she disappeared without a word, but with a backward-smiling look, between the golden curtains which hung over the recess.

But her lover stood motionless, the brief, fierce fire lit in his blood smothered for the moment by the utter downfall of his great and hazardous scheme. Who would have thought that the miserly hypocritical English . . . And now the child Queen . . . and others, too, perhaps . . . must die to no purpose.

Gaspard clung to the pillar of the bed, one hand pressed hard over his eyes. A voice said loudly: "It may not be too late to undo your work!" But it was, it was! How could he present himself at the Queen of Scots' apartments and warn her ladies without inculpating himself beyond hope of escape? It would be the sheerest madness. . . . And were not the chances evenly balanced that the "remedy" might never be given at all? Madame de Paroy might easily have forbidden its administration, the child have been asleep . . . or already better. Gaspard dropped his hand, then put it up again to wipe away the sweat. No, he could do nothing-nothing. Events must take their course now, for life or death.

And what indeed did the life or death of any man, woman or child, matter to him in this hour? All in white, with unbound raven hair, Eléonore de Saint-Cernin had come through the golden curtains.

PAR HEUR ET MALHEUR (2)

(June, 1551) —(1)

As the only two Scotsmen of importance in the little Queen's entourage (with the exception of her almoner) Arthur Erskine and Ninian Graham tended to seek each other's society. It was quite natural therefore, that in the packed little hamlet of Coray they should be sharing not only the same room, but the same bed. They were indeed lucky that they had to themselves this small and not overclean apartment, opening off the general living-room of the prolific peasant family upon whom, in an atmosphere of fleas and piety, they were quartered.

Immured on the farther side of the stuffy box-bed, the usual Breton *lit clos* , Ninian was drowsy to-night, perhaps from lack of air. Arthur Erskine seemed less disposed for sleep, being deeply disturbed by a rumour which he had that evening heard from M. de Curel of a reported plan to poison the little Queen made by a Scot in England, reputed once to have been an Archer, of the name of Robert Stuart. But Ninian, though agreeing that, if true, it was a dreadful business, was disposed to make light of the story. He remembered no one of that name in the Guard, and felt sure that no Scot, let alone an ex-Archer, would ever contemplate so terrible and unnatural a crime.

He fell asleep before his bedfellow, his last conscious impression being of the gabble of the family repeating the rosary in the next room. And when (he knew not how much later) he was dimly aware through the veil of slumber of some disturbance in the same quarter, he only thought sleepily that Breton devotions seemed to be quite unduly prolonged.

A moment later, however, he knew that it was certainly not prayers which were going forward on the other side of the wall. Arthur Erskine, as he could tell, had already raised himself in bed.

"What can be going on in there?" murmured Ninian, still rather sleepily, as the trampling of feet and the sound of a loud voice came through the crazy door.

"That is what I am wondering," replied his compatriot. "I fancied that I heard my name. I will rise and see." He leaned out and groped, but in vain, for the flint and steel; then gave it up, scrambled out in the darkness and presumably began to assume some outer garments.

"But what can be wanted of you at this hour?" asked Ninian, yawning. The yawn was not finished before the door was flung wide open, letting in the glare of torches, whose smoky light fell on the morions and accoutrements of men-at-arms. An officer strode forward.

"Is M. de Graeme there?" he demanded abruptly. "Bring a torch nearer. Monsieur de Graeme, I require you to rise at once and come with me. You are my prisoner!"

"But, in God's name, why?" cried Arthur Erskine incredulously. And as there was no reply he turned, half-dressed as he was, to his fellow Scot. "Graham, what means this?"

Ninian was out of bed by now. "I ask the same!" he said with indignation. "Prisoner! Is this some ill jest of M. de Montmorency's?" For he had by this time recognised the men-at-arms as those of the Constable's own guard.

"Pah, do not play the innocent like that!" retorted the officer in a tone of disgust. "Put on your clothes and come. Monsieur Asquin, you would be the first to turn from such a bedfellow. But I will ask you to witness something." Waiting only until Ninian had, in silence and with what dignity he could muster, pulled on his hose, he beckoned to a torch-bearer to approach still nearer, and then marched right up to his prisoner.

"Hold out your hands!" he ordered.

"If you intend to fetter me, at least let me finish dressing first," said Ninian, restraining himself with difficulty.

"Hold out your hands!" was the only response.

Resistance was as useless as undignified. Ninian complied, and the officer seized his right hand with an exclamation of triumph.

"Come here, if you please, Monsieur Asquin? Before I remove it, you see this ring on M. de Graeme's finger? You can testify that he was wearing it? . . . Now I shall take it off-by force if necessary!" For Ninian had involuntarily closed his hand to frustrate this intention; then, biting his lips, opened it again. The ring was wrenched off. "Look, if you please, at the device, Monsieur Asquin —a hand holding a rose, is it not?"

"But naturally," stammered the bewildered Erskine. "Naturally, since it is M. de Graeme's signet ring, bearing his crest. What is wrong with that?"

"You will soon hear-all the world will hear. 'Tis with this very ring," said the officer, holding it up, "that he sealed the letter!"

"Why should I seal a letter with any other?" enquired Ninian sarcastically. "Is that a reason for a midnight arrest?"

The officer loosed or rather cast his prisoner's hand from him. "Get on your doublet! And since we must hasten, one of you come and help him tie his points."

A man-at-arms came forward and began to assist in that rather lengthy operation. Ninian allowed him to do it. "I repeat," he said, still trying to control his anger, "that I shall be obliged if you will tell me plainly of what I am accused?"

The officer looked him up and down as though he could hardly bring himself to answer. "Of attempting to poison her Majesty the Queen of Scots in a posset."

Ninian gave a short and scornful laugh. "So wild a charge affrights me not!" And he added to the astounded and horrified Erskine, "This is some fever of suspicion which has seized on the Constable on account of that matter of which we spoke as we came hither. All Scots about her little Majesty may be under a cloud now. You will be the next suspect, Erskine, so have a care!"

"Monsieur Asquin has not sent poison to his wife with a letter instructing her to administer it to her Majesty!" snapped out the officer.

"Wife! letter!" exclaimed Ninian sharply, with a changed countenance. "What has my wife to do with this absurd story?"

"That is for you-and her-to answer," was the reply. "By morning, perhaps, we shall know the truth. Remove the prisoner!"

Brushing aside the gaping Bretons at the door, the armed men tramped out, Ninian unresisting in their midst, their officer following; and behind him again, pale and discomposed, Arthur Erskine, with his own points hardly tied, exclaiming that there was some terrible mistake, and that he would accompany the Grand Ecuyer.

But this he was not allowed to do. In haste, under that serene night sky with its gentle stars, the party got to horse again, their prisoner, his hands bound, in their midst. The ride back to Châteaubriant was like an evil dream to him-but, unlike a dream, it did not break. It continued into another phase, in another setting —a room on the ground floor of the château, where the Constable de Montmorency, fully dressed, stood like an avenger in front of the great hooded hearth. Before him, on a long table, lay upon a piece of green velvet a little contorted grey-brown body which Ninian recognised with a dull surprise as that of the Queen's monkey, Gris-gris. Near it, on a small dish, was a tiny empty phial with a broken end.

The officer went up to the Constable, made a report and handed over Ninian's signet-ring. Anne de Montmorency examined it closely, slipped it on to his own finger and strode forward. He was very far now from being the playmate of the royal nursery; he was his real self, fierce, competent and implacable, the man who had not scrupled, in the war of 1536 against the Emperor, to lay waste Provence as a measure of defence, so that French fields were strewn with the starved corpses of French peasants. And at the look on his face there leapt instantly into Ninian's mind the warning familiar throughout France, to beware of the Constable's Paternosters.

"You see your work, Scot!" His voice shook with rage and emotion, as he pointed at the dead beast. "It is only by the mercy of God that your own sovereign does not lie there!"

"Then there is no one who thanks Him more devoutly than I," returned Ninian boldly, "And if you will cause me to be told, Monsieur le Connétable, why I have been thus dragged from my bed, and why I am held responsible for that poor creature's death — —"

The Constable struck the table, his eyes blazing. "Mary Virgin, what effrontery! Here is your own letter, sending that phial there to your wife, for the little Queen's use. But before she could administer its contents the monkey picked up the bottle-with the results which you see!"

For the second time Ninian's head began to turn. "But I wrote no letter to my wife! Why should I? I had parted from her only at seven o'clock. And as for that phial, I never set eyes upon it before!"

The Constable said but one word. "Liar!"

"Monsieur de Montmorency, this accusation is sheer madness!" protested Ninian, with heat. "Why, I would gladly die rather than that my royal mistress should suffer harm!"

"By the mass, then, I think you are like to have your wish," retorted Montmorency grimly. "But we shall learn the truth first. Who are your accomplices? Or are you perhaps but a tool yourself, a tool of this man Stuart-again a Scot! —whom the English have arrested?"

"I tell you," broke out Ninian passionately, " — —and may God strike me dead within the hour if I lie-that I know nothing whatever of all this, nor does my wife, who cherishes her Majesty as though she were her own child. . . . And where is Madame de Graeme? Is she in custody too?"

The Constable sat down in the great chair at the head of the table. "She is not far away. You will be confronted with her when the need arises. But now, poisoner, before I send you to the dungeons at Nantes-for I have in my house here none deep enough for a crime like yours, nor any facilities for coming at the truth-tell me what you hoped to gain by your abominable attempt!"

"I repeat," said Ninian doggedly, "that I made no attempt. There has been some horrible mistake."

For all answer the Constable turned his head towards the officer in command of the guard, standing now by his chair. "Are his hands securely tied? Then, Marnier, you can lay his letter on the table in front of him."

A grave-looking individual, presumably a secretary, came round the table with an opened letter in his hand which he spread upon the table. His guards moved Ninian nearer, and in a dead silence he stared down at words in his own handwriting. . . *"Reinette"* . . . *"grandmother Hepburn"* . . . *"cough"* . . . In that paralysing moment he fancied that he must be going insane-for he had never penned them! Then the blood began to run cold as ice in his veins. God! what horror was behind this?

He found his breath at last, like one coming out of breakers. "It is a forgery . . . a close imitation . . . but not my handwriting!"

"Ah, a close imitation, is it?" repeated the Constable. "Close enough to deceive your wife, think you?"

"Not unless the light were dim," answered Ninian. And then, scenting something sinister in the question, and taken by the throat with anxiety: "You are not telling me that it did deceive her?"

The ironic creases on either side of the Constable's mouth deepened. He caressed his fine beard. "You will have the opportunity of learning that in due time. To resume. . . . Turn the letter over, Marnier, and show M. de Graeme the seal-the impress of this very ring of his which was on his finger half an hour ago."

Under Ninian's stupefied gaze two hands turned the letter over and spread it out again. There was the superscription, in that hand so deadly like his own: "A Madame, Madame de Graeme, aux appartemens de la Royne d'Ecosse," and there on the wax of the seal, broken through the middle, but coming together again neatly when once more the hands manipulated the piece of paper, the mailed fist and rose-branch of his family crest.

"Yes, that device is difficult to deny, is it not?" observed the Constable's voice, full of a terrifying satisfaction.

"That impression was never made by *my* signet ring," said Ninian hoarsely.

"You will be hard put to it to prove that! You have wax and a taper there, Marnier? Take the impress of this ring."

The Constable withdrew it from his finger. There was a scraping of flint and steel, and in a few seconds the fresh impression was lying side by side with the broken seal on the letter. They could not be told apart.

Ninian knew that he had turned paler. And, indeed, there was cause. He felt himself poised on the verge of some unfathomable abyss of treachery and mystery. Until the last hour his ring had never left his finger. But that ring, as he knew, had its counterpart. Oh, no, no, no! That was an unspeakable thought . . . and an impossible deed! Gaspard was in England.

Anne de Montmorency was watching his face closely. "I see, indeed, Monsieur le Grand Ecuyer, that you find what lies before you there difficult to explain away! But you will no doubt tell me that you had missed your signet-ring of late, but had found it again?"

But Ninian made no answer. He was dumb before what he was, after all, beginning to see at the bottom of the abyss-the shape of an unimaginable betrayal.

His inquisitor leant forward.

"By whom did you send this letter and phial to the château? We know who took them to the apartments of the Queen of Scotland."

"I have told you, Monsieur le Connétable, that I did not send them."

The Constable made a gesture. "You *took* them, then? Was it you in person who delivered them to the Archer, who conveyed them to your wife?"

An Archer? "The loyalty of the Archer Guard, as you must know, has ever stood above suspicion," answered Ninian hoarsely.

"That was so once," retorted the Constable with meaning. "Until, that is, the day when you came upon its muster-roll!" He stretched out his hand for the phial. "Chastain swears that he never compounded any specific for you at Blois or at any other place," he observed, holding it up.

Ninian looked him in the face. "That is perfectly true-and a proof that the writer of that letter was but guessing in his attempt to deceive my wife."

Anger ran over that threatening visage. "How can you persist in denying that you are yourself the writer? Who in France but you could know the name of your grandmother! Do you deny that the name written here is hers?"

"No! But the . . . the real writer . . . is sufficiently well acquainted with my family history to know it."

"One of your former comrades in the Archer Guard, you will say?"

"Never!" replied Ninian vehemently. "You must know that no Archer — —"

"Must I again put you in mind that you were an Archer yourself!"

"Yes," riposted Ninian haughtily, "and I am an Archer still, and have the right to appeal to the Captain, and above him, to his Majesty."

On that statement, M. de Montmorency made no comment. He reverted instead to an earlier question. "You deny, then, that you gave the packet in person to the Archer on guard?"

"I should have been a fool if I had done that."

"You were a fool!" was the uncompromising retort. " —Unless indeed he were in collusion with you. But the question of your wife's collusion comes first. Did you write that letter expecting to deceive her, or did she not require deceiving? In other words, was she already a party to your abominable plot, or not?"

Ninian clenched his bound hands. It was the peak of horror-that Magdalen should be dragged into this net of lies. "She could not be party to what did not exist," he answered. Then, physically half stifled as he felt by the fumes of treachery about him, he tried desperately to collect his wits. Was it better for her that he should say that the letter would have deceived her, or that it would not? How best could he shield her when he was entirely ignorant of what she had done or had not done on receipt of the forgery? Moved by the overmastering craving which he had for a word with her or even a sight of her he made a request which he had little hope would be granted.

"Can I not see my wife for a moment, even before witnesses?"

The Constable shook that fine head of his.

"Has she been arrested also?"

Montmorency looked at Ninian's ring, on his finger again. "Great consideration," he said slowly, "has been shown to Madame de Graeme. She is at present only confined to her own chamber. And if," here he looked very directly at Ninian, "if at your next interrogatory your replies are satisfactory, it may come to no more than that with her." He paused to let the meaning of this remark sink in, and then resumed: "Since, however, you are at present in so obstinate a frame of mind, I shall waste no more time on you to-night." He turned to the officer. "Take the prisoner to the lower room in the keep of the Vieux Château. You may loose his hands, but your men will answer for it with their own heads if he escapes."

"You need have no fear of my escaping," retorted Ninian proudly. "I am a gentleman of as good lineage as yourself, and my concern is to clear my honour of this monstrous charge. But am I not to have any person to assist me in this?"

"I fear me that's a thankless task for any man," observed the Constable. "But the matter shall be thought upon."

"I should desire," went on Ninian firmly, "to speak with M. Rutherford, of the Archer Guard, and also to know whether M. de Vernay, a gentleman of M. de Saint-André's suite, has accompanied the Maréchal on his embassy to England, or whether he is still in Châteaubriant."

The constable stared at the prisoner and shrugged his shoulders. "I know no gentleman of that name. But if you think," he added contemptuously, "that he can help you to prove your innocence"—here Ninian suppressed a wild desire to laugh—"I will have enquiries made. But my advice to you, Monsieur de Graeme, is rather to reflect upon the wisdom of making a confession—*of your own free will!* Remove him!"

2

Hour after hour of terror and bewilderment had passed over Magdalen's head, prisoner in her own chamber with a guard before the door, ignorant of what might be happening to Ninian, and unable to turn the eyes of her mind for more than a few instants away from that dreadful moment of the monkey's death-and of those which had followed it. Directly she had seen the little creature writhing on the floor she had known that Ninian could not have written and sent the letter which she had scarcely read . . . unless indeed the phial, with its deadly contents, had somehow been substituted for what he had actually despatched. For the seal was undoubtedly his.

Morning had come now, and still she lay upon her bed, her face disfigured with tears, her ruff all crushed, one self-reproach consuming her at last, so fiercely that she hardly knew how to bear it. Why had she not been quick enough to hide or to destroy the letter? Then nobody would have seen that Ninian-no, Ninian's *name* —had been in any way connected with this horrible affair. Yet there had been no time even for concealment before Madame de Paroy had rushed at her; she had herself scarcely understood the purport of the letter, scanned as it was by candle-light, before the Frenchwoman was gripping her. . . . Oh, had it only been Lady Fleming! *She* would not have believed the worst!

As to knowing whether she herself would have thought of employing the contents of the phial as a remedy for the Queen's cough-it had never come to a decision. Poor little Gris-gris! Yet suppose that instead of Gris-gris. . . . But that picture Magdalen's shuddering mind could not face.

And Ninian-they really believed that he was the writer of that letter! Yet she herself had thought so, at first. It bore his seal-that was the strange thing about it. But a signet-ring can be stolen. They had said: "We shall find out the truth." For the first time it came home to her what that phrase might cover. And as certain things she had heard about the preliminaries of French trials took shape before her, the girl uttered a little scream, and dragging herself off the bed went down on her knees. Oh, God, not that for Ninian-not torture!

She was still on her knees clutching the coverlet when she heard the door open, and got somehow to her feet. A man's voice-the guard's —said respectfully something about "Majesty"; and next moment Magdalen saw before her the tall form of the Dowager Queen of Scots.

Herself very pale and drawn, her hands clenched, Mary of Lorraine stood frowning at her; it seemed as though speech would not come.

"You vile and wicked girl!" she said at last. "You who were so greatly trusted!"

Magdalen took a few steps and fell on her knees before her. "Madame, madame . . . as God sees me, I was innocent of any ill intent!" And as Mary looked down at her with the fierce eyes of a mother whose child is threatened, Magdalen went on incoherently: "How could I think of harming her . . . I have loved her too dearly." Then sobs began to choke her.

"You would have me believe then," said the Queen harshly, "that you were the tool of your husband, deceived by his letter? —But no, no! You had conspired together-you are both equally guilty!"

In her desperation Magdalen reached up and, despite her resistance, caught hold of the Queen's hand. "Oh, Mary Virgin, how can your Majesty believe that the man who has loved and served our Reinette since she came to France, who was willing to delay our marriage lest it should be the means of taking me from her service, who risked injury to save her on board the — —"

"An affair made too much of, to my mind!" broke in the Queen curtly. "And, at any rate, it procured him his post about my daughter's person. Yet this is how he has fulfilled his trust!" She pulled away her imprisoned hand. "Whether the guilt lies upon him alone, or on both of you, the guilt is there, and the sooner it is expiated the sooner will there be one less anxiety upon the head of an unhappy mother. No, do not seek to detain me further! I wish never to see your face again!" And, as suddenly as she had entered, she was gone.

Magdalen dragged herself up from the floor. Why, she wondered dully, had the Queen Mother come at all? Once more her tormented thoughts went to Lady Fleming. Oh, if only she were still the gouvernante, how eagerly she would implore her to use her influence with her royal lover to get a hearing for Ninian-she who had once proudly declared that she would never sue to a king's mistress!

Suddenly catching sight of her tear-stained face and general disarray in a mirror, she thought, "I look like a guilty woman," and slowly bathed her face and repaired the disorder of her dress. Some instinct perhaps had moved her to this act, for it was scarcely finished before the door was opened again, and she heard with astonishment the words: "Her Majesty the Queen desires to see you."

With astonishment, and with thankfulness also. Queen Catherine surely could not have sent for her merely to condemn. Magdalen smoothed back a strand of hair into place under her headdress and said to the messenger, an usher of the Queen's chamber: "I am ready."

* * * * *

It was the same great chamber in which there had been dancing on the evening of Lord Northampton's arrival, only five nights ago. The Queen was seated in a high-backed chair, a small embroidery frame before her, two of her ladies attending to hand her silks and re-thread her needle. Spread out over a frame at her side was a much larger piece of tapestry of an allegorical nature, a landscape with posturing female figures grouped about a spotless and benignant unicorn-the Triumph of Chastity, as a scroll at the top indicated. Of this composition Catherine appeared to be copying some detail. She looked up for a moment when Magdalen was announced, bent her head again and took a few more stitches, then made a sign to her attendants, who removed the frame and themselves to a group of other ladies at a distance.

After her deep curtsey Magdalen had stood there trembling a little. The Queen sat very still, looking at her, her beautiful hands rather primly folded one upon the other in her lap. At last, after a long, unbetraying survey, she observed: "I believe, Madame de Graeme, that you are of kin to the late gouvernante of her Majesty the Queen of Scots?"

"Yes, your Majesty." Useless to deny it, though indeed the kinship could not but tell against her in Queen Catherine's eyes.

"She was a foolish woman, but not, I think, a wicked one. You, Madame, appear to be both!"

It was not a propitious opening. Yet there was not upon Catherine de'Medici's face the hostility which there had been on Mary of Lorraine's. Magdalen tried to rally her faculties. "May it please your Majesty, I may be foolish, as I am unfortunate, but indeed I am not wicked. I call all the saints to witness that I am as innocent of any complicity in this terrible affair as my husband is."

"That is not, perhaps, saying much," observed the Queen dryly. "How are you going to prove this innocence?"

"If we had been in a plot together, your Majesty, would my husband, who had parted from me only a few hours previously, have so rashly sent me a letter sealed with his own ring? He would have given me" —she faltered a moment —"instructions by word of mouth, for we were alone together in the ante-room before we parted for the night."

Catherine gave her another long scrutiny. It was always difficult to tell what went on in the brain behind that opaque gaze. What she said was unexpected.

"You married M. de Graeme against my wishes."

"We . . . had his Majesty's permission," replied Magdalen, her knees shaking under her.

"I am aware of that. It is for that reason that I have not shown you any displeasure, his Majesty's will being always paramount with me."

Magdalen clasped her hands together. "If your Majesty can display such generosity, then surely your Majesty sees that what I have said is a matter of reason; that my husband, had he been guilty, would not have written——"

The Queen held up a hand. "It is not necessary to point that out again, Madame. But, if he did not, who then wrote the letter and sent the poison?"

"Indeed, I know not, your Majesty. Someone, perhaps, who desired the death of . . . but who could desire it?"

The Queen leant forward. "What do you and your husband know of a Scot named Robert Stuart, now in England?"

The question meant nothing to Magdalen, who looked as blank as she felt. "Nothing, Madame."

The Queen leant back again. "I think," she said slowly, "that you may very well be innocent of this great crime-perhaps even your husband also. But it is not in my power to help you. His Majesty is terribly incensed, and it is never my practice to interfere in affairs of State. If you and M. de Graeme are indeed guiltless in this matter, you will not suffer. But rest assured that justice will be done."

The phrase rang sinister. As before to Mary of Lorraine, Magdalen fell on her knees. "Your Majesty, your Majesty-forgive me, but, a wife yourself, can you not intercede with his Majesty so that my innocent husband shall not be . . . forced to confess what is not true?"

The daughter of the Medici looked genuinely surprised. "But how," she asked, "can the truth be discovered otherwise than by force? And if your husband is able to point out the wretch who sent the poison-if indeed it was not he himself-then no doubt the question or the brodequins will wring the truth from that other person. But as I have just told you, I cannot interfere. You may retire, Madame."

But seeing that Magdalen, though she tried to obey, was at that instant scarcely capable of doing so, she beckoned to the nearest of her ladies.

"Madame de Saint-Cernin, be good enough to assist Madame de Graeme to the door."

A beautiful and haughty head bent over Magdalen; she was taken by the arm and helped to her feet and led away, murmuring brokenly as she went: "It was some enemy . . . but they will put him to the question, I know it!"

"But, Madame," asked Eléonore de Saint-Cernin in her cool, lazy voice, "why concern yourself so much about the sufferings of an enemy?"

Magdalen looked at her wildly. "It is my husband I mean . . . and the Queen will do nothing!"

"To meddle with justice is not her Majesty's custom," replied Madame de Saint-Cernin coldly, dropping the arm which she was holding, for they were now at the door, which the usher opened. And not troubling to see how the girl fared, once over the threshold, she returned with her swan-like grace of movement across the expanse of shining floor to her royal mistress.

Outside, Magdalen leant a moment against the closed door, breathing fast. Why had these two Queens, the Guise and the Medici, so desired to see her, since one was hostile and the other indifferent? Was it only to mock her agony? There remained a third, her own, her darling; but she, a child, was powerless. Nevertheless. . . .

"Take me to the Queen of Scotland!" she said desperately to her waiting guards.

But they shook their heads. "Impossible, Madame."

3

Only a greyish daylight could ever filter into the crypt-like apartment below the keep of the old castle, a place not so very unlike a dungeon, in spite of M. de Montmorency's disclaimer. Though it was nearly dawn when Ninian was led thither, and a few birds had begun to sing, its twilight had to be mitigated by a torch before he could see his way down the steps from the door which closed and was made fast behind him.

For some four hours thereafter he paced up and down under the low vaulted roof, or sat awhile motionless on the chipped and dirty stone bench which was the only object there. Now and again he found himself looking down at his own limbs and clothes in a kind of stupid wonderment; if he had had a mirror he would have looked in that to see what manner of man he was now become, a prisoner accused of an attempt on the life of his little Queen. There were moments when he really had a sickening doubt of his own identity, but they lasted no longer than the space of a lightning flash. What stayed, what paced with him during those hours was the phantasm of the man, his father's son, his own protégé, who had thrust him into this pit of incredible betrayal.

About seven o'clock some food was brought and set down on the stone bench. Ninian demanded urgently of its bearer that he should be allowed to see either the Captain of the Archer Guard, the Comte de Montgomery, or the Lieutenant, Thomas Stratton, or failing these, Patrick Rutherford. The guard said he would report the request.

An hour later the sound of the key turning once more sent his heart leaping up. But it was only the same man bearing a small table, followed by another with a stool, a standish and some sheets of paper. Ninian wondered whether he were shortly going to undergo another interrogatory in this spot. But when, the men having departed, he went over to the table, he saw that the topmost sheet of paper, otherwise blank, bore the heading: "*Confession of Ninian de Graeme, arrested for attempting to poison her Majesty the Queen of Scotland.*"

A flame of fury ran over him; gritting his teeth, he seized the blank sheets and was about to tear them across when he suddenly stopped, and with something like a laugh sat down on the stool and snatched the pen from the standish. These writing materials, which he had never expected to come by, should serve his own purpose, not his accusers'. And he began to write, using as little space as possible, to the Duc de Guise.

> *Monseigneur: On the day at St. Germaine-en-Laye two and a half years ago, when you were pleased to give me a chain from your own neck in recognition of the service which I had been fortunate enough to render to the Queen of Scots, your niece, on the voyage to France, you told me, if ever I needed help, to remember that the whole of your illustrious house was in my debt. Monseigneur, I am now constrained to recall this speech to you, for I need help most desperately at this hour, and unless you can give it I am lost, being most falsely accused of attempting to poison the very person I saved that day, my own sovereign. For the love of God, Monsieur le Duc, and for the sake of your promise, help me to prove my innocence before it is too late, and I am sent to the dungeons of Nantes. From the donjon of the Vieux Château, this 23rd day of June.*

Then he signed his name, folded the letter into a small compass, and put it into the breast of his doublet. How he was to get it into the hands of the Duc de Guise, he knew not; but if God were really omnipotent He would surely make an opportunity for an innocent man to save himself!

A further couple of hours, perhaps, passed, and at last he was summoned to come forth. Outside was an escort of several of the Constable's guards. When he asked them whether he were being taken to Nantes, they told him: Not yet; he was to be questioned further first.

Mixed with the daylight, which at first made him blink, there was a kind of warm mist, and a veil over the sun. The June green showed unnatural in it-but since last night the whole world had become unnatural. And, once outside the keep, Ninian perceived that he was not being taken back to the new château by the vaulted and portcullised passage through which he had been brought last night, but to some other portion of this half-ruined elder building. An uncontrollable shiver ran down his spine as he was led across the irregular square of the court-yard, of which the donjon occupied the north-eastern corner. Was it possible that there did exist here, after all, those facilities for "ascertaining the truth" for lack of which he was to be sent to Nantes-if François de Guise did not come to his aid?

He was ashamed of his fear, however, when he found himself entering a building which he guessed to be the disused chapel of the old castle, since in front of him was the arch of a chancel and beyond an apse with three narrow windows, in one of which still hung some fragments of ancient glass. In what had been the nave there sat at a table, with a clerk or secretary on either side, not the Constable de Montmorency, but some old man in lawyer's robes. A recently lighted brazier burnt on either side of him-no doubt against the damp of so neglected a spot. But once Ninian had realised that here, thank God, were no signs of what he had half dreaded, he was aware, with the most curious commingling of feelings, that the half-score of guards ranged along the pillars were not the Constable's but the King's Scottish Archers, and nearly all personally known to him. But not one of them would look at him; they stood with their halberds like statues, gazing straight in front of them. Patrick Rutherford was not of their number.

Colder at heart again, Ninian surveyed the aged figure at the head of the table, and recognised him then for Bertrandi, First President of the Parlement of Paris, who had just been made Garde des Sceaux. If the conduct of the case was in his hands, the proceedings would be likely to savour more of a trial than of an interrogatory-save that there was no one to defend the accused.

The old lawyer had looked up now from his notes and was smoothing his long, beautifully kept beard. He was eighty-one, and, though he did not know it, nearly at the end of his legal career and at the beginning of an ecclesiastical. The day was shortly coming when, on his wife's death, he should abandon Law for the Church, soaring upwards with singular rapidity through the hierarchy as Bishop and then Archbishop, to assume the cardinal's hat at the age of eighty-seven.

"Prisoner," he began in clear, flute-like tones, "the abominable crime with which you are charged merits the most speedy justice imaginable! You have attempted the murder of one who is not only a crowned Queen, but a young child as well —a deed from which the most hardened evil-doer might well shrink. And to choose for this outrage this place and time, when our sovereign lord the King is receiving an embassy from his dear brother of England, argues a hideous callousness. It is fitting on every count that you should be sent hence, as you will presently be, to the castle of Nantes, and it is at Nantes that your trial will take place. But I shall first put a few questions to you and to some other persons." He settled himself in his chair, and clasped his hands neatly together. "Your answer last night to this dreadful charge was, I understand, a total denial of your guilt. Do you still persist in that attitude?"

"I do," answered Ninian very steadily. "I swear before God that the letter is a forgery and that I never saw or sent any phial to the château. I would as soon plan to poison my own wife as her Majesty the Queen of Scots, my sovereign."

"Those are fine words, Monsieur de Graeme," answered Bertrandi, still in that clear little voice, and without any of the Constable's brow-beating manner. "They might carry weight if this were merely a question of rumour or suspicion. But look at the facts! If you persist in this stubborn attitude at your trial, I warn you that you can expect no mercy. But if, on the other hand, you make known without delay the names of your accomplices and reveal for what motive you undertook so terrible a deed, you will have some claim to his Majesty's clemency."

So the case was prejudged, he was condemned already. He might as well face that. But nothing should wring a lie from him.

"I can only repeat, and repeat it, Monsieur le Chancelier, as though I stood before the bar of God-that I am totally innocent. I made no plot; I had therefore no accomplices and looked for no gain."

"Come, Monsieur de Graeme," said the Chancellor good-temperedly, "because I am old, you must not take me for a complete simpleton! You deny that you wrote this letter here; you call it a forgery. Very good. How then do you account for your own seal attached thereto? Do not trouble, in spite of my age, to tell me that your ring was stolen from you, since it was on your finger when you were arrested last night."

"I do not tell you that, Monsieur le Chancelier, because it would be a lie," answered Ninian. "My own ring was on my finger. But that letter was sealed with another-its double."

"You would have me believe that someone stole your signet ring, copied it, and returned it to you?"

"By no means. The ring which was used to seal that letter is the property of the man who, I am constrained to believe, wrote that letter counterfeiting my hand and sent the phial to my wife in my name."

"And who, pray, is he?" enquired M. Bertrandi, almost in the tone of one humouring a child who plays at make-believe.

"A bastard son of my father's."

"Ah, another Scot-but you cannot mean the man Stuart, still in England?"

"No, he is a Frenchman."

"His name?"

Ninian drew a deep breath. Even then it seemed incredible. "Gaspard de Vernay."

"And you accuse this Gaspard de Vernay, who is the natural son of a Scot and yet bears a French name, of forging your hand of write, counterfeiting your ring — —"

"No, not of counterfeiting it. There was no need. He has-or had-its fellow."

"And you accuse *him* of the deed which is laid to your charge, and, moreover, of trying to lay the deed itself at your door?"

"With reluctance, I do."

The Chancellor put his fingers this time tip to tip. "A very strange counter-accusation to make, and one that will require much proving. But we will listen. Produce your grounds, Monsieur de Graeme, for making this charge, and in particular convince me of the motive which should lead this French half-brother of yours to attempt to poison the Queen of Scotland!"

To that question Ninian was aware that he could give no answer which would convince anyone. "I do not know his mind," he said slowly. "It must have been for gain of some sort."

Bertrandi shook his head. "That is easily said. Your whole accusation is too lightly made. Because this bastard kinsman possesses a ring like your own (if indeed he do possess it), I am therefore to believe that he wrote this letter? Why, pray, should he seek to fix so dreadful a stigma upon you? Had you quarrelled?"

"No."

"How and when, pray, did you come to be acquainted with him?"

Very briefly, Ninian told him.

"Ah, so you had him as your page for a while? He was therefore under an obligation to you, and the less likely to do you so great an injury. What chanced to him after he left your service?"

"He attracted the notice of M. de Saint-André and became one of his gentlemen."

"Then he is presumably with M. de Saint-André now, in England! How could he have sent the letter and phial last night?"

"I doubt whether he did indeed accompany M. de Saint-André to England, for I am almost sure that I caught sight of him here in Châteaubriant on Sunday night. And, therefore, in the name of justice, I ask that I be not sent to Nantes until search has been made for him-as M. de Montmorency undertook should be done."

"Search must certainly be made for him," said Bertrandi, with more sternness than he had yet shown. "He, too, has a right to know of what you accuse him, and to answer the charge! —I shall now continue my enquiries into the doings of last night. Call Madame de Paroy."

Stiff-faced and self-contained, the gouvernante entered, her skirts rustling with indignation, her hands folded on her stomacher. The Chancellor half rose and bowed towards her; she curtseyed and took her seat with dignity in the velvet chair which had meanwhile been placed for her at right angles to the table.

"Will you be good enough, Madame," said the old lawyer, "to relate again the events of last night as far as you know them."

The tale began, not a long one indeed, but so punctuated with his wife's name that Ninian tasted unlooked-for anguish as the brief pictures unrolled: Magdalen with the fatal letter in her hand, the monkey writhing on the floor, Magdalen brow-beaten, accused, dragged to her room, beset with charges against herself and him. . . .

He hardly heard the questions addressed to the witness. They were not numerous. His whole being was swamped with a longing to hold Magdalen in his arms, to reassure and comfort her-to tell her that that hard and vindictive woman should not harm her. . . . Alas, it might well be he would never hold her in his arms again, and what assurance was there anywhere now? The two of them were on a breaking bridge over a dark and swirling flood.

Her evidence finished, Madame de Paroy departed, fixing on Ninian before she went a long hostile stare which she terminated by hastily crossing herself. She was succeeded by Queen Mary's apothecary, Noel Chastain, short-sighted and nervous, but amply able to testify that he had never compounded any specific for a cough for M. de Graeme last winter or at any time. He was not accorded the honour of the velvet chair, nor was the Archer whom Ninian, with a catch at the heart, next beheld enter. Buchanan, an old comrade, to be dragged into these horrible toils!

Buchanan at least gave him a glance in which Ninian thought he could read a desire to re-assure him. Reluctantly, it was plain, but straightforwardly, he gave his evidence of the packet being brought to him by "one whom I took for a serving-man," and his delivering it himself to Madame de Graeme. Why had he done that? Had he thought it important? Had the "serv-ing-man" urged speed? Had he, Buchanan, recognised the seal? To all of these questions the Archer answered none too willingly, Yes. But when asked whether the "serving-man" might not have been the prisoner disguised, he replied emphatically that that was out of the question; he had been with Ninian Graham too many years in the Archer Guard not to recognise him anywhere. Could he then describe the bearer of the packet? No; he had taken no particular note of him, and the entrance was poorly lighted. In that case, how could he be sure that it was not the prisoner after all? But James Buchanan met that question scornfully. Of course he knew; for one thing the bearer of the packet, by the few words he had spoken, was a Frenchman, not a Scot.

"But," objected Bertrandi, "Scots who have been some years in France speak French. You are speaking French yourself at this moment, Monsieur, and M. de Graeme, like all the Archers of any standing, speaks French too."

"Yes, Monsieur le Chancelier, but we do not speak with the same ease and purity as the native-born."

"You are very critical," observed the old man, "for my ears have not detected much amiss with your speech, or with M. de Graeme's here. Is it not possible that you may have been mistaken-on the strength of a few hurried words-in the nationality of this unknown man?" But Buchanan would not admit this possibility.

He was dismissed, quite unshaken in his asseveration that it was certainly not Ninian Graham who had delivered the packet. And the next thing, thought his former comrade miserably, will be his own arrest as an accomplice determined to shelter me. However, there seemed no sign of this happening immediately. The Chancellor merely made a note that the unknown messenger must be tracked as soon as possible, and then uttered the command which drove any thoughts of Buchanan out of Ninian's head: "Bring in Madame de Graeme."

And there, two guards behind her, was his darling, pale beyond belief, in a dark gown which threw up that pallor. It was heart-shaking to see her and not to be able to go to her side. And she was evidently, though a woman, to stand —a culprit, not a witness. She gave him at once a desperate and half-guilty look, as though she felt that it was she who had dragged him into this appalling situation. At least, Ninian read it so, and tried by his own gaze to reinfuse courage into her-that quality which, in her own quiet manner, she had never lacked.

The Chancellor addressed her in the same gentle little voice. "I shall first read from my notes, Madame de Graeme," he informed her, "the account of what took place last night as given by the gouvernante of her Majesty the Queen of Scotland. You may interrupt me if you wish."

And he read Madame de Paroy's deposition, Magdalen listening with that shamed expression which so tore at her husband's heart. She did not interrupt. And then the questions began to pelt upon her in those flute-like tones; not terrifying, but as persistent as gentle rain. "Were you expecting to hear from your husband? Were you surprised to receive a remedy for the Queen? Had you spoken of it together before? Did you know that he used a remedy in the winter for his cough? Was this cough before or after your marriage? When you read the letter, did you recognise your husband's writing on the outside, or only within?"

Ninian saw her hands grip each other; she knew, the poor child, that any question about handwriting must be crucial. She drew a long breath. "I could not recognise it as his handwriting, Monsieur le Chancelier, since it was not."

The beard dipped benevolently in her direction. "But you thought it was his-you accepted it as his?"

"I . . . I had not time to do more than read the letter once before Madame de Paroy came in."

"Just so. But in that space you read it as being your husband's letter?"

"I . . . I suppose so."

She was beginning to look like a hunted creature. She probably guessed that his life might depend upon her answers now, and she knew not exactly how to answer. Useless, however, to try to prompt her, for it would only damn them both; moreover, he would never be allowed to get out more than a word or two.

Seeing that Bertrandi was waiting, looking at her expectantly, Magdalen began again after a moment. "The light, Monsieur, was not good . . . only . . . directly the monkey died I knew that the letter and the little bottle could not be from my husband . . ."

"But from whom else could they be?" enquired the Chancellor swiftly. "No, look at me-not at the prisoner!"

Her dear hands were so tightly clenched together in front of her now that Ninian felt sure the nails must be piercing the flesh. She was nearing breaking-point —and he could do nothing. "There is a bastard brother of my husband's," she got out. "It might have been he . . . he had served him as a page . . . might be familiar with his handwriting . . . know that he had had a cough . . ."

"And borrowed to seal the letter the ring which was on your husband's finger, returning it thither by magic when he had made use of it?"

Magdalen shrivelled at the tone and did not answer.

"My wife was not aware," interposed Ninian quickly, "that my half-brother had a ring identical with mine."

"And I am not surprised at her ignorance," retorted Bertrandi very dryly; and Ninian flushed with anger. "Now, Madame de Graeme," he resumed, "let us go back to the handwriting of the letter. When you read it you say that you supposed it was from your husband. I think it would be nearer the truth, would it not, to say that you had no doubt whatever that it was from him, since you did not know of these mysterious twin rings?"

There was a moment's silence. Magdalen unclasped her hands and put one over her eyes for a second or two. When she dropped it she appeared to have gained some fresh access of courage and strength, for it was in a firmer voice that she said:

"At the beginning I think I had no doubt, Monsieur le Chancelier, but when I came to the last sentence of all, wherein he made excuse for the ill writing, because he had cut his thumb in sharpening his pen — —"

But Bertrandi leant forward and interrupted her. "I do not remember any such sentence in the letter, Madame!" Nor, indeed, did Ninian. He stared at her, astonished, as she went on eagerly.

"It appeared to have been added after the letter was written. It puzzled me a little then . . . but I had no time to think about it. Now I understand why it was there; and if, Monsieur, you look at my husband's thumb you will, I am sure, find no sign of a cut upon it!"

The old lawyer, too, stared at the girl as one puzzled. "Give me the letter," he said to one of the secretaries, and taking it up scanned it closely. "Madame, you must have been dreaming last night. There is nothing here about such a matter."

"At the end, Monsieur, at the end!" urged Magdalen. "After my husband's initials, and that is not the way he is wont to sign his letters to me neither!"

"There is no such sentence here," asseverated the Premier President. And he held up the letter. "It ends thus, *Thine, N.G.* "

Craning forward a little, Magdalen flushed, then turned paler than before. "It was there, it was there! I saw it with my own eyes . . . It was added by the forger to cover the difference between his own handwriting and my husband's. There was a little mark as of blood also. And if there is no cut on my husband's hand when you look, it proves — —"

"Control yourself, Madame, I beg of you!" broke in Bertrandi somewhat sternly. "There is no postscriptum to this letter, or ever has been. You fancied it-or are of set purpose telling a lying tale!"

Magdalen carried her hand to her head as though she had been struck. Ninian wildly searched his memory. The glimpse he had had last night of the letter which had been such a thunderbolt was so brief, and he had been so stunned . . . *Had* there been such a sentence, or was Magdalen making a desperate and, it seemed, ill-judged effort to save him?

Then, suddenly, he saw her sway; she was near fainting. Clenching his hands, he made an effort to get to her; but he only accomplished a step before he was seized and held. As for Magdalen, her guards went to her at once, supported and removed her not ungently, the Chancellor directing them to deliver her with due care to the attentions of someone of the Queen of Scotland's women.

And so she was gone! Would he ever see her again? To preserve his self-control, he began to count the points of the dog-tooth carving on the arch high up behind the Chancellor's head. Then he became aware that the latter was addressing him, telling him that he must go to stand his trial at Nantes.

"And I would send you thither to-day," he said, "were it not for the serious charge you have made against your bastard brother-which I must warn you I consider one of the most unlikely accusations I have ever heard in my long life. Since, however, you have made it, it is only right that there should be sufficient delay to give him an opportunity of answering it, if he is in Châteaubriant at all. And the man who took the packet to the château must be found also-though your departure need not be postponed for that."

"And before I disappear into the dungeons of Nantes," said Ninian hoarsely, "is there no one to speak for me? None of my former comrades here?"

But the Archers all looked straight in front of them, save one or two, whose eyes were on the ground.

"Since you were once in the Archer Guard yourself," said the Chancellor reprovingly, "you must know that a soldier on duty is dumb. You will have full opportunity given you at Nantes of calling witnesses in your defence."

"Yes," thought the prisoner bitterly, "when they have finished with me in the dungeons, and my body only craves for death!" Aloud he said, throwing back his head: "Not only was I of the Archer Guard, but I am still of it. I claim the right of appeal to his Majesty whom it serves!"

Bertrandi shook his head.

"Then to M. de Montgomery-or to his son!"

"The Comte de Montgomery is ill. And neither he nor M. Gabriel de Lorges, in any case, has judicial status in this matter. You must stand your trial."

Here one of M. Bertrandi's secretaries leant forward and whispered something in his ear.

"Yes, yes, you are right," said his master. "The conference with the English envoys —I fear me I am late already. Paper and ink have already been taken to the prisoner's place of confinement, have they not? —Then, Monsieur de Graeme, since these materials have been given you, I advise you to use this respite in making the voluntary confession which, as I have said, may entitle you to some measure of clemency." Gathering his robes about him, he rose, little and bent; then paused to address Ninian once more. "In particular will there be a chance of this if you have any communication to make with regard to this Robert Stuart, who is being sent here by the English Council for trial, and about whom I have not time to question you now."

* * * * *

Out in that strange, lovely, misty sunshine again! He might not see much more sunshine after to-morrow. God! if only, before he quitted it for ever, there were some chance of taking by the throat the man who had brought Magdalen and him to this!

From that vain dream of vengeance he was brought back to wonder why, as they crossed the court-yard, the guard upon his left hand was holding his arm in so strange a grip, alternately pressing it and relaxing the pressure. It must be to attract his attention for some reason. Ninian turned his head, and found himself looking into the eyes of Patrick Rutherford.

A moment's bewildered amazement, and he divined that his friend had contrived to change clothes and places with one of the Constable's men. And in those eyes which he knew so well he read, without need of speech: "What can I do for you? Make it known quickly."

His head still turned towards him, so that the guard on his other side should not hear, Ninian said, scarcely moving his lips: "A letter for the Duc de Guise . . . in my doublet . . . when I stumble, thrust in your hand. . . . Get it to him for God's sake . . . my only hope!" And Patrick gave a nod.

A few steps more, and Ninian tripped convincingly over a piece of broken masonry not far from the door of his prison. "Hold up!" said Patrick roughly, seizing him with his free hand by the front of his doublet. The other guard took no notice-perhaps he, too, had been bribed; the officer leading the way looked round, but saw nothing suspicious. But the piece of paper which represented Ninian's last throw was safely gripped in his friend's hand, and when the door shut upon him two minutes later he knew that nothing short of sudden death would prevent its making its appeal to the gratitude of François de Guise.

(4)

Magdalen's half swoon had been brief. The open air and the water brought by her not unkindly guards revived her-but only to anguish. On the arm of one of them she walked back through the vaulted passage which led to the new château in a trance of despair. Ninian was lost, lost! She had pinned all her hopes upon his accusers realising the implication of that postscript to the false letter, which must surely clear a man whose thumb bore no mark of a recent cut-and they had denied that any such postscript had ever existed. Oh, how could such wickedness be allowed to triumph!

She hardly realised that she was in the new château once more, stared at by all she met. All places were the same. No, not all! After a while she became aware, with a pang, that her escort was taking her back to her room by a route which led through the ante-chamber where that dreadful scene had taken place last night-an unconsciously cruel action against which it was useless to protest. Very soon she was in that many-doored ante-room itself; she was crossing the floor where the phial-where Gris-gris . . .

Then through the unbearable memory came, like a shaft of sunlight from some happier world, the clear, childish laugh which she knew so well, the delicious carefree laugh of her little Reinette, whom she was like never to see again. For a moment she almost thought it was a phantom sound sent to torment her further. Then she saw that the door of the Queen's day apartment was ajar. And in an instant, propelled by some impulse which she could not have resisted had she wished, she had slipped from between her two companions and had run through that unfastened door.

The room was very warm, for a fire flickered there, pale in the June morning, and some kind of balsam was burning, too, against the Queen's cold. Even at that moment of extreme tension it was possible for Magdalen's brain to register the fact that the scent of this was unfamiliar-some specific of Madame de Paroy's, no doubt. But she herself, thank God, was not there; for in addition to the little Queen, there was only Jean Ogilvy, sewing on a window-seat, who sprang to her feet in amazement on seeing her-and one other person.

In a chair not far from the fire, a furred cloak over her shoulders, her feet on a footstool, sat Mary with a great book spread upon a table before her, while, bending over this book with its back to the door, was a tall scarlet-clad figure which could be no other than that of the Cardinal of Lorraine. The child, still laughing, seemed to have been asking him something about the engraving at which the book was opened, and to which she was pointing with one hand. Flying forward, Magdalen was on her knees by her before the young Cardinal had much more than turned round, or Mary's own laughter ceased.

"Oh, hear me, your Majesty, for God's sake-and my Lord Cardinal!"

Her guards were on her heels; but at a gesture from Charles de Guise they stood back respectfully. As for Mary, the colour sprang hot into her cheeks, and she cried, after a moment's surprise:

"My poor Gris-gris! How could you be so cruel, Mistress Graham! Did you indeed poison — —But why are these guards here?"

They have kept the full story from her, flashed into Magdalen's mind.

"I did not kill him willingly, Marie," she said, the name slipping out unnoticed in her desperation. "It was a mistake . . . But my husband . . . he is accused . . . of worse. They are sending him to Nantes-to the question. Oh, ma Reinette, save him-he loves you so!"

The flush had gone from the child's face. She had risen and now stood very upright, the cloak slipped to the ground. "What is this about Master Graham? They told me he was indisposed! Is that not true?" A door opened. "Madame de Paroy, why did you tell me a lie?"

It was indeed Madame de Paroy, not long returned from giving her evidence, who had appeared in the room, and took charge of the situation-or endeavoured to do so. "What has this wicked girl been telling your Majesty? As if it were not enough to have poisoned the poor

130

monkey! Who admitted her? Your Eminence will agree with me that no more should be heard of this. The Queen is not well. Let the guards remove — —"

But the Cardinal, holding up a hand to silence her, looked down at the "wicked girl," now clasping the royal child by the skirts and imploring her on her husband's behalf. "Marie, Marie, remember how he saved you from the dog that day-remember what care he has taken of you when you rode! Now they say he tried to poison you-and they will not listen . . . first the Constable, then the Chancellor — —"

"Silence, silence!" exclaimed Madame de Paroy, gripping her by one shoulder, and trying to drag her to her feet. "Come away at once!"

"Poison me!" cried the little Queen. "Master Graham poison me! He would never do such a thing! What is this tale?"

"A tale, Marie, that I think you had better hear," said her uncle composedly. "Wait without the door," he said to the guards. "And, Madame, if you will allow Madame de Graeme to rise — —"

Red with wrath, Madame de Paroy protested. "Your Eminence, is it wise to continue this? In her Majesty's state of health, I am responsible — —"

"I, too, am not without responsibility for my niece," interrupted the young ecclesiastic calmly, "and I consider that she must hear what has happened."

"Indeed, Uncle Charles, I mean to hear," said the small Queen with decision. "Did you know that Master Graham was accused of so monstrous a thing?"

The Cardinal shook his head. "It is the first I have heard of it. But Madame de Graeme shall enlighten us. Pray rise, Madame!" The shapely hand with the archiepiscopal ring was extended, assisted her to rise, and motioned her to a chair, the while Madame de Paroy, exclaiming: "I wash my hands of the results of this!" swirled out of the room.

From the conference chamber, where a further session of the chaffering over the Princess Elisabeth's dowry had just come to an end, there filed out by one door into a separate apartment the English commissioners, Lord Northampton, John Fisher, Bishop of Ely, Sir Philip Hoby, Sir William Pickering, Sir Thomas Smith, Dr. Oliver and Sir John Mason. And as the French members possessed a like convenient exit, they were able upon emerging to give untrammelled expression to their sentiments-as the Englishmen were probably doing also.

"A monstrous demand, although abated to half!" (For it stood at eight hundred thousand crowns.) "On my soul it is like bargaining at a fair!" "It would have been cheaper to let them have the little Queen of Scotland." "You are surely jesting," observed Gaspard de Coligny-Châtillon to the speaker, the Bishop of Soissons, "for you cannot rate the gift of her kingdom at so little!"

The Cardinal of Lorraine (who, for a good reason, had made a late appearance at the conference board) took no part in these exchanges. He was desirous of speaking to two persons only, and these were now deep in converse with each other by a window recess. From the Constable's expression Charles de Guise was sure that he was not discussing with Bertrandi the mercenary claims of the English. For one moment he thought of conferring with his brother about the affair he had in hand, but the Duke was just leaving the apartment, and moreover the Cardinal heard, at that moment, in Anne de Montmorency's gruff tones, the words "Nantes" and "early to-morrow." So, pulling out and opening his pocket-breviary, he approached the two in the embrasure, apparently absorbed in his Office.

"I doubt if he will confess to anything," came to him then in the Chancellor's silvery old voice. "He appears very stubborn."

At that the Constable gave a short version of his great laugh.

"My dear Premier Président, are there not ways of unlocking the most speechless lips? I know of at least three, and so do you!"

The Cardinal de Lorraine came to a stop, and raised his head from the psalm he was not reading. "You are speaking, I think, Monsieur de Montmorency, of this attempt upon the life of the little Queen —a terrible affair indeed, save that, but for heavenly intervention, it might have been worse!"

The Constable gave a grunt.

"My niece," went on the Cardinal smoothly, "refuses to believe in M. de Graeme's guilt, and says it is impossible that her Grand Ecuyer and his wife, for whom she has much affection, should be involved in such a crime."

"How did her little Majesty hear of the business at all?" demanded the Constable frowning. "Orders were given — —"

"Oh, my dear Constable, you know that a matter of that nature could not long be hidden from her. Rumours, too, take birth so easily and fly so swiftly. I myself have heard, how truly I know not, that the unfortunate Graeme most plainly accuses someone else of forging the letter supposed to have been sent by him. And there is also some story of a postscript to the letter —a cock and bull tale no doubt-of the writer having feigned to cut his finger in order to cover the difference between his handwriting and M. de Graeme's."

This time the Constable gave him an unmitigated glare. "Sang dieu! Where did you get hold of that, my Lord Cardinal? You were not at the interrogatory this morning?"

"No, my Lord Constable," answered the Cardinal, smiling to himself. "Should I have heard that tale if I had been there? Was there indeed such a postscript?"

"Ask the Chancellor here," muttered Montmorency, turning and gazing out of the window.

But when Charles of Lorraine looked at Bertrandi, the latter shook his venerable head. "No, indeed, your Eminence, there was no such thing."

"How untrustworthy, as well as swift, is rumour! How then could such a report have got about if it had no foundation at all?"

"Owing perhaps to some wild words of Madame de Graeme's. She affirmed that the letter contained such a statement-when it plainly did not. She was . . . overwrought."

"Ah, no doubt," agreed the Cardinal, who had had ample opportunity of judging. "Or she has a fertile invention. It was fortunate for you, my dear Chancellor, that no such postscript existed, since I imagine that you were anxious to get the case disposed of and the prisoner sent to Nantes as quickly as possible!"

"Most certainly. And to Nantes he will go to-morrow morning. . . . You will excuse me now, gentlemen? I have matters requiring attention in my chamber."

The Cardinal joined Montmorency in his study of the sunlit garden outside. "I think," he said appreciatively, "that I prefer this residence of yours, Constable, even to Chantilly. I am not so sure about Ecouen. Jean de Laval did well, in my opinion, not to pull down the old château entirely; the contrast between the two is piquant. To recur for a moment to this business of M. de Graeme's letter and the imaginary postscript, I suppose that, had such a thing existed, he could have advanced it as a proof that he did not write the letter-provided that he had no cut upon his thumb? But as I imagine that he undoubtedly did write it, it is proper to use all and every means that he should not escape justice. Is that not so, Monsieur de Montmorency?"

"Most undoubtedly," replied the soldier shortly. "And he will not escape it."

"As her Majesty's uncle," observed the Cardinal softly, "you will understand how glad I am to hear that. In fact, had there been at the end of the letter any statement likely to . . . to raise difficulties I believe I should have felt it only right to dispose of it . . . if I could have done so without leaving a trace. For in such a case justice must be served."

And as he spoke, his eyes fixed on the Constable's bearded profile, he knew that his half-suspicions were amply justified. The man beside him had taken exactly that view and resorted to exactly that measure.

But though Anne de Montmorency could not prevent the Cardinal from becoming aware of this fact, he was not going to acknowledge his action in so many words. He turned towards the cleverest of the Guises with his big laugh, the very slight obliquity in his gaze showing more than usual, and retorted, "I always said you Churchmen were unscrupulous above all others," and began to move towards the door of the room, now vacated by all but themselves.

The Cardinal accompanied him. "You call such an act unscrupulous! But, my dear Constable, I consider it praiseworthy! For, of course, you were convinced before you resorted to it that M. de Graeme was guilty, and your only wish was to bring him to justice as speedily as possible!"

Having an excellent, if narrow, understanding, the Constable probably realised that he had been driven into a trap; but he now submitted to enter it. "Naturally that was my wish," he growled, "and since the child against whom he was practising is your niece, the House of Guise should be a little grateful to me." And before the Cardinal had time to assure him of that gratitude he came to a standstill, and beating his fist vehemently into his open palm, added fiercely, "But we must have a confession, and the names of his accomplices, or of those who set him on to this attempt-what, for instance, is his connection with this man Stuart, whom the English have arrested. And he is obstinate; I saw that for myself last night-or rather early this morning. It has but just occurred to me that the swiftest way to make him open his mouth would be to threaten his wife with the question-although Bertrandi thinks she was but a dupe-and to let him know it."

Even the Guise blood ran a little cold at that. "My young niece the Queen would be most averse to that measure," he said quickly. "As I say, she is affectionately disposed towards Madame de Graeme, and greatly esteems her Master of Horse also. She should, I think, be considered."

"I did not say 'put to the question,' " retorted the Constable impatiently. "I said 'threatened with the question'!"

That heartbroken girl upstairs? No, not if he could prevent it! But Charles de Guise said no more on the point; it was time for him, if he wished to put a spoke in the Constable's wheel, to seek the King. But before parting from his companion he judged it not amiss to raise one more objection.

"There is a point which puzzles me in this affair, and makes me a trifle less sure of Graeme's guilt. It is this; why, seeing that for the past two and a half years he has had countless opportunities of causing her little Majesty, when she rides, to break her neck, should he have given them the go-by and now send poison and an incriminating letter?"

But Anne de Montmorency found no difficulty in answering that conundrum. Pausing, his hand on the doorhandle, he answered confidently: "Because the time was not ripe for her death. Now, for some reason which we have not yet discovered-but which we shall get out of him at Nantes-it is judged ripe. And there is more," he added, his little eyes gleaming. "I have come to believe that the attempt was originally planned much longer ago than appears: that it was with the object of getting rid of the little Queen, when the moment arrived, that Graeme contrived to secure a post in her household at the end of '48, and that-against the royal wish-he married one of her maids of honour in order to be in closer touch with her Majesty. Some deep and deadly intrigue is here, I am convinced, Cardinal-but I am going to unravel it before many days are out!"

Charles de Guise gazed at him and said nothing. Indeed it was high time that he saw the King. With so much animus against that unfortunate Scot as to be able to distort his every action into a preparation for crime, the Constable was likely to stop at nothing. He had already gravely tampered with justice: did he think that he was master of France?

A rather steely gleam was in the Cardinal's blue-grey eyes, a slightly heightened colour on his delicate fair skin, as he said a few words commending the zeal of this rival of his house, took farewell of him, and, after making sure that he had not been followed, made his way towards the King's private apartments.

Nine years ago, at the mature age of seventeen, Charles de Guise had been made overseer of the household of the Dauphin Henri, six years older than himself, and he had always the privilege of entrée to the King. But when he came now into the royal ante-chamber, thronged and humming with courtiers, English lords, nobles and gentlemen waiting to play tennis with his Majesty or to watch the game, he was informed that the King was already changing his clothes in readiness and would probably in a moment or two come forth ready to go down to the open-air court (for in fine weather he preferred the *jeu de longue paume*). The Cardinal was vexed to find that he had missed his opportunity, for there was scarcely even any great affair of state for which Henri would consent to postpone a game of tennis or a hunting party. Nevertheless, he asked admission, hoping that the King was at least alone.

Save for his pages, he *was* alone, standing up in his bedchamber in a loose white silk shirt and haut-de-chausses of white linen, a costume which both set off his athletic figure and threw up the dark pallor of his features. A page holding the special shoes for the game stood just behind him.

"Ah, Cardinal," he said, on seeing his visitor, "and how went the conference this morning?" But the question was perfunctory; he would not, as the young churchman knew, attend to a detailed answer if it were given, wherefore, he did not give it.

"Tolerably well, Sire," he replied. "Could your Majesty grant me a moment or two in private? It is an urgent matter."

"Afterwards, afterwards," said the King rather impatiently, and sat down to have his shoes put on.

"Afterwards, your Majesty, may be too late. Two minutes now — —"

"Cordieu, is so much at stake?" asked Henri, as a second page lifted up his foot for the shoe.

"A man's life and the reputation of French justice!"

" —Not those shoes, imbecile!" exclaimed the King angrily. "The pair I wore the day before yesterday. —Who is the man?"

"The unfortunate Graeme, Grand Ecuyer to her Majesty of Scotland."

Henri II's brow grew dark. " 'Unfortunate,' you call him, that abominable miscreant!" Colour sprang to his sallow cheeks. "That the life of a child so precious should have been attempted by a man of my Archer Guard! You cannot mean to tell me that you are interceding for him, Cardinal!"

But the suppliant stood his ground. "Near of kin to the Queen though I am, I do intercede for him, your Majesty, for I am convinced that there has been a grave miscarriage of justice." He was tempted to add, 'devised by the Constable,' but this was a delicate matter to handle even in private, and certainly could not be touched upon in the presence of attendants.

But already the anticipation of tennis was smothering the flame of the royal indignation. "As to that, the affair is in the hands of the Chancellor," said the King, in a tone of dismissal. "In any case I cannot hear more now. When I return, perhaps. —My other shoe, quickly!"

When, early on that morning of sunshot mist, Gaspard de Vernay had slipped out from Madame de Saint-Cernin's chamber with her last kiss warm on his lips, and warmer still on his finger the ruby ring which she had transferred to it from her own, it was to emerge from an enchanted bower to a region where-as he had naturally foreseen-he must for a few days walk with extreme caution.

He had indeed foreseen the hazards of his own position, since he was himself the author of them-but he had never foreseen that they would have to be encountered to no purpose. There was no reward after all to be expected from the English for making away with the Queen of Scotland . . . rather the reverse! . . . The first question for him was, therefore, Had she been made away with?

This was not a question which he dared ask of anyone. But the answer was not long in coming to his ears. By ten o'clock or so the whole château, the whole town, was ringing with the news of the attempt on her life, which had however failed because a lapdog or a monkey had drunk the poison before it could be administered. And Gaspard drew a very long breath of relief. To have removed the royal child with no advantage to himself would have been stupid. Here at least his luck had held.

About the identity of the would-be poisoner and his fate, diverse reports were going round. In some mouths he was an Englishman, in others an Italian; in a few, a woman-perhaps even Madame de Paroy herself. It was said that he had been run through on the spot by the guards, that he had drunk poison himself, that he was still undiscovered. But at last the one man in Châteaubriant able to sift true from false did learn of his half-brother's arrest, interrogatory and probable despatch to Nantes. Luck again-his carefully-selected scapegoat already in custody!

Back in his attic with this harvest of information, Gaspard sat down to review the situation. Ninian would almost certainly make a counter-accusation against him, for it was inevitable that he should guess whose hand had penned that letter, and whose ring had sealed it. But would his charge be listened to? If it were, Gaspard's own course was quite plain, and of a commendable simplicity. He would merely oppose a blank and horrified denial to a charge which it would be almost impossible to prove. His father's ring, the only dangerous piece of evidence against him, was hidden away in the rafters above his head until he could dispose of it more permanently still-if he decided to do so. Now he had only to deny and deny and deny. It might at need be made to appear that at the very hour of the delivery of the phial and letter he had already entered Madame de Saint-Cernin's apartment; a bribe to the waiting woman would ensure that. And no search on earth would ever discover among all the *valetaille* of Châteaubriant him who had handed the packet to the Archer on guard.

And Ninian, uselessly sacrificed? Gaspard had thought himself better armoured against remorse, but it was impossible entirely to avoid thinking of his half-brother and of what was likely to be his fate. This affair of the man Stuart in England-which was evidently a fact, since there were whispers of it going about this morning-would not improve the chances of that acquittal which he had vaguely assured himself that his victim would, somehow, obtain . . . after an interval. In the circumstances which were now so much altered, Gaspard would willingly, he told himself, have put out a hand to save him, if he could. But that was difficult without extreme hazard to himself; in fact, it was impossible-and doubly so if Ninian made a counter-charge. Bon Dieu, one must defend one's self!

Yes, if Ninian did accuse him, he would only have himself to thank if he went to the scaffold. One cannot be expected to succour a drowning man if he tries to pull his rescuer under also! In the same way that grasping old Marillier would only have had himself to thank if the poison had gone down his throat instead of down the Queen's monkey's. Gaspard only wished now that it had. (And by the way it was strange, after what the vendor had told him of the stuff, that the animal had, apparently, died almost instantly.)

The thought of Marillier reminded the young man all at once, and most agreeably, of something learnt yesterday, which the more urgent claims of murder and love had put out of his head. Was not the Prior of Lincennes reputed to be by this time almost at death's door? And here on his own finger, glowing like lit blood in the sun now streaming through the skylight, was the means (and more) of finally buying off the old Baron! But the ruby should not be sold yet, for to-night again he was to wait in ecstasy to see that golden curtain sway and part. . . . Standing admiring the jewel, he decided to put on his orange cloak and go to show himself awhile at the château. It was not, in any case, good policy to seem to be in hiding.

* * * * *

Like many in the closely-pressed little town, the house where Gaspard had his lodging looked out into-in fact leant over —a narrow alleyway, dark, winding and malodorous. Along this the young man in his finery had not gone many yards when he saw advancing towards him the white surcoat with the crowned H and crescent of a Scottish Archer. His heart gave an uncomfortable twist. Arrest? No, impossible! Moreover, there would have been two of them. He went on as one expecting to pass, for which there was room and to spare, but the Archer, placing himself directly in his path, addressed him curtly and sternly by name.

"Monsieur de Vernay, I want a word with you!"

"I do not know who you are," answered Gaspard, looking him up and down-had he seen his face before? —"but if you make your request in a more civil manner — —"

"This is no time for civility," interrupted the Archer, frowning. "It is a reckoning that I have come for."

"But, my good Scot, I do not owe you any money!" responded Gaspard rather insolently, though his heartbeats were quickening.

"Money! It is a man's honour and liberty, perhaps his life, that you have stolen! I am Patrick Rutherford; we have met once before, and you are coming with me now to the Chancellor to confess, vile serpent that you are, what you have done to the brother who befriended you!"

So Ninian *had* accused him! " 'Brother' —'befriend'!" he exclaimed. "I do not know what you speak of! Give me passage, Archer, or I will take it!"

And he laid his left hand warningly on his rapier hilt.

Tall and menacing, Rutherford came still nearer. "You will come with me," he repeated, "and tell M. Bertrandi what you have done before it is too late!"

"I will go to M. Bertrandi and ask protection from a bully!" retorted Gaspard with a blaze of anger. And as, on that, Patrick's hand came down heavily on his shoulder, he cried: "Loose me, or I will use my dagger on you!"

He had plucked it from its sheath behind him before Rutherford, to save himself, sprang back and drew his rapier. Gaspard's was out nearly as quickly, and in a moment the little alley was alive with the click-clock of angry steel. In fury and skill the two men were fairly matched, though the Scot had the longer reach. But this was of little advantage in so narrow a space, where a weapon of such length as a rapier was not too easy to handle well, and where the daggers in the combatants' left hands would actually have served them better alone.

For a few moments thrust and parry went briskly on, while a casement or two was opened and from one a head looked out, to be withdrawn as quickly as a tortoise's. But the ruelle, littered as it was with domestic garbage, was too treacherous underfoot for prolonged sword-play. Actually, it was a rotting fish-head which brought it abruptly to a close. By the time that Gaspard had recovered from his slip and stagger, his rapier, twisted from his hand, was lying a couple of yards away in a puddle, and Patrick Rutherford, who might have transfixed him, but wanted him sound and alive, was forcing him at his sword's point back to the wall.

"Drop your poniard!" he said between his teeth, for Gaspard was trying vainly to parry with it. "Drop it, or I'll run you through!"

Gaspard's shoulders were now against the wall, the point of his adversary's blade actually pricking through his doublet and drawing blood. Snarling with useless rage he let the dagger fall. Still with his point in position, Rutherford sheathed his own dagger in order to have his left hand free, and then seized the young man by the right wrist in a grip there was small prospect of shaking off.

"Now," he said grimly, "*now* , liar and assassin!"

Gaspard looked him defiantly in the eyes. "You call *me* an assassin!" he retorted, his left foot feeling about until he had ascertained the exact whereabouts of the handle of his dropped poniard. Then, with a lightening dive downwards, he grabbed up the discarded weapon, and before Patrick, still gripping sword and wrist, had realised his intention, had driven it in to the hilt just below his right collarbone.

(8)

The business in his chamber to which M. Bertrandi had alleged he must hurry away after the conference was neither more nor less than the light collation which was waiting him there, and of which he felt himself in justifiable need. After all, he was an octogenarian who had had several hours' hard mental work that morning.

Of this quite frugal meal, consisting chiefly of broth, a little bread and some Anjou wine, he was slowly partaking, while his secretary Benoît wrote out his notes of the recent proceedings, when there was a commotion outside the door, it was flung open, and there rushed in without any announcement, a young, well-dressed gentleman, heated and discomposed. Uttering a sound of protest, the secretary sprang up from his seat.

"Pardon me, Monsieur le Chancelier, but I must speak with you!" said the intruder breathlessly.

"This is not a convenient moment, sir," said the startled Chancellor, also a trifle breathlessly, having nearly choked over a spoonful of soup. "My secretary will hear what you have to say."

But Gaspard had pushed past that individual. "Only you can hear it, Monsieur Bertrandi, since it concerns the attempt upon the Queen of Scots. And it is on account of it that I ——"

Bertrandi laid down his spoon. "Ah," he said in a different tone, "if you know something of that I will hear you in a few minutes. I see that you have made commendable haste hither. Benoît, conduct this gentleman ——"

But the gentleman was not to be dislodged. "In God's name, Monsieur Bertrandi," he pleaded, "suffer me to remain in your presence! There is safety here from would-be murderers. Unless, indeed, it was by your orders that the Archer attacked me."

"Murders! Archer!" exclaimed M. Bertrandi, leaning forward in amazement, his noble beard in some danger of immersion in the half-empty bowl.

Gaspard de Vernay tore open his doublet. There were two or three small scarlet stains on his shirt. "Death was as near to me as this a few moments ago!" he exclaimed, pointing to them. "That is why I ask protection from the friends of that man who has already tried to poison the Queen of Scots, and who now sets others to seek my life, I know not why." Not Machiavelli himself could have guessed that three-quarters of his discomposure was assumed.

The Chancellor pushed away the bowl of broth, took a gulp of wine, and said: "Do I understand that you have been set upon, Monsieur, and by an Archer of the Scottish Guard? That is extraordinary!"

"No, not extraordinary. The Archer is a friend of M. de Graeme's, who was once of the Guard himself."

"And where is he now-following you?"

"No," answered his visitor, dropping his eyes; there was a smile in them. "He will not follow me. I was forced to defend myself, and I left him lying in the ruelle where he assaulted me, and came hither as fast as I could to claim the protection of the law."

"I imagine," said Bertrandi, fixing his eyes upon him, "that you must be that bastard brother of M. de Graeme's of whom I heard this morning?"

The petitioner, in his turn, looked absolutely bewildered at this. "I, a bastard brother of Graeme's!" he exclaimed. "But, Monsieur le Chancelier, what tale is this? My name is Vernay, Gaspard de Vernay!"

"That was the name," said the secretary softly.

"Yes, I remember, Benoît. And you are not, you say, the prisoner's half-brother?"

"Most certainly I am not! I am no kin of his, I thank God —a Scot and a traitor to his sovereign! I am a Frenchman like yourself... But the Archer who attacked me said something about 'confessing.' What in the name of all the saints am I expected to confess?" asked Gaspard, a picture of bewildered innocence. "There is some vile plot against me here!"

"Indeed," said the old lawyer gravely, "it begins to look like it. Remove this bowl, if you please, Benoît, and bring your ink-horn and paper over here. Now, Monsieur de Vernay, sit down and let us go into this matter in order."

M. de Vernay, obeying, was careful to leave his doublet still gaping. Evidence of violence is always impressive.

"You are not, you say, Monsieur, a bastard brother of M. de Graeme's. Then it is also untrue that you were recently in his service as page?"

Never deny what it is not safe to deny. "No, Monsieur, that is true. Last May, owing to a family misfortune, I had but little money at my disposal, and when the position of gentleman page was offered to me I thought it not beneath me to accept it."

Bertrandi nodded. "But why," he enquired, "was it offered to you in particular rather than to another?"

A slip to admit that it had been offered! He ought to have said that he had applied for the post. But Gaspard hardly hesitated at all as he replied: "Because, when we met by chance-it was in the park at Anet —I happened to warn M. de Graeme of an unseen danger, a viper in the grass."

"And that was the reason why he took you into his service, and not, as he stated this morning, because you were his father's son?"

"Do I look like the son of the same father, Monsieur Bertrandi?"

The old man caressed his beard and considered this. "No. No, you do not." A pause and then he appeared to sink into a reverie, for he went on as if to himself, "And yet he might be of other than French parentage-that hair, those eyes — —"

Hastily Gaspard broke in as if he had not heard this soliloquy. "With all respect, Monsieur le Chancelier, I should like to remind you that I am still at a loss — —"

M. Bertrandi came out of his reverie. "True, I forgot. I have not yet told you of the astounding charge which Monsieur de Graeme has made against you, and which would have made it necessary for me to have you sought out, if you had not come here of your own free will. Briefly, it is that it was you, and not he, who sent the phial of poison to Madame de Graeme last night, copying his handwriting and using, to seal the letter, a ring the counterpart of his own."

His visitor drew a long breath of horror and fell back in his chair. "I . . . I attempt to poison that adorable child who is to marry Monseigneur le Dauphin? Chancellor, the man is mad!"

"It is possible," said Bertrandi dispassionately, observing him the while.

The pained horror on the face opposite him deepened.

"And in addition he accuses me of trying to make it appear that he was the criminal! My God, as if I should so stab a benefactor in the back!"

"I have known it done," said the old man.

"Why," ejaculated Gaspard with increasing vehemence, "was it not I who induced M. de Saint-André, my patron, to use his influence with his Majesty to give his assent to Graeme's marriage? You can easily discover that it was so. That is how I repaid him for befriending me!"

"And yet it is true," observed Bertrandi reflectively, "that while in his service you had excellent opportunities for learning of his family circumstances, studying his handwriting, perhaps even of copying his seal."

"But do you not see that is just why he has tried to fix this guilt upon my shoulders? He was cunning enough to see that such things could be said of me as you have just said. It is a wicked plot against me!"

"It is a wicked plot against her Majesty the Queen of Scotland," retorted Bertrandi with a note of reproof in his voice. "That is the fact which must not be forgotten. And now, what of these two signet-rings bearing the same crest? You wear a ring, Monsieur de Vernay?"

Without hesitation M. de Vernay spread both his hands upon the table.

"That is not a signet-ring," remarked the Chancellor, looking at the remarkably fine ruby which gleamed upon the right hand.

"The gentlemen of my house do not wear them," answered the young man, with the faintest touch of mystery and hauteur. "That is not to say that we are without armorial bearings."

He was certainly not without a splendid jewel. That ruby, computed the Chancellor, would purchase quite a well-rounded little estate. M. de Vernay's clothes, too, had certainly required a purse of some depth. So, argued the old lawyer to himself, he is certainly not now in need, whatever he may have been; hence the only likely motive which could have driven a Frenchman to an attempt on the life of his future queen is lacking. Yet he quietly stretched out his own old hand, and laying hold of that young one with the ring, turned it palm uppermost and scrutinised the thumb and first finger-its owner looking greatly puzzled meanwhile.

"Thank you," said the Chancellor, laying it down. "I thank you also, Monsieur de Vernay, for saving me the trouble of having you sought for-in which indeed I had anticipated a little difficulty, since it seemed uncertain whether you were in Châteaubriant or no. And why, by the way, did you not accompany M. de Saint-André to England?"

The question nearly took Gaspard by surprise. He had thought himself by now clear of peril. But he gave, composedly enough, the reason already given to his associates that morning in the encampment. "A sad family bereavement on the eve of setting forth prevented it."

Once again the old lawyer's eyes strayed over his festive attire, to dwell perceptibly upon the cloak which so little suggested this event. Gaspard could read his thoughts this time, and was not thereby rendered more comfortable. A short period of silent beard-stroking then ensued; after which M. Bertrandi appeared to come to a decision.

"You may now withdraw, Monsieur de Vernay. I am glad that you came to vindicate yourself." His tone-but only his tone-seemed to show that Gaspard had succeeded in this. "As to the question of the Archer who attacked you-do you know his name?"

"He told me that it was Rutherford."

"The question then of this Rutherford must be taken up with M. de Lorges or his lieutenant. You say that you left him lying on the spot. Was he severely hurt?"

For a moment Gaspard hesitated. "I did not kill him. And only, I vow, in self-defence did I — —"

"Yes, yes, I understand. I will myself take steps about the matter. Meanwhile, if you are molested, go instantly to the captain of the Constable's men-at-arms and ask for a couple of them as guard. I shall write to him. Good day to you, Monsieur de Vernay."

The young man gone, the Chancellor sat nibbling a piece of bread from his interrupted repast. This interview had cast a still more sinister light on M. de Graeme, and his attempt to fasten his guilt upon another man's shoulders with a tale of a forged letter and a ring exactly similar. His possible connection with the man Stuart must be thoroughly examined. As for his wife, she was most probably merely his dupe, for had she been an accomplice no such letter as she had received would have been necessary. Still, it would be better policy not to make that opinion clear yet, especially to the prisoner himself.

As for the question of the postscript to the letter and what Madame de Graeme had declared it to contain, M. Bertrandi scarcely knew what to think. He now made Benoît bring him the letter, and for the first time looked closely at the lower edge of the sheet. It did indeed appear as though some words had been cut off. But one could not be sure, and since the letter had been committed to him in its present state by M. de Montmorency himself, he did not propose to concern himself with its previous experiences.

Now that this missing Gaspard de Vernay had come forward of his own accord-the last thing he would do, one would think, were he guilty-there was really no reason for delaying further the sending of Graeme to the dungeons of Nantes. With all these English here it was desirable to get him out of Châteaubriant as quickly as possible. Nevertheless, it would so greatly assist enquiries if he could be induced to make a written confession before departure, that it was worth while giving him further time to reflect on the advantage to himself of this course. Yes, he should have the night in which to think it over.

"Have that cold broth removed, Benoît," said the Chancellor of France, "and tell them to bring me some hot. And then take your pen and write to my dictation a letter for me to sign."

He had never played better, and the compliments presented to him by the Marquis of Northampton and other English lords had almost led him to forget their excessive demands in the matter of his little daughter's dowry; he was still sweating most agreeably, and the only companionship lacking to make this sojourn at Châteaubriant completely satisfactory was now to be given to him.

So, clad in a loose robe, the Most Christian King entered his bedchamber from his cabinet de toilette, where his pages had been rubbing him down and changing his shirt, and finding a tall scarlet figure standing by one of the windows, laughed instead of showing annoyance.

"Your persistence, Cardinal, should earn you another hat, if that were possible! Do not tell me that you have remained here for two and a half hours!"

"Indeed, no, your Majesty," said Charles of Lorraine, smiling. "I returned some twenty minutes ago. And if my persistence be laudable, as you are gracious enough to hint, all the reward I crave is five minutes of your Majesty's time."

"Têtedieu, there is no turning aside you Guises!" remarked Henri good-humouredly, as he threw himself into a chair, while a page placed at his elbow a draught of warmed wine and water. Since that fatal draught of cold water from the well at Ainay which fifteen years ago had carried off his elder brother, François, the first Dauphin, after a game of tennis, Henri had been careful never to risk a repetition of the tragedy (though it was true that the water in question was said to have been poisoned). "I have been playing against your brother the Duke."

"I heard as much, Sire," said the Cardinal, who had wasted some time seeking for François in order to consult with him. And he stood there waiting.

"Pray be seated," said the King. "For, by Saint Denis, I see I shall have no peace until I give way to you. Is it always this disgraceful business of the poison and the letter? But why in God's name are you not satisfied with Bertrandi's conduct of a case which is plain enough?"

"Because," replied the Cardinal, pleased at so favourable an opening, "the Chancellor had not the full facts before him. Moved (naturally) only by his zeal, M. de Montmorency (as he avowed to me after the conference this morning) cut off or caused to be cut off the postscript of the letter which accompanied the phial—a postscript which only a forger would have written. Had the phrase remained it was sufficient, in my judgment, to show that M. de Graeme was not the writer-since he had no cause to use such a plea, unless he had indeed injured his thumb."

The King took a drink of the wine and water. "Your Eminence's speech is dark; I pray you expound it."

His Eminence did so, carefully explaining the exact bearing of the mutilation with just the right shade of implied criticism of the Constable's action.

"So Montmorency cut off those words-and admitted it!" To the Cardinal's annoyance Henri began to laugh. "By my faith, that was, perhaps, going too far! But what, in the name of all the saints, would you have me do, Cardinal? Have Graeme's right thumb examined? I will order——But no, cut or no cut, 'tis all the same now."

"Exactly," said the Cardinal dryly. "Nothing can be proved or disproved by the state of his thumb now that M. de Montmorency has . . . made away with the other portion of the evidence. And that fact, your Majesty, if it got about, would scarcely redound to his honour nor to that of the justice of this realm."

The King frowned. "Yet I do not perceive what, at this hour, I can do."

"Are you not the King, Sire? Though you cannot indeed restore the destroyed evidence so that M. Bertrandi can weigh it, you can prevent an innocent man being hurried off to Nantes, where he may well be forced to confess to a crime which he has not committed."

"But he may not be innocent-he may have committed the crime," retorted Henri, in a tone which suggested slight accesses both of boredom and irritation. "All the appearances are against him."

"If your Majesty would deign to put yourself to a little trouble you could soon ascertain the guilt or innocence of your former Archer. Your Majesty has no doubt heard of the Ear of Dionysius?"

"Never," returned Henri. "Who was he, and of what importance was his ear?"

In less than a score of words the Cardinal imparted the required information about the tyrant of Syracuse. The King appeared interested.

"I think that device has been put in practice later than the days of the Sieur Dionysius," he remarked. "There was King Louis XI for instance. . . . Yes, it would undoubtedly serve as a test. I will reflect upon it; but now it is time for me to complete my toilet and to pay a visit to the Queen." And gathering his robe about him he clapped his hands for his pages.

"Graeme will be sent off to Nantes early to-morrow morning, your Majesty," the Cardinal reminded him.

"My dear Cardinal, I must have time to reflect upon this plan of yours," said Henri a trifle testily. "And also," he added with disconcerting shrewdness, "upon what has caused you so to champion the case of a man whom you ought to abhor for his attempt upon the life of your royal niece!"

"The cause," replied Charles de Guise, not at all anxious for any other to be discerned, "is my niece's own petition. The child is much distressed, and she hopes that your Majesty, who is as a father to her — —"

"Yes, yes," broke in the King as he rose, "but you will not deny that the first duty of a father is to protect his children. And until the real criminal is discovered, how can Graeme be cleared? But your scheme shall be thought upon, I promise you." And he went towards his cabinet.

The Cardinal stood there tugging angrily at his little fair beard. He had as good as lost the game, for if the King said he would "reflect," that was like to be the end of the matter. Charles of Lorraine knew him and his indecisions by heart; knew too how he was always swayed by one or other of the great influences of his life, his mistress or his friend-both so much older than himself. And at this moment the wrong influence-from the Cardinal's point of view-was at hand, while the right was absent. If the matter were mentioned to the Constable, as it might well be before to-morrow morning, it was all over not only with the unfortunate Graeme, but also with the hope of dealing a shrewd blow at the credit of the Constable himself.

"Ah, by the way," said the King, turning at the door, "I forgot to tell your Eminence a piece of good news which I received a short while ago. Mme. de Valentinois has at length allowed herself to be persuaded to pay Châteaubriant a visit. An express arrived from her while I was at tennis. She is, in fact, upon her way, and will be here to-morrow about noon."

A gleam came into the Cardinal's eyes.

"That is indeed excellent news. She comes from Anet, I suppose. Does your Majesty know where she will lie to-night?"

"At Château-Gontier, she says. Some special entertainment must be devised for her —a masque perhaps. A pity Saint-André is not here. You have never given your mind to such trifles, Cardinal?"

"Never, your Majesty," said the Cardinal, smiling. "But on this occasion . . . who knows, I might put pen to paper!"

It was exactly what he did. Half an hour later a rider on a fast horse left Châteaubriant by the eastern gate and made at top speed for Château-Gontier, thirty-three miles away, carrying a letter sealed with a Cardinal's hat above the cross of Jerusalem, which was one of the Guise quarterings. It was addressed to Madame la Duchesse de Valentinois.

(10)

The pool of dried blood in the middle of the ruelle looked very dark when, as dusk was falling, Gaspard returned to his lodging. He had no qualms over the question of its shedding, as he stepped carefully to avoid it. It might have been his own.

Of his late assailant there was no further trace, but enquiries revealed that he had been removed, in a serious condition, by some other Archers. Well, the Chancellor was attending to that matter; so Gaspard went cheerfully to his garret, using the rickety outside staircase to avoid the Englishmen who were laughing and drinking below. Since he had learnt of their Council's attitude over the accused man Stuart he felt that his loathing for all that nation was too intense for politeness.

He sat down to write a letter to old Marillier, undecided, however, whether to send it or to set out for La Sillerie himself. Having done so, he cast a glance at the rafters above his head. For that query of the Chancellor's about a signet-ring had left him a trifle uneasy. Although he had half-resolved to keep his father's seal, since it might conceivably be of use some day, he began now to revert to his former plan of throwing it into the river. As far as he could gather he had impressed old Bertrandi with his complete innocence-how marvellously well inspired he had been to take the bull by the horns and go to him, instead of waiting to be fetched! —yet who knew whether after all the Chancellor might not cause search to be made, and the ring, though so small and well hidden, discovered wedged into a cobwebby beam. Best get rid of all traces of this perilous episode, this scheme which had gone so doubly wrong, and for which he might, but for his careful planning, have paid so dear. Even so he would not feel safe until Ninian was lodged at Nantes. Nothing, fortunately, had been said about a confrontation.

The light had failed sufficiently now for him to make his way unperceived to some place outside the little town where its river, the Chère, was deep and lonely enough for his purpose. There would be just time to commit the ring to its keeping before making his way once more to his rendezvous in the château with his brilliant mistress. Gaspard climbed up and extricated the ring, but, since caution demanded that he should neither wear nor carry it in his doublet, he slipped it into the toe of one of his wide-ended shoes where, the leather being soft, it lay without inconveniencing him too greatly. Humming an air, he ran down the stairway and plunged into the narrow streets, shadowy already with twilight, but crowded as never before in their history. He threaded his way along through the bustle, taking little note of anyone or anything. To-night Eléonore in his arms again; to-morrow, the scapegoat despatched to Nantes, whence, if ever he returned, it would certainly not be to a post at Court . . . so they need never meet. And in addition, the near prospect of the revenues of Lincennes to remove him for ever far above the fear of penury.

Wrapped in these rosy dreams he followed the Chère westwards until he was clear of the town, going farther indeed than was necessary, as he recognised after a little. There were certainly no houses to spy upon him in these meadows, edged with occasional wind-blown willows among the grass and wild flowers. The grey dusk was torn here by a strong and fitful breeze, presaging rain to-morrow, and ruffling the river, which had begun to slide along with a noise out of all proportion to its speed and volume, a noise suggesting falling waters. Gaspard soon guessed the cause of this; there must be a weir farther on. If so, it would be an excellent place in which to commit the crest of the Grahams to the Chère's keeping.

He went on, therefore, facing the last streaks of a lemon-coloured after-sunset, until he came to the weir, a sloping wall of grey water slipping smoothly down into a tossing pool some fifteen feet below. What would be more appropriate to this occasion than to walk out along the top of the rough sluice and cast the ring into the very middle of the pool? It could be done easily and safely enough, since the upper part of the stout old wooden structure was double, and the water-at least in summer-flowed under, not over the topmost beams, and there were in addition some projections at intervals to which one could hold on-the handles no doubt of some sort of sluice gates. And next moment, driven by a subtler intoxicant than wine, Gaspard was clambering along without difficulty, for sliding water beneath his feet did not make him giddy.

The timbers proved to be damp and spray-worn, and not so wide as he had thought, and it was very much windier in midstream than on the bank; the gusts came almost chill. Arrived about the middle of the sluice he turned and faced the pool below-and only then remembered that the ring was not in his doublet, but in the toe of his shoe. However, he could extract it easily enough by merely unfastening a strap, and he stooped to do this. No, he could not get the ring out without removing the shoe altogether; so he knelt upon one knee to do this, slipped the ring on to a finger, and replaced the shoe. It was the last completed action of his life.

Thinking how chilly it was this evening . . . but in an hour's time he would be warm enough . . . he began to get to his feet again. He was not yet upright when a really violent gust of wind caught his short orange cloak from behind in an inimical grip, and blew it clean over his head. Clutching at the beating folds, Gaspard instinctively turned, cursing, to face upstream, whence the wind came, but, half-blinded as he was, lost his footing on the slimy timber, tried frantically to regain his balance, failed, and went over backwards down the weir.

Unfortunately he had never learnt to swim.

It had been going on for hours now, this suspense of waiting for some message or messenger from the Due de Guise, but Ninian guessed that he might have to wait as many more. The Due would probably send-perhaps with merely some message of encouragement-one of his gentlemen, who would almost certainly be able to command admission to this place, unless the Constable or Bertrandi had given absolute orders against it.

Yet when at last the door at the top of the steps opened and a man came in, the time of waiting was forgotten, and as the newcomer descended Ninian even said to himself how speedy Patrick must have been! Then his heart fell; it was one of those two secretaries whom he had seen taking notes in the chapel a few hours ago. In his hand was a letter.

"From the Chancellor," he said in dry tones as he held it out; then turned without further speech and went up the steps again.

But was it really? Ninian turned the letter over with a wild hope that——But no, the Due would not have employed Bertrandi's secretary as an emissary. With unsteady fingers he opened and read:

> To Monsieur de Graeme, prisoner in the Vieux Château. This is to inform you that M. de Vernay has just of his own will come forward and cleared himself to my satisfaction of the monstrous charge you made against him. Nevertheless, I am still delaying your departure for Nantes until to-morrow morning, in order that you may have full time to write a complete confession of your guilt and that of your accomplices. If you do this it will not be necessary to proceed at Nantes to sterner measures for that purpose. You will also by confessing remove the shadow of complicity which at present hangs over your wife. — Bertrandi, Garde des Sceaux.

"To my satisfaction," "monstrous charge." How the gods must be laughing! Ninian found himself tempted (but not greatly) to laugh also. He began, against his will, to picture the scene, imagining without much difficulty how Gaspard would carry it off, and equally against his will a ribbon of little miniatures began to unroll themselves, beginning with that fatal day in the Salle des Gardes at Anet, and the more fatal one in the park. He sat down at last on the stone bench and remained staring at the blotched stone wall so long that he could fancy himself back in the hall at Garthrose looking at his father's picture and saying, "I befriended him for your sake, for your memory-and this is what your son has done to me."

Could physical torture be actually much worse than the increasing tension of waiting now, while the dim stone chamber grew gradually dimmer, and the outlines of the vaulting were lost, for some result of the appeal which Rutherford surely could not have failed to deliver? (For François de Guise must certainly have been in Châteaubriant this morning at the conference over the little princess's dowry.) It was Magdalen whose image was with him now, Magdalen, his own for so short a time. What was happening to her in these hours, after that strange effort which she had made to save him? Had she, poor child, dreamt that phrase about a cut thumb, or had she invented it? He could recall nothing of the sort in the letter, and the Chancellor had affirmed without hesitation that there was nothing. But if there had been. . . . Ninian found himself looking at his right thumb reflectively, trying meanwhile to conjure up a true picture of the whole letter as it had been spread out before him last night. But it was of no avail.

Slowly the light drained away still farther, and the vaulting overhead became loaded with menacing shadows. If they leave me in the dark, thought the prisoner to himself, trying to jest, how do they expect me to read le Balafré's message if he sends a written one?

Steps at last! The door was unfastened and two men came in, one carrying a lantern. The other must be the Duke's messenger. Now he should know what measure of hope was to be his.

For the second time his heart sank again; the men were both guards. The second man was carrying a basket containing food, for the light showed, projecting from it, the neck of a stoup of wine and the end of a loaf of bread. Lantern and basket were set down upon the table without a word. Yet Ninian thought, or imagined (since his whole being seemed at that moment concentrated in his eyes) that the guard who had brought in the basket looked at him in rather a curious manner.

"Have you any message for me?" he asked them in a voice which seemed to belong to some other man.

The guard with the lantern shook his head. "There is your supper. I am leaving you the light." Then he and his companion turned and went to the door again, the key rasping as its bearer tried to fit it into the lock in the obscurity.

Ninian stood for a long time staring at the lantern. No message yet. It must be between ten and eleven o'clock by now. Then he roused himself. Though he doubted whether, strung up to this pitch of expectancy, he could swallow any food, he thought that he had better try.

As he took the bread and wine out of the basket he was instantly struck by the weight of the long loaf. He looked at it, and saw that it had been slit along its length and pressed together again, being in one place secured thus by an almost invisible piece of cord. And there was something inside-something of a certain weight. When he had wrenched the loaf apart he found himself looking at a short dagger.

And at first Ninian did not understand. Had Patrick, failing after all to deliver the letter, contrived to smuggle in this weapon to him in a wild hope that by its means he might break out and escape? But Patrick knew as well as he that, even if he managed to stab a guard or two, he would never get clear. No, that was not the explanation. The weapon did not come from Patrick.

Unbelievable as it was, the bitter truth came upon him quite soon, like a stab from the weapon at which he stared, whose pommel ended in a great topaz, and whose exquisitely-chased blade bore . . . yes, the eaglets of Lorraine by the hilt, the lilies of Anjou nearer the point. This smuggled poniard was the Duc de Guise's response to his desperate appeal; and it was more eloquent, if more sardonic, than any written words. "I can do nothing for you but help you to take the only way out."

And that was all the gratitude of his great House amounted to! *Take yourself off, and be thankful that I send you the means of cheating the torture-chamber and the scaffold.* The bridge was broken now which had so frailly spanned that dark and suddenly-racing flood. With a curse, Ninian threw the weapon from him; it rang upon the stone floor at a distance. Then he began to laugh-and continued to laugh until the sound of his own mirth, echoing in his ears like the hysterical laughter of another, made him catch at his self control. To stop himself he snatched up the stoup of wine, poured out a draught into the horn cup which accompanied it, and toasted his benefactor.

"To the princely house of Lorraine," he cried aloud, "and Duc François de Guise in particular! May he never know what it is to ask promised help in vain!" And when he had drunk off the wine he went across the chamber and picked up the dagger, its golden eye of a jewel cracked across in two places.

So great and precious a gift to be treated thus! It was sharp enough; he ran his fingers over point and edge. What a privilege to be able to slay himself with the Duc's own poniard, to have his blood, that of an obscure and now dishonoured gentleman, running over quarterings such as these!

But there was something to be done before he could turn this key to freedom in its lock. Ninian went slowly back to the table where the lantern shone not only on the bisected loaf and the emptied wine-cup, but also upon the untouched surface of the sheet of paper waiting to receive his confession of a crime which he had not committed. Before he took his way through the door of which this dagger was the key, he had to save Magdalen, if he could, even by sending down his own name to all ages as the would-be murderer of the royal child whom he had loved and served, at the cost-until recently-of his own happiness. And even if he wrote no word of actual confession (and by that abstention destroyed his wife's chance of escape from the shadow of complicity), the very use of the weapon on himself would brand him as guilty. He was in a trap indeed.

Opening his doublet, he concealed the Duke's answer in his breast, and sitting down began to try to eat a piece of the loaf which had concealed it. He could swallow only a few morsels; and he was soon back once more at the interminable pacing to and fro of captivity.

He had the whole night before him in which to review all the yesterdays in the life of up-rightness and fidelity that was ending like this. Fidelity and compassion also-had he never, and against his will, pitied the man who had brought him here, never held out a helping hand to his father's bastard, just because he was Malise Graham's son, that son, passing at once out of his life, would never have had the power to do him this mortal and unimaginable injury. And while Gaspard had-what did the Chancellor write? —"cleared himself to my satisfaction of the monstrous charge you made against him" —had there ever in the world's history been a situation more horribly ironical? —*he* stood stripped of everything, his good name not least, on the brink of this black, plunging, starless sea where he must leave Magdalen behind to believe him guilty.

No, he could not do it! He could not confess to a crime of which he knew nothing in order to save himself from torture (for the scaffold was nothing in comparison with what would come first-unless, indeed, they meant to employ that new and lingering death to which the Constable had condemned the rebels of Bordeaux, breaking on the wheel). He could not write himself down there at that table a traitor and a child-murderer. . . . Yet suppose, since one was but human and there were limits to endurance, suppose that in the end they succeeded in wringing a confession from him in those dungeons at Nantes into which he would vanish to-morrow? Was not the best course to admit nothing, use the poniard on himself before morning-and cheat them all?

But then, what of Magdalen? The Chancellor had seemed to say that only his confession could save her. He must leave her, in any case, to become a widow bearing an execrated name-leave her unprotected to these wolves. The flood of his love and tenderness for her came choking about him; and he suddenly flung himself down at the table and buried his face in his hands.

He was still for so long that at last a mouse ventured out from its hole and ran like a shadow towards some crumbs of bread fallen from the table. Then, more swiftly still, it vanished again-for the man sitting there had moved. He had put out his hand and taken up a pen.

(12)

Though the windows of the Cardinal de Lorraine's quarters in the Château looked out into the now rain-drenched cour d'honneur, the clatter and bustle between seven and eight o'clock that Wednesday morning, when a horse-litter with a number of mounted attendants entered it, went unheard by him, for he was already at his prayers in his oratory. To him thus occupied, however, there soon tiptoed in an apologetic secretary, who whispered in his ear that the Duchesse de Valentinois was come and was asking for him.

The Cardinal got up so quickly from his prie-dieu that he dislodged his breviary. "Madame de Valentinois here herself! Impossible!" For his letter had but besought her to write at once to the King.

The impossible, however, had happened. Looking very tall in her long black travelling-cloak edged with ermine, its hood still over her head, Madame Diane awaited him in the outer room. At his evident astonishment she gave her usual tempered, practical smile.

"I judged it best to come in person," she said briefly. And then, for she was rigidly orthodox, she kissed the young man's ring before seating herself.

"But the distance you must have travelled all night, Madame!" exclaimed he. "I had never thought — —"

"A small matter," said Diane, putting back her hood. There was indeed no trace of fatigue visible on her unsullied complexion. "I feared lest a letter should miscarry. Moreover, I can now see his Majesty myself, and move him to-to play Dionysius as your Eminence proposed. For, as you wrote, the Constable's disregard of the principles of justice is so outrageous, his assumption of omnipotence so intolerable, that it must be curbed! He shall be taught a lesson. To suppress evidence in so high-handed a fashion!"

Nor, to judge from the expression of virtuous indignation round those tightly folded lips of hers, would it have been easy to guess that, had circumstances demanded it, she would have done precisely the same thing without a tremor, and Charles de Guise also; and that their conspiracy to save an innocent man was far more a conspiracy to damage a rival. Yet the Cardinal's motive at least had a strand of altruism in it.

"You will go, then, to the King without delay, Madame?" he urged. "His Majesty, as you know, is always afoot very early, but he will not yet have gone to Mass. But I must remind you, Duchesse, that little time is left, since M. de Graeme may set out for Nantes at any moment now. I have unfortunately not been able to ascertain what time was fixed for his departure."

But a frown had crossed the mistress's high, white forehead, and her whole face seemed to close up, even as her figure stiffened. "Monsieur de Graeme, did you say, Cardinal? The Queen of Scots' Ecuyer? Is it he who is accused of this crime? I read your Eminence's letter so hastily — —"

"Small wonder, Madame," interposed the Cardinal quickly, "when you graciously hastened to leave for Châteaubriant with so little delay! But the identity of the accused is truly of small importance, is it not, for we are agreed that what is at stake is the . . . the first principles of justice?" —"And the domination of the Constable," added his eyes.

But Diane de Poitiers was the last woman in the world to forgive a slight to her authority. "M. de Graeme married against my wishes and those of Madame Catherine," she observed, the words falling thin and bitter from her compressed lips.

"But had he not his Majesty's permission?" hazarded the Cardinal. "In that case, he must have supposed that he had yours also, Madame."

"That he never had!" declared she, sitting very erect. "And his Majesty has too good a heart, which is sometimes taken advantage of. I repeat that this man Graeme took to wife (always against my expressed wishes) that one of your royal niece's attendants who is akin, I believe, to that trollop Mme. de Flamyn, now expelled from the Court."

"Of that kinship I have no knowledge," said the Cardinal uneasily. "But you will surely not let it, or the marriage, stand in the way of frustrating M. de Montmorency's design?"

"I am not sure," returned Madame de Valentinois, very haughtily, "that I care, after all, to interest myself in M. de Graeme's affairs. I think that he had best go to Nantes for trial-both he and his wife. It would teach him a lesson."

Charles de Guise suppressed a very impatient exclamation. Was the scheme to be wrecked, at the eleventh hour, for this petty rancour?

"Yes, Madame, he would undoubtedly learn a lesson. But in that case, a greater than he would have to go without one. Is it not, as I had the honour to write to you, a rare opportunity to administer this?"

The long, gem-laden fingers of Madame Diane's left hand drummed upon the table beside her, while her eyes, under frowning brows, went straying round the room. The Cardinal forced himself to patience. On this woman's will depended not only the fate of that Scotsman in the Vieux Château over there-if, indeed, he were not gone by this time-but the chance of giving a sound rebuff to the Montmorency ascendancy. How could the mistress, with her cool head and calculating heart, allow herself to be kept back from dealing that blow by such a trifling grudge?

"That is a pretty thing you have there," observed she suddenly, her eyes coming to rest upon a richly jewelled crucifix of Spanish workmanship standing on a table at a little distance.

The Cardinal followed the direction of that chill, appraising glance. "It is remarkable, is it not, Madame, and is indeed reckoned a masterpiece. I commonly carry it with me, though it is somewhat too ornate for devotion." He hesitated a moment, then took the plunge. "If, Madame, you thought it worthy of joining the treasures which you are amassing at Anet, I should be most happy . . ." And with an inward malediction, for he valued it, he took the symbol and placed it on the table at her side.

As with most Spanish crucifixes, its realism was extreme, though tempered in this case by the fact that the wounds on the tortured ivory figure were of rubies, the nails diamonds, the leaves of the thorn-wreath composed of tiny emeralds, and the spikes of gold. Madame Diane took it up and studied it with her head on one side.

"You will honour me by accepting it?" asked the young churchman.

"You are too generous, Cardinal," was the reply. "But I shall greatly value a sacred emblem as coming from your Eminence." And with that, the frost gone from her visage, Madame Diane rose from her chair. "I perceive, upon reflection, that the opportunity is too good to miss. Pray have me conducted to his Majesty's apartments. There is, as you say, no time to lose."

* * * * *

No, there was indeed no time to lose. Madame de Valentinois gone, the Cardinal summoned his discreet secretary and instructed him to go down to the court-yard of the Vieux Château, glean what he could there, and return to report. Then he forced himself to the rôle of impotent waiting, for matters were in the capable hands of Madame Diane now. . . . It was monstrous and inconsistent that she should have required bribing to undertake a mission which she had already considered worth that hasty night journey from Château-Gontier! Charles de Guise gazed with annoyance at the treasure which he had been obliged to throw into the scale to save M. de Graeme. By Saint Denis, he could not be more concerned about that unfortunate gentleman if he had really felt a personal interest in his fate!

In five long minutes the discreet secretary was back, more out of breath than he had been for years.

"The escort is ready and waiting in the court-yard, your Emminence, and I think, indeed, there must have been some delay already, for I heard the men grumbling at having to sit their horses in this heavy rain instead of setting off. But I saw no signs of any change of orders."

Frowning, Charles of Lorraine bit his lip. "Go down again, and when they bring out the prisoner, do your best to hinder his departure. Say that an order to stay it is on its way from his Majesty-say anything that may cause delay!"

She could not surely be going to fail with the King, thought the Cardinal, beginning to pace impatiently up and down. Was it possible that she had not found him, that he was hearing Mass already? If he were himself to go down to the court-yard he could achieve nothing-if he were to seek the King (where he had failed already), he could not persuade him as Madame Diane could do. But the minutes were sliding by! And he smote his hands together, his light eyes darkening with anger. So priceless an opportunity of dealing a blow at that immense prestige to be allowed to slip at the eleventh hour!

Hurried steps at the door; there was his messenger again, more breathless than ever, but clearly bearing different news.

"They were on the point of bringing him out, Eminence, when an Archer-three Archers — —"

"Ah!" said Charles of Lorraine, with a long sigh of relief and elation, "she has succeeded then!"

And as a royal page suddenly made his appearance in the open doorway, he said, without even waiting to hear what message he brought: "I am coming to his Majesty at once."

(13)

Magdalen had fallen asleep at last; and it was Jean Ogilvy, who had inveigled the guard at the door into allowing her to spend the night with Madame de Graeme, who was standing looking out at the rain. She did not know at what hour the prisoner in the Vieux Château was to be taken off to Nantes, but she half hoped that he would be gone before his wife awoke. Since the latter was not, apparently, to accompany him, would it not be less agonising for her thus?

Jean, who in her short and merry life had never seen grief like Magdalen's, stole after a few moments to the bed and looked at her lying there, in her clothes, like something cast up by the tide, her face almost as white as the pillow against which it rested. But the door was opening. The girl tiptoed to it quietly, and asked, as one speaks from a sick-room: "What is it?"

"Madame de Graeme is to come forth," responded the sentry.

"For what purpose?"

"I do not know, Mademoiselle."

His voice had wakened Magdalen, and she raised herself quickly on her elbow. "What is it? Perhaps I, too, am to be taken to Nantes?" Her tone showed how much she hoped it.

Jean helped her to put her attire quickly in order and, going with her to the door, gave her a long kiss. "Courage, courage!" she whispered.

But courage or despair were all one to Magdalen now-names, names! She traversed the fatal ante-chamber once more without emotion. Something dreadful had happened there, she knew, but it was thousands of years ago. Presently, however, she did perceive that she was not being taken out of the new château at all, and knowing that Ninian was in the donjon of the old, the last faint hope of saying farewell to him flickered out. During that interminable night Jean had said to her more than once: "My dear, why do you lay so much stress upon taking leave of your husband? He is not a condemned man, he goes but to trial, and after his acquittal-for he *must* be acquitted-you will be able to greet him again!" And at last Magdalen had forced herself to give words to her fear: "Aye, but shall I know him?" And Jean had gone pale and turned her head away.

Perhaps, thought Magdalen now, as they paused at a door on the ground-floor, I am to be interrogated again by that old man, and he will then send me to Nantes with Ninian for trial. Oh, God grant it!

The door had an Archer in front of it. The garb was a little comforting to her, though she did not look at his face. She entered-prepared to encounter the Chancellor, perhaps even the Constable —a handsome, lofty and rather narrow room of some size . . . empty save for one person, her husband.

He was standing, his eyes upon the ground, by the high window, whose glass was set with blazons, and as he lifted his head she felt a pang of alarm at the sight of his face, so sad and stern was it. It made him seem a great way off.

"Ninian!" she cried.

And at the sound of her voice the icy look melted, the distance was bridged, and she was in his arms.

* * * * *

Afterwards she was to find it hard to recall exactly what they had said at first, save that he had thanked God that she was not (so it seemed) to be sent to Nantes, while she as fervently lamented it. On that, with what she realised was a strained cheerfulness, he reminded her that he was an innocent, not a condemned man; though, indeed, he had added, looking at her rather hard, until the real writer of the letter could be found. . . . And she had broken in, unable to contain herself: "But we know that it was Gaspard-hard as it is to believe such wickedness! Cannot they find him, Ninian, cannot they make him confess?" To which he had replied that it was no matter of finding him now, because he had been found already. He *was* in Châteaubriant, he had seen the Chancellor privately, and had satisfied him, God alone knew how, of his innocence.

That proved the downfall of her last stronghold of hope, and she learnt only in that moment how high she had built it. "Innocent! Innocent!" she said, with a bitter cry. "Then who is guilty? It is he, Ninian, it is he . . . And how do you know that he has convinced the Chancellor?"

"By a letter from the Chancellor telling me so, and urging me to confess," said her husband, his face hardening again.

"Confess!" she gasped, gripping his arm. "How could you confess to what you would have died rather than do?"

He looked away at the coats-of-arms in the window. "Bertrandi used a very potent weapon, Magdalen. Tell me, have they threatened you in any way that, if I did not — —"

Her clutch became almost fierce. "Oh, God, say that you have not! What would threats . . . and none have been made to me . . . Ninian, Ninian, you have not lied, thinking to save me?"

He looked at her a moment sombrely, and his hand went to his breast. "No, I have not. I could not bring myself to do it, even for your sake. Yet . . . Magdalen, I was tempted, I own it, in the night. Ink and paper were ready, the Chancellor had said that it would help you, and in the end — —" He stopped abruptly.

But she had broken in. "How could it help me, my darling, when we are both as guiltless as-our little Reinette herself!"

A spasm of pain crossed her husband's face. "The Queen-does she know of this?"

"I saw her yesterday and I told her-in spite of Mme. de Paroy. And the Cardinal of Lorraine, who chanced to be there, promised to do what he could."

"The Cardinal of Lorraine!" exclaimed her husband scornfully. "Put not your trust in princes, whether of the Church or of the world, nor, above all, in those of the house of Guise. I have good reason to know how worthless are their promises!"

Before she could ask him what he meant, they both turned round quickly at a slight sound for which, in that empty room, there seemed no cause. Only, high up on the wall above their heads, a great damask curtain swayed a trifle as though some draught had caught it.

"Moreover," finished Ninian in the same hard voice, "the Constable is set upon my condemnation. But I may yet escape him," he added, almost inaudibly.

Magdalen caught the words, however. "How, how?" she asked eagerly. He seemed not to hear her, for he was saying hotly how vile was the plan to poison a child. And though, indeed, Magdalen felt this with all her heart, yet now that the horrible scheme had failed, it was the ruin which it had brought to Ninian and to herself which overwhelmed her. And she recurred to what he had said about escape. If only the postscript which she had seen at the end of the forged letter . . . yes, yes, a thousand times was she sure that she had seen it, because on reading it her thoughts had at once gone to her own father, so prone to that mishap with his pen-knife. But now, since the Chancellor denied its existence, either he was lying, or it had been removed, cut off— —

And Ninian said, his face very dark: "Yes, by some person who saw that it might prove evidence in my favour! You perceive how little chance of justice I have!"

* * * * *

It was at that point that the miracle took place. There came a sudden sharp jingling noise, as of rings being drawn along a rod. And looking up whence the sound came, Ninian and Magdalen beheld, to their petrifaction, two figures standing in a recessed gallery, flush with the wall, which the curtain had concealed. The foremost was the Cardinal of Lorraine; behind him, incredibly, was the white doublet, the black cloak, the whole figure of the King.

It was the Cardinal who spoke. "You may, Monsieur de Graeme, have a better chance of justice than you think," he said calmly, looking down upon them. "Knock upon the door of the chamber, and the Archer on guard will conduct you hither to kiss his Majesty's hand, and to learn to what pains he condescends to put himself to discover the truth."

* * * * *

On the couch at the end of the gallery to which he had carried her after his stammered words of gratitude over the King's hand, Magdalen was recovering from her swoon. All Ninian's attention had been for some time bent upon her alone, yet he was not unconscious that a conflict was going on at the other end of the gallery. The Constable de Montmorency was there now, having apparently come in search of his missing prisoner. Ninian could hear him arguing brusquely, imperiously, with his royal master.

"You are too tender-hearted, Sire! Whatever you have overheard, it is only natural that the man should protest his innocence to his wife. God save us all! That is no proof of it! She is his dupe. Why, he dare not avow his guilt to her, even in private, lest she should reveal it if she were questioned. Your Majesty has been disgracefully imposed upon!"

Yes, a battle was raging over him, Ninian Graham. But it was too late now; the King himself, convinced, he said, by what he had overheard, of his and Magdalen's innocence, had set him free. He heard the Cardinal of Lorraine observe coolly: "My dear Constable, if he were guilty, would he have denied having seen the postscript which might have saved him? . . . I do not know at what stage in the proceedings you saw fit to remove it?"

Ninian had just time to savour once more this miracle within a miracle, a Guise coming forward to champion him, when Magdalen's eyes opened.

"Are you better, my heart?" he asked tenderly. She smiled up at him, pressed his hand and closed them again. She was not ready to move yet.

As he knelt gazing at her, a fourth voice joined itself to the three at the other end of the gallery, the unmistakable flute-like organ of the old Chancellor.

"Pardon me, Sire, if I intrude! I had sent to see whether the prisoner Graeme had yet set out for Nantes, and was relieved to find that he had not, for a very strange matter has come to light, and I was anxious to speak with the Constable, who, I was told, was here."

"What is this strange matter?" asked the King. "M. de Graeme, as you perceive, is here also-but no longer as a prisoner."

It was perhaps Ninian's presence which caused Bertrandi to lower his voice, so that whatever tidings he brought did not reach his ex-prisoner's ears. But not long afterwards Montmorency was heard to laugh his rough, contemptuous laugh and say: "I'll not believe that! You are become a weaver of romances, Chancellor!" on which the Cardinal observed smoothly: "Perhaps his Majesty will see fit to command that he be brought — —"

But at that moment Magdalen not only opened her eyes again, but tried to raise herself on the couch. Ninian took her in his arms, and as their lips met in a kiss such as might, he felt, scarcely be given and received save by those reunited in Paradise, King and Chancellor, Guise and Montmorency passed from his mind as though they had never existed. And when, after a while, he looked round, it might, indeed, have been so, for the gallery was empty save for Magdalen and himself.

He raised her to her feet. "Let us go, beloved!" he whispered.

Still in that hushed rapture they moved slowly away from the end of the gallery. Voices, indeed, came up from the room below, and the tramp of feet, sounds as negligible as those which might float up from earth to the ears of the blessed. Whatever was going on down there was no concern of theirs now. His wife's head was on his breast-not so far from the dagger, his last resource, never now, please God, to be used; and thus they came to the spot whence King and Cardinal had looked down upon them. The curtains were still drawn aside. Half unconsciously Ninian, too, glanced down . . . and went no farther.

Not for his staying his steps so abruptly did Magdalen raise her head, but because she was aware of the sudden racing of his heart. She looked up quickly at his face, where the bliss which the last few minutes had written there was all shattered; then she followed his downward gaze, and saw what he saw.

On the floor of that room where they had lately stood in the anguish of farewell was a litter, and upon it the motionless body of a young man in grey, partly covered with a stained and sodden rust-coloured cloak from which a little water was slowly dripping. Water still darkened also the disordered bronze hair. King and Cardinal stood side by side looking down at this sight, with the Constable de Montmorency, frowning heavily, his arms a-kimbo, a little behind them. On the other side old Bertrandi, stooping with evident difficulty, had lifted one of the passive hands, and was examining something upon it-something which he had already tried to draw off and could not.

"Is it . . . is it Gaspard?" came Magdalen's horrified whisper. Ninian bent his head.

But the momentary silence below was broken by the King. "What is troubling you, Chancellor?"

The old man looked up. "This, Sire, this ring. The device is familiar to me. Its counterpart lies in my chamber above —M. de Graeme's seal. And this is the young man whom he accused, and who came to me yesterday denying that he possessed — —"

"And how comes he here thus?" interrupted Anne de Montmorency gruffly.

"He was found in a weir-pool of the Chère this morning by some peasants who guessed him, from his attire, to be of the Court. Bringing him here, they chanced to fall in with one of my secretaries, who recognised him, as I do also."

At that moment Henri II, looking up, saw the drowned man's victim standing transfixed in the gallery, and beckoned him to come down.

Like an automaton, Ninian put Magdalen from him and obeyed; and presently stood speechless among these great ones, conscious only that his father's son lay lifeless at his feet, a long tangle of waterweed across the heart which had devised a Queen's death and his brother's. After a moment he put a hand across his eyes.

"The river has sent M. de Graeme his completest vindication, has it not, Constable?" asked Charles of Lorraine in suave but exultant tones.

"And so," said Arthur Erskine, "you are returning to Scotland? It grieves me to hear it, and I know not why you should take this step, now that you are cleared of all suspicion, and that the Queen continues so much attached to you and to Mistress Graham?"

Stared at by a group of solemn Breton children, he and Ninian were standing outside the peasants' cottage whence the latter had been dragged on the night of his arrest. The two men no longer shared that inner room, for Erskine had given up his claim upon it in favour of Magdalen, whom her husband had brought hither from Châteaubriant immediately after his vindication three mornings ago.

Ninian Graham smiled rather sadly. "There are many reasons. It is plain that the King thinks it better that we should both resign our posts about her Majesty, though he does not insist upon it. And I see well that if we remained Mme. de Paroy would make my wife's existence a burden to her, while I should always have M. de Montmorency for enemy."

"You believe that he will always bear you a grudge because you escaped him even after the 'precaution' he took with the forged letter?"

"Yes; and a still deeper grudge because this action was the occasion of the King's openly showing favour, at his expense, to the Cardinal of Lorraine, who brought it to light."

"But," urged Erskine, "why not return to the Archer Guard, which you say his Majesty was anxious for you to do?"

"Yes," answered the elder man slowly, "his Majesty was most gracious. . . . But life in the Guard would no longer be the same now. Rutherford, as you probably know, died yesterday evening of his wound, sacrificed on my behalf. I have finished with France. We will go back to our own country."

Erskine looked hard at him. He seemed a man ten years older than he had been a week ago. And his wife, of whom the Queen's cup-bearer had had a glimpse when she came out of the cottage just now-but she was young, she would recover her looks.

"We have only one wish now," resumed Ninian, beginning to move away from the group of cottages, "but I know not how it can be compassed. It is, to take leave of the Queen not under the eyes of Madame de Paroy-nor under those of Madame de Curel either, for that matter."

Erskine nodded comprehendingly. "It is possible that it might be contrived, with the aid of Mistress Ogilvy, for example."

Silently, after that, they walked along under the ringed chestnut trees, giants in girth, some of them, which bordered the rough road leading to Châteaubriant, Ninian's eyes dwelling upon the figure of a horseman who was rapidly coming towards them.

"I shall never take the child riding again," he said suddenly, as if to himself.

"Yet you could if you chose," retorted the younger Scot, with some vehemence. "Your honour is unharmed, you are not dismissed from your post of Grand Ecuyer. He who wrought that abominable design — —"

"Who comes in such haste?" broke in Ninian Graham, so obviously with the object of changing the subject that Erskine bit his lip and was silent. Through the alternations of light and shade the rider cantered easily towards them, finally pulling up his horse upon its haunches with an exclamation and a flourish of his plumed cap. It was no other than M. Charles de Pontevez, Chevalier de Brion.

"Gentlemen, your humble servant! I am in luck, Monsieur de Graeme, to come upon you with such ease, for I have ridden over-stolen away, indeed, like a truant scholar-to offer you my congratulations." He swung out of the saddle. "I have been absent for the last ten days from my post, as you know, and upon my return yesterday was shocked to hear of the monstrous charge against you, of which I would as soon have believed myself guilty as you!"

Ninian took his outstretched hand and thanked him; and after a few more speeches the young Frenchman prepared to mount again, for the Queen of Scots, so much restored in health during the last few days, was shortly going to take the air in the château garden, and his presence might be required. Was there any message that he could bear to Châteaubriant, any service that he could render?

"Yes, Chevalier," answered Ninian, "there is. You would be doing me a great kindness if you would tell Mistress Ogilvy how greatly my wife and I desire to take leave of the Queen-alone. Is it possible, think you, that she could contrive — —"

"I wager there is nothing she would more willingly undertake," asserted her admirer promptly. He put his foot in the stirrup and withdrew it again. "Nay, Monsieur de Graeme, why not take horse now, with Madame de Graeme, and follow incontinently after me, and, with Mlle. Ogilvy's connivance, your desire may be fulfilled this very morning. What better place than a garden for giving a duenna the slip?"

(15)

Not far from the end of the long alley where Madame de Saint-Cernin had walked that evening with her two English admirers was a small secluded pleasance full of sun and butterflies, and it was here that Magdalen and Ninian waited to take farewell of their Queen. The particular reason for which the ingenious M. de Brion had chosen this spot in which to station them was its proximity to a labyrinth of clipped box of which he remembered the Queen had heard, and in which she had shown all a child's eagerness to adventure herself. It would not be too difficult for his fair accomplice to carry her off to visit this maze without either her gouvernante or her dame d'atours, to neither of whose temperaments, mental or physical, would the prospect of wandering round its convolutions at her Majesty's heels hold out any attraction.

About three sides of this little square garden ran a hedge of roses and lavender; from the fourth a short, straight path led between borders of heartsease and carnations to the mouth of the labyrinth. In the centre of the grass stood a sundial older than Jean de Laval's habitation. *Umbram jacio: umbra ipse es*, proclaimed its gnomon, but the letters were so nearly effaced that no one troubled to read the warning now. Perhaps in earlier years it had met the eyes of his beautiful wife Françoise de Foix, she whose reign as the mistress of François I had ended so abruptly in favour of Mme. d'Etampes. But the sundial itself was not so old as the days of that other châtelaine too greatly, not too little, faithful to her lord, that Sybille de Briant, who had died of joy when her Crusading husband returned from captivity. And by it now the husband and wife, given back to each other, as it were from the dragon's mouth, waited sadly, yet with fingers intertwined.

It was not long before the sound of excited children's voices heralded their invisible owners- evidently the whole brood of little Maries must be on their way hither. And in another moment the flight of children burst through the entrance in the hedge, brilliant, chattering little birds in azure and almond green and rose-colour. "Where is the maze, Mistress Ogilvy? Where do we go in?" they called, looking backwards. Then they perceived the entrance, and without paying any attention to the couple standing by the sundial, went helter-skelter along the path between the heartsease, and with little cries plunged into the labyrinth.

But the eight-year-old Queen of Scotland, coming last, with Jean Ogilvy a little way behind, did not follow her four playmates. She stood a moment in her stiff, tight-waisted saffron gown against the white and red roses and the blue-grey spikes of the lavender, the sun seeking, as it always did, the red-brown of the hair round the high brow left exposed by her close-fitting, jewelled head-dress. So Magdalen and Ninian saw her as they came forward, so they would always see her; and they knelt to her not only as to their sovereign, but as to a dear child whose features one desires to imprint more closely on one's memory.

And she, the rose-petal hue of her cheek a little dimmed, gave a hand to each of them.

"Must you go away?" she asked rather piteously. "Must you go because you were falsely accused, Master Graham? All the world knows now that you were innocent. I . . . I always knew it," she added, lifting her head proudly.

Magdalen kissed the small hand passionately again and again. Then she perceived a tear glistening upon it-her own. There should be no tears on a child's hand. She kissed it off, and rose, as Ninian had already done.

"It is better that we should depart, your Majesty," he was saying, in his deep, grave voice. "Some day perhaps we may return to France, and pray our Queen to receive us. And whether in Scotland or in France, we are your servants always, to our lives' end."

A slender curving brooch set with three pearls clasped the child's high diaphanous collar at the throat. She took it off and put it into his hand, and smiled a little tremulously at them both. "That is to keep you in mind of me," she said.

She had hardly spoken before there came a shrilling of voices out of the maze. "Marie, Marie, when are you coming?" But at the same time Mary Seton reappeared from its entrance, and running towards the Queen, panted out, half crying: "Pray do not go into that place, Marie!

It is dark, and one cannot see where one is going . . . and I think that one might perhaps never come out again!"

The challenge restored Mary of Scots at once to good spirits. "Fainéante! You are afraid of everything! Come!" And seizing her by the hand, she set off instantly towards the mysterious green tunnel and its dangers.

One instant only did Jean Ogilvy pause to fling an arm round Magdalen's neck, kiss her and whisper in her ear: *"My* gift, when the time comes, shall be a cradle!" before she followed her royal charge.

But the Queen, overtaken at the entrance to the maze, motioned to Jean to precede her, and turning, waved her hand in a last farewell to her departing servants. Then, with that one of her childhood's companions who, for all her shrinking now, was to cleave to her for two and thirty years, walking by her side along more tortuous paths and through deeper glooms than this mock mystery would yield, she vanished into the labyrinth. Voices and laughter, heard at first in the distance, grew fainter and fainter, until at last the only sound which came to the ears of the man and woman standing there looking after her was the steady hum of the bees as they rifled the lavender.